THE
DATE
FROM
HELL

ALSO BY GWENDA BOND

THE
DATE
FROM
HELL

GWENDA BOND

ST. MARTIN'S GRIFFIN
NEW YORK

First published in the United States by St. Martin's Griffin, an imprint of St. Martin's Publishing Group

THE DATE FROM HELL. Copyright © 2022 by Gwenda Bond. All rights reserved. Printed in the United States of America. For information, address St. Martin's Publishing Group, 120 Broadway, New York, NY 10271.

www.stmartins.com

Library of Congress Cataloging-in-Publication Data

Names: Bond, Gwenda, author.
Title: The date from hell / Gwenda Bond.
Description: First edition. | New York : St. Martin's Griffin, 2021.
Identifiers: LCCN 2021048555 (print) | ISBN 9781250771766
   (trade paperback) | ISBN 9781250771773 (ebook)
Subjects: GSAFD: Romance fiction.
Classification: LCC PS3602.O65648 D38 2022 | DDC 813/.6—dc23
LC record available at https://lccn.loc.gov/2021048555

Our books may be purchased in bulk for promotional, educational, or business use. Please contact your local bookseller or the Macmillan Corporate and Premium Sales Department at 1-800-221-7945, extension 5442, or by email at MacmillanSpecialMarkets@macmillan.com.

First Edition: 2022

10 9 8 7 6 5 4 3 2 1

For Bill and Gretchen, Yanni, and the gang—I'd definitely go through Hell for you

CHAPTER ONE

CALLIE

THE GRAY KEEP, THE KINGDOM OF HELL

I stand on my tiptoes to slide a book with a thick black spine adorned with golden skulls—*Being the Rules of the Kingdom of Hell, Vol. 99*—back into its place on the shelf. The candle in the nearest sconce gusts flame.

"That *is* where it goes," I say. "Between ninety-eight and one hundred."

The invisible demonic wraiths who keep these tomes in tidy condition are rightly finicky. Another burst of flame crackles in answer. *Fine*, I interpret it as, *if you say so. But we're checking later.*

I'm a certain way about books. I get it. My useless undergraduate history degree was motivated in part from a deviant level of enjoyment in research. The near-apocalypse by misunderstanding I helped save the world from came from my love of books too, in a roundabout way: I accidentally bought a real grimoire for my family's escape room business, a cult showed up to steal it, then conjured Luke, prince of Hell (now my boyfriend), and chaos ensued.

Anyway, I always knew that one day I'd walk into a library, the *perfect* library, and it would instantly be my favorite place on Earth. All the other libraries I'd flirted with would just be warm-ups.

The Earth part turned out not to be true. But the warm-up part's truer than I ever imagined. Hell's library tried to drive me to madness the first time we met, but after a few weeks with open access, it feels almost like . . . home.

I turn and take it in for a breath. An actual breath, a deep inhale of old-book goodness. The stacks loom thirteen stories tall up to the domed ceiling mural of Lucifer presenting a book—aka access to knowledge—to a horde of falling angels. Typical Lucifer overstatement. The population of this library is usually low.

I have it to myself for the moment, though Luke should be here anytime. And, of course, there's the only person who the library truly loves back.

"Milady!" Porsoth says by way of greeting as he clicks in from the corridor. He's trotted out this overly formal hello the past couple of times I've been here.

"Just Callie. I'm not a lady. Well, I am, sort of, but you know what I mean."

"I do," Porsoth says. "I merely hold you in high esteem."

A month ago, having a conversation with an owl-faced, pig-bodied scholar of a demon would have been odd. Today, we're arguing etiquette.

"We're friends," I say. "Friends don't need to call each other fancy things."

That sets Porsoth back on his heels. I forget how sentimental he is. He stops and puts a wing with a small hand on the end to his breast. "Friends," he repeats. "Oh, milad—Callie. We are friends."

He has a suspicious shimmer like tears in his eyes. He's a good friend to have. Especially as I'm reminded that he can also be several stories tall with a frightening manner when he summons his more booming voice, "Agnes! Don't dawdle! *Callie* needs help with a book."

I know he's trying to be helpful, but Agnes hates being ordered around. Given that she's one of Hell's lost souls, a former human, she spends a lot of time grumpy.

Scowl in place, she stomps into the doorway in a tunic and boots. Her face is small and heart-shaped. Her dirty-blond pigtails droop. She's still an eleven-year-old girl, at least on the outside.

"I can get it myself," I say, and pluck volume 100 from its spot.

Agnes stalks over and puts her hands on it too. "Allow me."

"It's fine."

We have a brief tug-of-war, in which I *feel* about eleven. She has this effect.

Agnes glances down and sees what book it is. She lets go. "That my last chance? Good luck with that, *milady*."

Maybe I'm making it up, but I think I detect an emotion other than crankiness buried underneath the words. Besides sarcasm.

"Agnes, I meant what I said. I'm going to find a way. What happened to you is unfair—and Porsoth says you're far from alone."

"Most people would be grateful at such a generous attempt on their behalf," Porsoth says to Agnes.

"Perchance, I won't get my hopes up," Agnes says dramatically. "She's on the last book of rules and nothing. I am doomed to remain here. Hell is forever. You brought me here, you should know."

Porsoth's head dips. "I had no choice."

When I first met Agnes, it took me a few days to pull her story out of each of them. Agnes stole the illuminated Bible from her town's church, high up on the sin scale. "I wanted to spy the pictures up close! But girls weren't allowed!" she said, defiant, telling me about it. She promptly ran into the street and got mowed down by an ox cart. Yes, she essentially got hit by the equivalent of a bus in the Middle Ages. At the time, eleven was plenty old enough to be considered an adult—and so she came here, to Hell, by way of Porsoth. When he left his job torturing and assumed his current form, he brought her to the palace with him as a library assistant. She says it's just torture by another name. Bottom line is, even a demon understood she doesn't deserve eternal punishment.

And my idea of second chances for Agnes and people like her was born.

Porsoth says I'll never get anywhere with a new policy without a precedent to cite. A time when such a major change has occurred. I've been combing over the rules and regulations ever since, searching for something to help make our case.

Assuming Lucifer will even hear us out. But we'll cross that burning bridge when we come to it.

I feel like I might finally be about to find a purpose in life. Beyond dating Hell's most eligible bachelor. Porsoth says I've got fresh eyes from not being part of the system. And I've gotten the sense lately that Lucifer might even be the tiniest bit pleased with Luke's new, somewhat more focused approach to the afterlife—and that maybe he's impressed with my not seeming (too) afraid of the devil. This formerly aimless book-worm is starting to have *plans*.

I settle into a leather chair that looks severe and straight-backed, but is surprisingly comfortable, with the volume. Por-soth sends Agnes for tea and she returns with a tray for him alone. I don't take it personally.

I've gotten used to the way these books are constructed, and I can afford to skim. They aren't written by any one wraith, but linked to Lucifer's will and changed automatically whenever he adds or—I'm praying—takes away or changes an operating principle. So far the text has been additions. I'm about halfway through the book when I sigh and lean my head back against the chair, frustrated.

Hands cover my eyes gently. I inhale a scent even sexier than old books. Luke. With a grin, I slide my fingers up Luke's arms and tug away his makeshift blindfold. I stare up into his impossi-bly handsome face, crowned with a shock of tousled blond hair. His blue eyes nearly make me forget we have an audience.

He seems to get more gorgeous with every passing day. It's seriously insulting.

Or it's because you've fallen in love with him. But we haven't said *that* yet. Neither of us.

"How long have you been here?" I ask.

An affectionate smile plays at the edges of his mouth.

"Watching you read? A while," he says. The smile grows lazy, flirty. "It is *one* of my favorite hobbies."

I fight a blush. "How'd you keep Agnes from tipping me off?"

We look over and she holds up half a cupcake from the kitchens. "Bribery," she says around a mouthful.

"I take it you've had no luck?"

Luke assures me he's behind my idea all the way, but he pitches in on the reading lightly at best. I suspect this talk of souls and redemptions hits close for him. He admitted to me the other day that he's still not sure what *his* having a soul means. Long-term. I'm not sure he believes he has the ability to change, that his demonic nature doesn't define him.

"I told her it was a fool's errand," Agnes says.

"But Callie doesn't give up because someone tells her to," Luke says. "It's one of the—first things I learned about her."

Was he about to say something else? I search his eyes, but his expression is back to contained beauty.

"Lucky for *you*—" I say to Luke, and then to pouty Agnes with chocolate frosting on her cheek. "And it will be for you too."

I go back to skimming my book and the next two pages are more new rules. And then.

Then I nearly stop breathing as I turn a page and see one single heading, followed by a long list afterward. I decide it might be the most beautiful word in the English language:

AMENDMENTS

My finger trembles as I run it down the list and confirm that I'm right. A date followed by the adjustment to an existing rule: 1327, no consumption of human flesh on Earth, it spreads disease (Black Plague era, well, duh); 1684, changing a lake of blood to a lake of vomit for the torture of the particularly squeamish (gross); 1908, the exact punishment of damned souls taken under the age of fifteen will be considered on a case-by-case basis (wait a second!).

"Porsoth," I try to keep my voice level, "when did you move to the Gray Keep with Agnes?"

"Ah, I believe in your time, it would have been in the early 1900s," he says, and presses his glasses up his beak.

"Could it have been 1908?"

"Yes, I believe so. Why?"

"There was a rule change then to allow it. Why didn't you tell me?"

Porsoth blinks. "I had no idea."

Aha. Because no one reads these books but me. Lucifer had to allow Porsoth to bend the rules, and, as usual, he didn't bother to tell anyone.

I think through what this means. There's already been an exception made related to Agnes, that included other children. The reminder of the other children in Hell—like Agnes, taken during times when they would've been considered adults or close enough—would be enough to convince me this is something we *have* to make happen. Porsoth says the damned can't just be released. But I can argue that this rule should be expanded for *all* the damned who deserve case-by-case treatment. All who could be worthy of a second chance.

"I found it," I say. "The precedent is Agnes."

I vault out of the chair and Luke moves fast enough to catch me in his arms. "What? Obviously, I mean of course you did. I knew you would."

"Nice try," I say, but my entire body feels like it's floating. *I found it.*

"Me?" Agnes's skepticism is unsurprising.

I squeeze Luke. "Yes! We're going to save—all the people we need to save! Porsoth, you've made this possible, by bringing Agnes here, and you didn't even know!"

Porsoth puts his hand to his breast, astonished.

Luke spins me around, and we both laugh. Though I can tell there's a nervousness to his.

"What's wrong?" I ask.

The spinning slows. "We still need Father's approval."

He's right. Too soon to celebrate. But . . .

"Don't worry," he says. "You want this. I'll secure an audience with him."

"Prince," Porsoth says, "be careful of overpromising."

Luke raises his eyebrows. "I'm not."

"I believe him," Agnes says. Why do I never get this confidence from her? Because she adores Luke, that's why.

Luke leans in closer, speaks into my ear. "I'll go see Rofocale right now."

"We can do this, right?" I ask it, low, just for us, not our eavesdroppers.

"Yes. You can do anything." He rubs his cheek against mine, probably to distract me from the fact he didn't say *we* can.

I'll have to prove it to him. I'm willing to do the work.

The work.

Oh no. I suddenly realize I wasn't supposed to be here all day. Luke was late, and I got absorbed in saving the underworld (some of it) and . . . "Does anyone know what time it is back home? On Earth?"

"Nine of the clock," Porsoth says.

Crap. I start for the door. I'm an hour late to the Great Escape. I'm supposed to help Mom prep for a weekend-long citywide game—our first venture outside the business's physical space—themed as Good vs. Evil. A tie-in capitalizing on the near-apocalypse that most people think was a mass hallucination. But surely she'll understand?

"Let me know what happens," I say. "You got this."

"I should see you home first," Luke says.

I can move freely between Hell and Earth, using Luke's handkerchief, through one specific entrance behind the business. It's an unusual arrangement, but it doesn't seem to have any side effects like the zappity variety of travel did.

"No, you go use your charm. And if that doesn't work, play the prince-and-heir card. I'll see you later." I can't keep my excitement from showing. I press my lips to his—wishing I had time to linger, amazed that I can kiss him casually, just because I feel like it—and then go.

We're close. We might actually do this.

Change Hell forever.

CHAPTER TWO

LUKE

As soon as Callie's gone, Porsoth clicks his tongue in his beak in concern.

"I know you'll give me that look until I hear you out, so go on." I motion that he has the floor. "What's got you so worried? I thought you were encouraging Callie on this."

My tutor rises. "I am, of course, in awe of what Callie has achieved. Her vision and education about our kingdom in such a short time are breathtaking to behold . . ."

He doesn't need to remind me. I admire her dedication more than I could express. But I admit I've been longing for more time for us to learn each other. "What's the 'but'?"

"But your father can be, as you know . . ." Porsoth crosses the dark library marble. "I'm afraid an audience might be premature and provoke him to plot against you. The two of you. You know how he feels about loyalty." He lowers his voice. "She challenges yours to him."

The suggestion I have any loyalty to Father, after he was ready to unmake me weeks ago for not living up to his low standards—that's rich. "He's probably plotting against us already."

Porsoth sways from side to side.

"He is, isn't he?" Of course. How did I not assume this? "Maybe we'll throw him off. Distract him."

Porsoth mumbles something and examines a bookshelf as if it's the most interesting thing in the entire universe.

With my enhanced senses, I believe I understand, but I make him say it again. "You'll have to speak up."

"He already knows. About the idea."

I take this in. "How?"

"Occasionally Rofocale and I have tea. I told him I expected discretion, but I'm afraid . . ."

"You expected discretion from Rofocale and you're lecturing me on what Father's capable of?" Rofocale is my supervisor, technically. For now. He's Father's second-in-command. "Cheeky. Looks like the student has surpassed the teacher on reading the room."

"I just worry, Prince."

Agnes has her arms crossed. She's been quietly watching our exchange up till now. "Am I hearing this right? Are you truly discussing whether it's worth pissing off the devil for a chance at my freedom?"

Unlike most denizens of Hell who'd consider avoiding Father's wrath top priority, Agnes is peeved.

"It's politics, my dear." Porsoth flutters his hands. "You know we value you."

"I have no interest in politics," I say.

Agnes snorts.

"What?"

"You're a prince. You *are* politics." She immediately gapes like she wants to take back the words. Then, "I speak out of turn."

"You're not going to get in trouble with me for that—" I give Porsoth a look. "Or him. How can I not try for this audience when Callie has so passionately combed through the archives? When Agnes might get to return to Earth?"

"I fear for you," Porsoth says. "For all of us."

I fear he's correct to. The same way *I* fear that when Callie realizes who I really am—soul or no soul—and understands the true nature of this place . . . I fear I will lose her.

"You're supposed to be fighting that impulse," I say. "So fight the fear. Or don't. This is our project."

"Is it?" Agnes slips the question in like a dagger. "Or is she your project?"

"The distinction doesn't matter. I'll do what I promised her. We *will* have an audience with Father."

I'm no fool, though. Before I call upon Rofocale, I send an urgent message to Mother through a demon messenger. Then, I go to my chambers and wait for her to arrive.

My mother swans into the entrance of my apartments precisely half an hour later, which means she's invested in this. Otherwise, she'd have taken her unsweet time, as is her usual way.

Her black skirts swirl around her, her hair an unruly tangle, her face a goth masterpiece. "Is it true? You're ready to take the concept to your father?"

"Yes, but you know I'll need your help. Rofocale will need convincing to even ask him."

Mother grins. "Let me handle him."

I don't point out that's the entire reason I sent for her.

"I'm impressed Callie has gotten this far. Do you think it can work?" Mother asks. She has her own opinions, always, so she's fishing for a glimpse at my inner workings. My parents are exhausting.

But Callie and Lilith have developed something like a grudging mutual admiration society. I suspect because Callie saved my life. My mother may not be sentimental, but she likes—all right, loves, in her unique way—me enough to be pleased I still exist.

"Father is too unpredictable to say. I'm afraid she doesn't realize how unlikely it is he'll go for any of this."

Mother presses her lips together. "No, I was asking about the concept itself. Do you believe these people will prove themselves worthy of redemption? If given the chance?"

"Callie believes so."

"And you? Do you want to do this?"

"Yes." Or, at least, I hope I can. If second chances are possible, if humans can become better, avoid their past mistakes—perhaps I can too. Perhaps I can have a life of my own choosing.

"Let's go then," Mother says with a practically ravenous smile.

I link my arm through hers and we make our way from my quarters to Rofocale's office in the working wing of the Gray Keep. If he's not at Father's side, this is where he's most often found—hard at work in the large, over-warm stone room. Where Callie's passion makes observing her at a task into a wonder, Rofocale's foul humor makes watching him a torture all its own.

With scaly gray skin, he's in one of his usual flashy tailored suits, scratching away with his bone pen in the hide-bound ledger on his enormous wooden desk. He sees me first and the curl of distaste on his face is delicious. Even more so when he discovers Mother is with me.

Rofocale hops to his feet and sweeps into a bow. "To what do I owe this honor?"

I can't resist poking at him. "Now this is how a prince should be greeted. Thank you. You're finally understanding the hierarchy."

He frowns, red pupils glowing. "You know that I was not referring to you—"

Lilith raises a hand. "I'm here on my son's behalf. I need you to help him. I would consider it a personal favor."

The strain on Rofocale's face is magnificent. Truly.

Mother keeps her hungriest smile trained on him. She isn't a legendary witch and vanquisher of men for nothing. Rofocale raises his hand to the back of his neck, as if he's hot under the collar. Is he fidgeting?

I have to bite back laughter. "You wouldn't disappoint my dear mother, would you?"

Rofocale remembers I'm here. He speaks carefully. "What is the cause?"

"I understand from Porsoth that you know what it's about. We're ready for our audience with Father."

A burst of heat is our only warning before Father, Lucifer Morningstar himself, strides into the room, his gray-tipped white wings nearly as wide as the span of it.

"You require an audience with me, my boy?" he says.

His icy gaze drifts between Rofocale and my mother. My parents haven't been an item for as far back as I can remember, but they do have a strange bond.

Mother raises her eyebrows to him, but doesn't curtsey. *Mother, you're supposed to be helping.*

Rofocale has gotten better control of his reflexive flirting. "Sire, I was just about to tell them that you would need time to consider your schedule and—"

"Proceed," Father says. "I'm here."

Oh, he's the worst. Can't say that, though.

"I need an audience for Callie *and* myself. We have an idea to present. Together."

A slow smile crosses Father's face. "Done," he says. "Shall we say . . . Saturday? Hangman's noon?"

That was far too easy. Lilith and Rofocale's expressions confirm they think the exact same thing. What's he up to? It doesn't matter. There's only one possible answer.

"We'll see you then." For Callie's sake, I add, "Father . . . thank you."

"My pleasure."

Well, that's never good.

I brace myself before I leave to go see Callie. I know she'll either be waiting up or spending a sleepless night wondering. The only kind of sleepless night I want her to have is with me. But we haven't taken that step yet, because I'd never rush her.

I'll wait until she's ready, and die a little every time I have to stop touching her.

No, it's not her I'm dreading. She said she was working late with her mom.

At first, her mom seemed to be on board with the whole concept of me. Lately, I get the distinct feeling that is ceasing to be the case. I can't truly blame her. I'm not *good* enough for Callie, that much is plain.

That I don't care and want her anyway is more proof.

I let my mind's eye find Callie, and then I zappity into the control room at her family's escape room business.

Monitors and workstations line one wall. Callie is on the floor in front of them, surrounded by envelopes and sheets of paper. Alone.

I keep my sigh of relief inside.

"I come bearing good news," I say.

She peers up at me without the joy I'd expect. "I could use some."

I reach a hand out to her and she sets aside her papers. I pull her to her feet and she nestles her head under my chin against my chest. She keeps her hand in mine. The contact feels so good, so right, I don't dare move except to ask, "What's wrong?"

"I was late."

"Yes."

"Mom was already gone. Left me a note about what to do. It was very 'not mad, just disappointed.' I'm screwing things up here."

Ah. "I've screwed up far more things than you could ever begin to. She'll understand." I pause. "Besides you have a few days to concentrate on things here before . . ."

She pushes back a bit, shaking her head at my tease. The hint of a smile appears. I made her feel better. I give myself a gold star.

"Before?" she asks.

"We meet with my father on Saturday. One p.m. sharp."

"He agreed? Already?"

I decide not to tell her that might not be such a positive sign. "It'll still be an uphill climb over burning mountains to get him to say yes to the ask. But he did."

Callie's smile widens and . . . changes. "I have an idea," she says.

"Really?" I say in a mockery of being shocked. "You? An idea? Never."

"Very funny," she says. "I know I've been spending . . . a lot of time on this." She holds up her hand before I can say anything. "A hundred books can't read themselves. But, uh, what if we spend the whole day together? A big date after the audience."

Her ears are scarlet. That's her tell when she's embarrassed or interested, or both. I'm too on the edge of my proverbial seat to say anything.

"And then, you know, I could stay over." She hesitates. "If you want."

I settle my pulse as best I can. She hasn't yet spent the night. "I want. Oh, I want."

As I pull her in close and press my lips to hers, we greedily melt into each other and it's a preview of what's to come.

Yes, Callie Johnson, I want you. Forever. I only wish I deserved it.

ANOTHER 48-72 HOURS
(AND UNTOLD MILLENNIA)
ON THE CLOCK

DAY ONE

A HOT DATE

"When I used to read fairy-tales, I fancied that kind of thing never happened, and now here I am in the middle of one!"

ALICE'S ADVENTURES IN WONDERLAND, LEWIS CARROLL

Hell is empty,
And all the devils are here.

THE TEMPEST, WILLIAM SHAKESPEARE

CHAPTER THREE

CALLIE

On Saturday morning, I stand at the edge of the counter and do everything but a tap dance. My arms are folded, body tight with tension. My posture screams, "I have to get going—you KNOW this," and yet my mother is taking her precious time photographing the group of four teenage girls who just successfully completed the Chamber of Black Magic in front of the lock-shaped metal GREAT ESCAPE sign to post on our social media.

We do it with everyone who manages to beat our escape rooms in sixty minutes or less. And I'll give her one thing: they are cute.

Meanwhile, my brother, Jared, and best friend forever, Mag, are holding back my freckle-nosed dog, Bosch, and our knob-kneed fainting pygmy goat, Cupcake—it's a long story, he used to be a human cult leader—so they don't crash the photo.

A girl with deeply cool oversized glasses asks, "But can't they be in it too?"

Little did we know that Cupcake would turn moderately famous and bring in new customers enchanted by the magical friendship between him and my rescue pup. Mom nods. Jared and Mag both shoot me apologetic looks and release the creatures. Who canter over and, I swear, strike poses.

It's adorable, as are the squeals of the girls, but I still want to growl with frustration. Today is the day. Our audience with Lucifer, followed by a big date. Not the stuff legendary dates are usually made of, except this time I'm hoping it is.

And I've spent the last three days working nonstop here. Which means I'm more eager than ever to get to Hell to see Luke.

The girls finally finish the photo op, and drop to pat an appreciative Bosch and Cupcake.

"All right, gang, I need to get moving," I say, as sanguine as possible.

My mom gives me a look that lets me know she's fully aware and refusing to hurry. The other day she came this close to questioning what kind of future I could have with a demonic crown prince.

It's not like I haven't caught myself wondering the same thing. But . . . then I firmly cross back into denying-it's-a-problem land.

"I'm going no matter what," I add. I'm not about to miss this chance. I can only imagine what it must have cost Luke to arrange it. And then there's Agnes.

My words apparently get through. Mom nods to Jared and Mag again, who surge forward to keep Bosch and Cupcake clear as she herds the customers to the front door and out.

After she waves good-bye, she turns to me.

"You know you are scheduled to work here today?" she asks, leveling a carefully neutral expression at me. "Even with the extra folks I'm bringing in, I need you."

At twenty-two years old, the effects of disappointing my mother should be waning, but, alas, her guilting still works gangbusters. Yes, I spaced that I was working on Saturday when Luke secured the audience.

"I promise I'll be back in time to work our station. With Luke in tow." A weird date all around, but that's us.

I glance at Jared and Mag for support. Jared is so clean-cut his polo and jeans might as well be a uniform, and Mag is dressed in their usual casual weekend flare in glittery lip stain, swirly Doc Martens, and a rainbow T-shirt that says Y'ALL MEANS ALL.

Mag chimes in to answer Mom. "We're here to help," they say. "It'll be fine."

Jared loops his arm around Mag. The two simply work as a couple, despite their surface differences. Not that I understood that right away. At first, the two of them dating freaked me all the way out, mainly because they kept it secret from me.

"This is to make up for the repair bills, you know." Mom has a small frown.

Jared coughs. "Did Mom tell you we helped her write the clues?"

Mag can't keep in a laugh. I could hug them both for the distraction attempt.

"You're all so funny," I say. "I can't wait to see how specifically the mockery targets me."

"Oh, and Luke too," Mag says, still laughing. "The answer is very."

"Wonderful." I shake my head. "But I really do have to go."

"Good luck," Mag says.

Mom cuts in. "I hate to say this, Cal. But this is your job. This is a big day for us."

The mood in the room changes in an instant. Her face is as serious as when they killed off Wash in the *Firefly* movie.

I should've helped more than just the past few days. Instead I was busy inhaling Hell's library. In my defense, I've been catching up on millennia of history normally forbidden to mortals in an attempt to change it. But suddenly I feel like the crappiest daughter and employee of all time.

"Callie, say something," Mom says.

My mind whirs at top speed. We're a tight-knit family unit, always have been, and I know everything she does comes from a place of love. And anxiety for me.

I've admittedly been a mess ever since I graduated and discovered no jobs exist for history majors. Pitching in at the business is the one thing I've always done well. Now I'm making a mess of that too. But my relationship with Luke, the possibilities that have opened up . . . I can't turn my back on them either.

"I have to go," I say. "Luke's waiting. I *promise* I'll be back as fast as I can . . . I'm sorry."

She leans in to hug me. "It's not you I doubt," she says in my ear. "It's the devil."

"Fair," I tell her.

I release Mom, scratch Bosch and Cupcake each behind their fuzzy ears, wave to quiet, sympathetic Jared and Mag, and then I leave.

I make my way around the back of our building to where there's a new, permanent long rivulet of water running down the alley. As I stride along it, I reach into my jacket pocket and pull out the handkerchief with the monogrammed initials L. A. M.

Luke Astaroth Morningstar.

In a few more feet, a large gate made of knobby, charred bones emerges out of sudden mist. If only we had special effects that looked this good at the business. Not that ours aren't great, they are. But this gate *is* real. When I reach it, I cover the back of my hand in the cloth and trace the solid lock made of finger bones linked with brass.

The gate creaks open. I step through—

And almost barrel into Luke's solid chest, where he stands waiting for me.

My body transforms to electrified anticipation between one heartbeat and the next.

While I know technically my blood still pumps at roughly 3 to 4 mph, walking speed, just like anyone else's, it doesn't feel that way. Right now I'd clock mine at more of a sprint.

Luke's insanely handsome face lights from a fire within when he sees me. He reaches out like he *needs* to touch me to be sure I'm really here and settles a hand on my shoulder.

"Am I late?" I ask.

"Never," he says, and gently tugs on the end of a strand of my hair. "I just couldn't wait to see you."

His hand slips around the back of my neck and we exchange a soft kiss, a simple touch of lips on lips that deepens into something that could get out of hand in moments. Am I on fire or is the prince of Hell just happy to see me? I could swear *I'm* burning from the inside out. Melting, even. It's hard to remember what I'm here for.

Oh right, it's this.

Us.

We're an us. A new, fragile us.

I push back. *Can* this work out? I keep asking myself the question, even though Luke and I are good together. This feels right.

I want to blurt out the news that Mom is even more upset with me. That it's time for me to finally get my act together. I shouldn't even still be living at home. I'm *twenty-two*. But . . . then he'll want to talk it out or race back home reporting for duty. Something has to happen right today.

Luke tilts his head in question. "I must be losing my touch. I can see the wheels turning in your head. What about?"

That obvious, huh? It's like he can read my mind. (Thanks to the universe, he can't do that. No demon or angel can.)

"Nothing." I reach down for his hand. "We should go. We can't keep your dad waiting."

Luke lifts one shoulder in elegant fashion, folding both his hands around mine. "You're technically incorrect. We could keep him waiting for hours. I'm sure I could find a way to entertain you."

My mouth goes dry. *Yes, please.*

I manage to say, "We have to get back for the big game."

"As *usual*"—he draws it out, grin widening—"you're right on the metaphorical money. We should go."

I roll my eyes at him. "Charmer."

"So they tell me." He drops his lips softly to my cheek, which basically combusts in response, then puts his hand into mine. "You're sure everything is okay?" he asks. "You're not nervous about today?"

"Of course not," I lie. I plan to stay with Luke. All night. For the first time. Oh, wait, he probably meant about proposing a huge change in Hell's protocols to his dad. It's a yes to both.

He accepts my answer and we pick our way across the charred landscape of bushes with vicious thorns. They now part for us and avoid sticking me like they do Luke; since they're familiar with me they no longer view me as torture-bait.

After a short stretch, we reach the chasm that separates the giant tree-shaped castle known as the Gray Keep, the heart of Hell, from the rest of it. I can't deny that even though traveling here has become slightly familiar, the castle never fails to impress. The stories those walls could tell . . .

I'm glad they can't speak.

"Let our big date begin," Luke says.

He waves his fingers and a bridge forms and drops from what was solid stone moments before and we walk inside the shadowed entrance.

Flickering candles against obsidian stone create the perfect ambiance for the kingdom's brooding master, Lucifer. We make it halfway up the first dark, empty corridor before a familiar clatter of hooves rushes out of the library to meet us. Agnes follows, her expression unreadable.

"Are you two prepared for the meeting?" Porsoth hurries to catch up to us and then continues speaking without waiting for an answer. "You realize this would be unprecedented." Porsoth makes a worried *tsk*ing noise. "I'm not sure it's possible, that kind of permission from him."

Luke snaps his fingers. "You're supposed to be on our side."

"Oh, right!" Porsoth flutters his wings and the hands at the ends of them. "Pardon. My apologies, master! I am!"

Luke winks at me. "It's okay."

Porsoth lets out an audible breath, relieved.

"Wings out, Prince," Porsoth says as we approach the wide entrance to the throne room. "It reminds him how far you've come."

In a blink, ebony wings stretch tall from Luke's back. I'll never get so used to his wings they don't inspire awe. They're stunning. They catch shadows as well as light, gleaming like a beautiful oil spill filled with rainbows even in the dim castle. He folds them in close behind him so we can continue up the baroque nightmare corridor.

"And Callie," Porsoth says, "I'm not asking you to be meek, but could you be a smidgen meeker? You and I may not stand on ceremony—as dear friends—"

I bite the inside of my cheek lightly to keep from laughing. We've gone from friends to dear friends like that.

"But the sire does very much like it when people seem afraid of him. You'll try?"

"I'll do my best." I turn to Agnes. "We're going to convince him. I swear to you."

Agnes shrugs.

In reality, Lucifer terrifies me. I'm only human. But the way Lucifer whips out his overblown masculinity and plays the bully with Luke makes me never want to give an inch in his presence. I also have a theory it's why he seems to semi-respect me.

Or maybe I'm fooling myself.

"You should also remember that he has eons of experience manipulating . . . er, mortals," Porsoth says.

"Thanks, Porsoth, got it." *Live human walking.*

"Hey," Luke says, sensing my change in mood. He squeezes my fingers lightly in his. "This is going to be a good day."

Luke can be distracted by his own good looks. I count on it. I admire his wings. "You're cute."

"Cute?" he sounds scandalized. "Cute is what Cupcake is. Cute is what kittens are. Cute is . . . an apple-cheeked cherub. I am . . ."

I smile at him. "If you say it, then you're definitely not . . ."

"Smoking hot," he says, and extends his other hand with a, yes, smoking ball of flame hovering above it.

"Show-off," I say.

He lifts a lazy shoulder and then tosses the ball of fire from one hand to the other. "If you've got it, flaunt it."

I consider my options and reach a hand around the ball of fire, going for his rib cage. Time to find out if Luke is ticklish.

"Luke, Callie." Porsoth's tone is a warning.

"Playing games, I see," Lucifer says.

The warning was too late. Lucifer appears beside us, next to the entrance. His wings take up every inch of space, blocking our view of the hall behind him. His brows are lifted above his ice-chip eyes.

This would be the *one* time he decides to enter the throne room from the main doorway. I wonder how much he's overheard. The problem with having bluffed that this immortal being doesn't scare me is that I have to stick to pretending it's true in public.

"Father," Luke says, recovering and getting rid of the flame.

I straighten and do my best to get my voice to sound casual. "Lucifer."

"Shall we?" Lucifer gestures.

He's reminding me of my position in relation to him.

Thanks to Porsoth's lessons, I know enough to drop to a knee instead of taking the bait and entering in front of him. He's the one playing games.

What a good omen for the conversation we're about to have. Sarcasm alert.

CHAPTER FOUR

LUKE

When Callie arrived, she was in prime distraction mode and acting like she wasn't. I know she's all in on this plan, so the logical conclusion is that she's having doubts about our relationship.

Now I'm the nervous one. Father showing up like he did is not a good sign. To say the absolute least. Hopefully even if Father says no (as he almost certainly will), it won't ruin the rest of our day. And night.

"After you," I say to Callie, doing my best to conceal my nerves. I sweep a hand to the grand arch carved with frolicking demons.

Callie hesitates only briefly before she enters Father's den.

I pause for a second and reflect on how different this feels from my many previous times in Father's throne room. This time I'm not being summoned by my lonesome. Not being dragged in to be informed of all the ways I am a disappointment or of my desperate need to plumb greater depths of evil or face an unmaking. Even the last time I was here with Callie it wasn't an unfortunate accident on my part that we bumped into him, but his design.

This time not only am I not alone, I'm not lonely. I asked to come here.

Getting to know Callie is changing me, *challenging* me, and that scares me. Maybe more than I'm scared of Father.

But I'm also grateful. And I'll never say any of this to her. How seductive would it be to know someone is fawning over you? Telling you that you've *changed* them for the better?

No. Way.

I need to show her that there's more to this place and me (and, frankly, to show myself). But it turns out a lifelong habit of hedging my bets isn't so easy to shrug off.

Porsoth fidgets. His usual state is extreme worry. "Should we wait for your mother?"

Mother is not known for being punctual. She'll be here when she intends to.

"No, better not."

"Then go on before Callie makes him angry," Porsoth says quietly. "Crack some skulls." The phrase is Hell's equivalent of *break a leg*.

I tug my leather jacket the tiniest bit crooked and saunter in to join Callie.

She swallows when she meets my eyes. This I'm certain of, our physical chemistry. Sauntering is a devastating look on me.

I gaze back at her, the reason I'm here risking Father's wrath. Those vibrant stormy eyes, a lift of that determined chin. Her presence steadies me.

Father sits on his ostentatiously large obsidian throne, wings thrust out wide on either side, his knees sprawled open in the way that drives Callie up the proverbial wall. Thin gray light streams in through the tall windows with stained-glass portraits of demons slaughtering angels. The tactical table Father uses to represent our forces, the Above's, and humanity languishes in one corner. It hasn't seen that much action since the near-Armageddon Callie and I thwarted.

Father still isn't aware how close I got to archangel Michael and the pearly gates. That I held the Holy Lance and survived. Or is he? It's hard for me to believe his spies wouldn't have gathered every scrap of intelligence they could for him. In truth, I wouldn't be surprised to learn that he and Michael secretly play chess every Tuesday at midnight. Father is nothing if not unpredictable.

Porsoth click-clacks in. He and Agnes take a spot behind Callie and me. Once we're assembled Callie hesitates, then opens her mouth to speak.

Father lifts his left hand and commands: "Wait."

She closes her mouth with a grimace. I give her what I hope is a "hang in there" look.

We wait.

And wait.

Eventually, after staring at Father and likewise for too long for comfort, my mother breezes in witchily on Rofocale's arm.

Father studies the two of them, and Rofocale drops Mother's arm as if he's been scorched by it. *How interesting.*

She comes to me, ignoring Father, and lifts her hand. I kiss it and say, "Mother, you're looking beautiful enough to bewitch any human or demon, and also right on time."

"Am I late?" she counters with a bat of her kohl-rimmed eyes that tells me she knows precisely how far past the appointed hour her arrival is. "Rofocale and I got to talking about old times."

She tosses Rofocale a sultry look over her shoulder and he shifts uncomfortably from foot to foot. He's in an overly slick black suit, looking like Hell's version of an investment banker or maybe an administrator in the "Church" of Scientology.

"About what old times?" Lucifer asks, voice chilly as the grave. He's possessive to the core.

"Oh, all about the boy," Mother says dismissively. "Of course."

Father's lips gather and then he smiles at her. Mother preens.

"*Our* boy," he says, "is a man now. And so he has come to present us with his first idea for the realm. And brought his consort along."

Nice way to help me out, Father.

"Consort's a little old-fashioned," I say. Not to mention we haven't precisely consorted yet.

"Are you going to present this scheme of yours to me or not?" he counters.

I hesitate and Callie gives me an encouraging smile. Here goes . . . my heart.

"As you know, the customs of soul-gathering are well established . . ." I should have practiced this. I don't know how to say it. "You have always said understanding humans should be among our goals and . . ." I check in with Callie and see her brow crease in concern.

"If you want something, you must ask for it," Father says.

He's right. It's now or—

"We're here because we want your approval to try something." Callie blurts it. "Something revolutionary."

Father's lips quirk to one side. He lifts a brow at me. *Am I going to let her speak for me?*

He gives me my moment to object, which I don't, then waves. "Okay, I'm prepared to have my mind blown. Proceed."

Rofocale has his brows raised at me too, but snorts at Father's humor. Father shoots him a quelling glance. Agnes has her hands clasped in front of her, studying the floor. Porsoth shifts from hoof to hoof, as nervous as Callie must be. As nervous as I am. It takes all my effort to not show it outwardly.

Mother crosses her arms, and I'm mostly with her. This is a disaster.

But Callie, as Callie does, seizes her moment. "I've been learning about the kingdom . . . your kingdom . . . from Porsoth and Luke. And then I met Agnes."

"Agnes?" Lucifer asks, though he certainly knows exactly who she is.

"Agnes, Porsoth's library assistant." Callie looks over her shoulder at Agnes, and then back. "A damned soul. How can it be that an eleven-year-old is stuck in Hell? I began to ask how exactly people end up here. Not all of them. Obviously I know for murderers, thieves, the worst. But what about people who *might* change if given the chance? Or the only kind-of bad people? Who make a bad decision in the heat of the moment and then die suddenly, like Agnes? The ones who make a mistake and lose their soul, because they're convinced to?"

"Our entire business model, you mean," Lucifer says.

Callie lets that pass. "Once Luke told me that the reason he had trouble with taking souls is because the real offense for most of the inhabitants here—"

I cough because I didn't realize this would ever be aired with my father. His eyes have narrowed.

"Some of them anyway," Callie says, "is just that they're human. The whole system—the business model—doesn't seem fair."

Lucifer is stone-faced.

"I've found evidence that you have changed procedures in the past. There's an entire section of amendments in *Being the Rules of the Kingdom of Hell, Vol. 100* and—"

"Someone's been studying," Rofocale says with irony.

"And one of them related to Agnes herself. You allowed Porsoth to tailor her punishment. Why not expand that rule so that she and others like her can have a second chance?"

Father stays quiet.

"Lucifer, king of Hell," Callie says, and gestures at everything around us. "I know you're not afraid of change. You didn't start out here."

She's invoked the fall. The thing Father hates most is any implication that his current state is worse than Before, when he served his own Father. The one Above.

"I might then remind you," Father says, "that it was not me who created the hierarchies between humans and celestial beings. The rules were mostly established by then. We play within them."

"But you also help create and enforce them," Callie says.

Father steeples his fingers and leans forward. "Your idea is that we stop enforcing them? You've been here for a month and you're proposing we stop competing for souls and let bad people float in the void instead of having any afterlife at all? Interesting. I didn't realize you had this cruel streak."

Callie's mouth has dropped open. "No, that's not—is that—"

"Very funny, Father," I say, stepping in. "I know Rofocale told you about this idea. It could work."

Father nods. "And you agree with this plan? You want to do this?"

Callie is confused. "Why wouldn't he?"

"I'm with Callie." I redirect my attention to a smug, smirking Father. I've heard Callie talk about this enough that, now I think about it, outlining her plan is easy. "We simply want the ability to select a few test cases—starting with Agnes—and return them to Earth and see if they might have a different outcome, soul-wise. They'll remember their time here but be unable to speak of it. We'll monitor them carefully."

"To what end?" he asks. "That's what I don't understand."

"Fairness," Callie says. "Giving them a second chance. Adding a little fairness to the universe."

"Adding a little fairness to the universe." Father rolls the words over his tongue. I can't tell, but he might be considering this. That surprises me. In truth, I'm not sure *I* believe that it's possible.

Callie has so much faith. I wish I could borrow some. So I am, by supporting her. She wants this and I don't know what I want—besides her. The combination was a good enough reason for me.

"What if fairness is the one thing the universe can't withstand?" Father asks. "It's not something Above was very good at including in the so-called intelligent design."

"Let's keep this focused," Callie says. "We're asking for a simple experiment, to prove this can work."

Father looks down his nose at her. "What if your idea is

unfair at its premise? How is it fair for you to give some second chances and not others? How do you know who's capable of this possible redemption and who isn't?"

Callie squares her shoulders. "Well, I—"

Father cuts her off. "I can't help but feel you asking me for this experiment and me simply granting permission for something that's such a fundamental upheaval of our ways isn't fair at all either. But I will allow this to proceed. On my terms."

"Which are?" I ask.

Father ignores that part. "To prove to me how committed to this idea you are, how serious about it *both* of you are, I'm going to ask you to prove it can work by showing me a particular soul can be redeemed. You'll have your experiment, if you can. Do you agree to these terms?"

He's so pleased with himself. Every shadow in the room seems to creep toward me.

Callie looks at me. I want to say *No. No way. We should leave.*

She gives me the slightest nod, a request. I could say no to Father, but I can't say no to her.

I close my eyes rather than see Father's face switch to gloating. We're waltzing into a trap. I'm certain of it.

"Fine," I say.

Callie drops her hand into mine and it's almost worth it, whatever nightmare he's cooked up for us in the burning fires of his mind.

"Excellent," Father says. "I want you each to fully understand the ecosystem you're proposing to throw out of balance. To understand the difficulty of truly reforming someone. To answer the age-old question of whether some people are simply incompatible . . . with redemption."

Porsoth raises a wing and blurts, "Sire, if I may—why not let them begin with the young lady—"

"Would that be better than the person I've chosen?" Father asks.

Porsoth stumbles. "Sire . . ."

The throne room goes quiet.

"Who is it?" I venture. We might as well get this over with, see how bad it is.

Father glances at Rofocale. "Bring him forth."

Rofocale's lips split in a wide grin. He lifts his hand and snaps his fingers, emitting a puff of smoke.

Or not. The smoke emerges from the back of the chamber, where a fiery seam opens in the floor and a rush of heat fills the room. Two small, round, pointy-winged demons are flying a man out of it, each holding an arm. His face and ragged jeans are streaked with soot, sweat running down his cheeks. His broad, muscled chest is covered in a tattered black T-shirt.

He's not my type, but even I recognize that he's somehow making the look work. The look of being fresh from torture and carted around by demons.

Callie's mouth has fallen slightly open.

The demons drop him unceremoniously on the floor in front of us. Rofocale lifts his chin and they depart, smoking seam closing behind them. Lilith fans herself, despite the heat having dissipated.

"Who is he—a missing Hemsworth brother?" Callie asks.

The man in question stands and scans his new surroundings. He winks at Callie and speaks in a posh British accent. "They wish."

"Meet Sean Tattersall, a man known by many names," Lucifer says.

Sean opens his mouth to speak and Lucifer raises his hand. No sound emerges from this Sean's lips. I find I can't access basic information about him, a bit of editing on Father's part to make this more difficult, no doubt.

"Sire . . ." Porsoth manages nothing else.

"What good is a test if it's not a difficult one?" Lucifer asks.

He focuses in on this Sean character. I don't like how Sean is staring at Callie. His lips curve knowingly and I want to punch him. I've never liked the idea of punching someone before.

Callie slips her hand gently from mine and stops staring back at our mark.

"So," Callie says, "you're setting us up to fail?"

"Think of how many souls you might save if you succeed," Lucifer says. "How much fairness you might create?" He lets that sink in. "Do we have a deal or not?"

Callie says, "But it seems so . . . unfair. For you to pick."

"You have no idea," I say under my breath. This is bad news. I can feel it.

"There's just not much fairness in the universe right now," Father says. "Sorry. Take it or leave it. You have ten seconds to decide."

"We'll take it," she says immediately, sounding uncertain, before I can tell him he's won and we'll regroup with another idea.

Father settles his gaze on Sean, who's watching this with a studied boredom. "You may go."

He flicks his wrist and Sean disappears.

"Wait," Callie says, "where did you send him?"

"Earth," Father says. "I wanted a few more words with you two."

The throne room goes quiet, all of us calculating the odds this audience is a colossal mistake. Father is a stickler for the spirit, if not the letter, of the law.

"Can you tell us any more about him?" I have to try.

"That's part of your test. And this will be a good test of your affections, as well," Father says, and settles his gaze on me. "Of how well you can pursue your common goals."

The task he's given us, I am certain, will be so hard as to be almost impossible. I understand what he's about. He's chosen a way to drive a wedge between me and Callie. He has no intention of letting us upend his rules. He knows this is her idea more than mine. He thinks this maddening task will force me to give up, and her to see me for who I really am, and leave. Then he can get back to remaking me in his image.

I refuse to let any of that happen. We're going to have to do this. Save Sean Tattersall.

I cover up my misgivings with a cocky grin. "Game on."

"You have forty-eight hours," Father says.

"Why give us a time limit?" Callie says. "Two days isn't enough."

She sounds worried. I imagine she's trying to figure out how we manage to pursue Sean and redeem his wayward soul *and* work for her mother all day.

"I get bored," Lucifer says. "Seventy-two is my final offer."

"No problem." I'll figure that part out. I'm excellent at getting out of tight spots.

"Oh," Father says, and bares his teeth in a smile directly at me, "one more thing . . . since we're indulging revolutionary change and all." Still smiling, he flutters his hands around in the air.

A shift happens inside me, a lessening of sorts. My body feels like a cage made of bones and skin. I'm not a fan.

Looking over at Callie's gasp, I watch as my wings—*my wings!*—extend from *her* back.

He's made me human. He's made her a demon.

Even for Lucifer himself, this is low.

CHAPTER FIVE

CALLIE

I twist and crane my head around, trying to see if what I feel can possibly be true.

The answer is yes. There they are. Luke's wings. Rising out of my shoulder blades and extending wide on either side of me.

"As I'm sure you've now gathered," Lucifer says, "I've given you each the other's powers, just to make it interesting. To allow you to fully understand each other's perspective."

Luke seethes. "Father, is this truly necessary?"

I give the wings a gentle, experimental flap and my feet hover off the ground. "Oh my—"

"Don't say it," Luke says, anticipating that I'm about to invoke the heavenly father.

I swallow the word, barely. Having wings is strange and . . . and . . .

Incredible.

I should be more worried about what Lucifer sprang on us. But my brain and body sing in unison: *I have wings I have wings*

I have wings. I take off and do a circle overhead. The throne room takes on new dimension and depth as I rise above it. My wings carry me gracefully through the room's upper reaches and I let out what even to me is a bananas-sounding laugh.

"We are finished here," Lucifer says, cranky as ever, though he's successfully arranged for us to go on a wild soul chase at his behest.

Hovering near the demonic war scene on the painted dome of the ceiling, I grapple with what we've agreed to. But if we manage it, we can help Agnes and more damned souls. The whole plan. That's a real purpose in life. I'll start saving up and I can get my own place, dog-friendly, so Bosch can come along. Although Bosch will not want to live in a place without her best friend Cupcake. Are there dog- *and* goat-friendly apartments in Lexington?

That reminds me of my actual job, which I can't bail on today. Wings or no wings. The Great Escape is the family business and always will be.

Just like Hell is Luke's family business.

"You are *dismissed*," Lucifer says.

"Callie," Luke says. He holds his hand up and waves me down, the gesture tight. "Let's go."

Both of them are so far below. My head swims deliriously with it.

"Right." Swooping down, I do my best to contain my glee at being able to *fly*. Which was frankly the coolest even when I was hanging on to Luke.

I land beside him. "This is so weird," I say.

"You're telling me." His voice remains strained, and I can understand since he's getting the short end of the power stick. As in nada. Nothing. Human zip.

Lucifer gives an irritating wave of his wrist. "You don't have all the time in creation, you know."

"Callie," Luke says, and slides his hand down to take mine. "Let's go."

"Right," I say and force myself into a farewell curtsey to Lucifer. The unfamiliar weight of the wings nearly makes me tip over. Porsoth sighs in relief behind me at my observation of protocol.

"Good luck," Lucifer says with a lazy grin, crooking one finger to tell me to stand.

"You're going to need it," Lilith puts in, always helpful.

"I'm feeling lucky." Not my best retort.

Luke frowns at her as he offers me assistance in getting back to a fully upright position.

That's when I realize none of them think we can pull off this test either. I already picked up that Lucifer isn't worried in the slightest. But the rest? Rofocale, Lilith, Porsoth, Agnes . . . Is Luke doubting too?

The Sean Tattersall guy who Lucifer picked must be impossible to save.

I hate being underestimated. I hate knowing that Luke is *used* to being treated this way.

We'll have to do it. Then, I'll have proven to myself that I know what I'm doing and can make a life of my own out of all this weirdness.

Luke leads me back to the door. But when we reach it my— well, Luke's—wings are thrust out too wide to get through. I think of them disappearing, but nothing happens. At last, after a throat-clearing from Rofocale, I turn sideways and shuffle through into the hallway. A few gleaming black feathers are lost in the process. They drift to the marble floor.

Luke and Porsoth follow me much more gracefully. Agnes stomps alongside them.

My ungainly winged shimmy earns some amusement from Luke. "You know you can zappity now, correct?" he asks.

He means travel instantly from any one place to another.

"That reminds me." Because, no, I didn't and I can't wait to try it out—does this mean it won't even hurt now?—but first I take the handkerchief from my pocket that I use to travel between Earth and Hell and present it to Luke. This way he can go back and forth, if I'm not with him for some reason.

Luke stuffs it into an inside jacket pocket and hesitates. "How can she have my powers?" he asks Porsoth. "Is it safe?"

"She's, ah, stronger than you think."

I ruffle the wings. My shoulder blades tickle at the move. "It must be weird for you too, seeing me with your wings."

"You're a vision," he says quickly. "And, yes, deeply." A wicked gleam appears. "I don't hate it though."

"Down, boy." Agnes still looks more thoughtful than usual, so I go for as chipper as possible and pretend it's smooth sailing. "That actually went better than I expected."

That's almost true. I was prepared for a flat-out no. Sure, it's less than ideal to have to run around and be toyed with for Lucifer's amusement, but this is for our larger goal.

"It did . . . what did you expect?" Luke looks at me again and I catch a flash of anxiety before he masks it with his usual veneer of confidence.

"I don't know." That much is true. "Not that."

Porsoth, meanwhile, is pacing, which is the opposite of soothing. I ignore him.

"We should start by locating Sean Tattersall," Luke says.

I shake my head. "We can't. I can't bail on Mom. We have to show up for work."

"Are you sure we can't skip out just for today?"

Misgiving at the careful way he phrases the question shoots through me. I shift from foot to foot. "My mom gently read me the riot act. Right before I came today."

He blinks. "What?"

"She isn't a fan of me being involved with all this." I gesture widely and hope he doesn't ask if that includes him.

"Or with me?"

Of course he picked up on that. "I'm my own woman. But . . . she's right. I've been phoning it in at work and I need to make a life plan. So now it's new plan time. We can do all this. Can't we?"

"All right," Luke says. "All right."

Mayday, Houston, going down in flames here . . . "I'm not—you don't have to make some big commitment just because . . ." *I want you to.* Why can't I stop talking?

"Don't worry," he says, and it's gentle.

The words comfort me, his innate skill at saying the right thing. Or almost. I cling to the sentiment like a blanket in a snowstorm in Hell. Then it occurs to me he might be telling himself what he needs to hear too.

Porsoth has continued to pace and wring his wing-hands through our entire conversation.

"We got this, right?" I ask. "It's possible?"

Porsoth keeps pacing.

"Luke? Porsoth?" I prod, when neither responds. "We *can* do this, can't we?"

"Not only can we, I'm looking forward to it," Luke says, not at all convincingly. He turns to Porsoth. "Can you tell us anything about our quarry?"

"I fear he's set you up to fail," Porsoth says, and peers at us. "My dear charge and my dear friend, you must not. I fear he must have . . . plans . . . if you do. I'm . . . troubled. I find I cannot reveal what I know about Sean Tattersall to you."

"Great," Luke says. "No pressure then. And three days."

Lucifer's words come back to me. We don't have time to waste.

"We have to get going. I'll zappity us to Earth."

Agnes moves forward, and touches my arm to stop me. "Callie . . . You . . . You were so brave. In there. I didn't think . . . I didn't expect you to mean it."

I have to swallow over the tightness in my throat.

Then she finishes, "I still don't know if you have a chance in Hell."

Okay, Agnes wasn't going to get *that* sentimental. I try to touch her shoulder, considering a hug, but she takes two big steps back.

Fine. I wave at Porsoth and take Luke's hand and try not to grin at the shriek he lets out as we travel across time and space back to Earth, the alley behind the Great Escape, to be precise.

This is going to be some date, all right.

Luke falls to his knees in the alley behind the Great Escape and I remember the horrible sensations from my first long trip by his method.

"It'll pass in a minute," I say.

I start to get concerned when it takes five.

He straightens, shaking out his arms and legs, expression hangdog. "I'm so sorry I did that to you."

I shrug. "You didn't know." Then I realize, "But *I* did. And I did it anyway."

He considers me, heat in his gaze. "Getting into your new role already, I see. Torture becomes you."

"No, it doesn't." But he's right. I gave him a taste of his previous medicine—only *he* didn't mean to do it. My wings have vanished en route, but there's a flutter like them in my belly at the thought. I do my best to banish the hint of glee in it.

I thought I'd enjoy our positions being reversed, but instead I feel guilty.

"I'm sorry," I say.

He moves to put his hand on my cheek. Still unsteady, he almost misses. But he recovers by sliding a palm around my neck. I lean into his touch.

"You're forgiven," he says. And with a squint, "Also, your senses are not at all acute."

Funny, because my senses right now are so acute every nerve in the skin of my neck is on fire at his touch. "Rude!" I protest, instead of saying that.

"Try them," he says. "Try mine."

I take a look around and understand what he means. Here on Earth, his vision is a different experience. I can focus in on the sparkling water droplet about to fall from the roof next door. If I concentrate, I can hear each bird individually singing. I'm suddenly overwhelmed by the brilliance of every color and texture and smell. The smells, so many of them. Rain puddles and garbage dumpsters and cloying flowers . . .

"Take a breath. You can tune it out," he says. "Or in."

I take three in-out, slow and easy breaths, and then I sort of push the world to arm's length. The ability to focus in more deeply is still there, but I don't *have* to pay attention to everything. So I don't.

"Better?" he asks.

His palm on my skin is an acute burn, but a nice one.

"Yes." I nod. "Your father is a jerk."

He smiles. "You like the flying part, though."

"I think that may be the only part I like." *Lie.* Every tiny division around Luke's perfectly blue irises is apparent to me. I could drown in them like an ocean.

I could lose my mind, drawn into the details by the devil. I shake my head.

"We need to find out more about this Sean Tattersall," I say.

But we're interrupted by the back door of the business opening. Mag rushes out and grabs my arm. "It's about time. Your mom is ticking like a bomb, looking at her watch every two seconds. Get in here. Oh, and hi, Luke."

"Hi. How did you know we were here?" Luke asks.

Mag holds up their other hand, which has a phone in it. "Find my friends. Plus, Cal always comes back this way."

"You're okay?" I check with Luke first.

"Right as rain."

A saying between us that means something like, "I've been better, but I'll live."

Mag looks between us. "I don't have time to figure out what's going on here. You can explain later. Now . . ." They step to one side and hold the door open. There's nothing to do but go in.

I wish hard for my wings to stay hidden and nothing else to give away the current change in my abilities. I won't be able to explain that without setting off Mom, even if it's temporary.

We travel up the hallway from the back entrance and find Mom busy at the front desk and Jared preparing stopwatches and paperwork. Outside, there's a line of people already waiting, many of them in clumps of black or white T-shirts. A few sport elaborate cosplay—horns, wings, slinky red demon outfits, and flowing white angel robes—which automatically earns them extra points in the competition.

"They're here," Mag announces.

Mom exhales and bends at the waist before rising to shake a finger in our direction. "I thought you decided to ditch us."

"Mom," I say, offended.

Luke offers an easy grin. "What better possible way would we have to spend the day?"

Mom ignores his charm offensive and hustles over to me with a thick folder in her hands. "Here's your packet. I have you at Thoroughbred Park, okay? Anyone who arrives with the correct password gets the next clue. No hints. No leaving your checkpoint unattended. You should be able to take turns going to the coffee shop next to the park for lunch." She thrusts the paperwork at me. "Get going. The instructions should be self-explanatory."

"Mission accomplished," I say to Mom with a salute.

"Mission what?" She tilts her head.

"I mean, message received," I say.

She gives Luke a speaking glance next. The thought occurs to me that my mother is wondering if my trip to Hell involved sexytimes. I really do not want her questioning that in any way. Mom and I are close, but we're nerds. Discuss the latest *Dr. Who* scandal? Yes. Discuss my sex life? Not since "the talk" in high school and a box of condoms packed next to my *Chicago Manual of Style* when I went to college.

It's only then I notice her T-shirt is for the Good vs. Evil competition. Jared and Mag are wearing them too.

Distraction time. "We were in a rush to get here. And now we're in a rush to leave. Are we supposed to have shirts?"

"Shirts! Yes!" Mom rushes over to a box on the floor behind

the counter. She tosses one to each of us. I catch both without meaning to because my reflexes are better than normal. Oops.

I hold one up. They're baseball shirts: half black and half white, with a haloed version of our logo and the word GOOD on the front and a horned version of the logo with EVIL on the back. One sleeve is bloodred. The other is sky blue.

"These are great," I say.

"I ordered them from Mag's design," Jared says, and the two of them do that sweet moony thing where you can see how much they like each other even from across the room.

"You see what you miss when you're not around?" Mom says, and pointedly goes back to work.

I manage not to protest that I've worked on this nonstop for the past week. When I go to pass Luke his shirt, he puts out a hand to stop me, moving to take off his jacket. He's about to strip and change right here. Now I do feel like I have a fever.

"Wait," I manage.

"If you insist," he says.

"I do." I drag Luke out the front door by his arm and through the crowd of people who mill and cheer, taking our appearance as a sign the start time is about to come. Once we're mostly out of sight, I zappity us to our station at the park . . .

And completely forget to warn him first.

CHAPTER SIX

LUKE

The early afternoon sun blazes down on me as my knees threaten to buckle and send me to the concrete—wait, make that cobblestones. The part of the park we're in is cobbled with life-size statues of racehorses and jockeys running across it, a fountain tossing up water behind. I consider dunking myself.

A busy street borders the other side, drivers honking at each other. Callie stands hesitantly at my side, her hands hovering like she's afraid to touch me.

I avoid sinking to my knees, preserving some dignity. "Callie dearest," I say, "please stop doing that."

"I know, I'm so sorry, I didn't think." She's the picture of concern. "I just wanted to get out of there."

"Why didn't you tell your family what we're doing? I'm sure they'd let us out of this if they knew that—"

"That we're also pursuing a prisoner from Hell? You didn't hear my mom this morning. I told you she doesn't think I should be doing any of this. And then there's—"

A pair of skateboarders glides straight at us, separating to go wide on either side of us and high-fiving once they're past. They're the only other people in the park, save an older male couple reading the paper on a bench two dozen feet away.

"What?" I ask.

"I can't disappoint her." She holds up the folder. "We have to channel our inner Tim Gunns and make it work."

Our task from Father is going to be impossible enough on its own. But if this is how she feels . . . What can I do but relent? I take another sweep of our surroundings and miss my enhanced senses. I'm not entirely useless though.

"Doing both will be hard, but I have an idea. What does this entail? Our job here, the game."

I heard what her mom said, but I want to make sure I'm not missing any nuances. Like the ones my enhanced mind usually fills in for me.

Callie shrugs. "We have to be stationed here for six hours. People competing will be racing around to different checkpoints today and tomorrow—we'll be somewhere else then—and we give them the clue to find the next place." She pauses. "We just have to take their password first, obtained from the previous site. And that's . . ." She flips through the folder while still holding the T-shirts in the crook of her arm. "Ha."

"What?"

"The password is 'Enemy of Lucifer.'" She sniffs. "Very funny. The clue must be to find a certain church."

"They better hope he doesn't show up at his name being said so often."

Callie blinks—and I admit to liking the fact I can tell it's difficult for her not to stare at my face now that she can fully appreciate its glory. "Is that a possibility?"

One I shouldn't have raised based on the tone of the question. "Extremely unlikely. Anyway, back to my idea."

She tucks a stray lock of soft brown hair behind her ear. "What is it?"

I crook my head over to the two gentlemen, who've just switched sections of the paper. Sports for the crossword from the look of it. "Them."

"I don't think they're here to play."

"Watch and learn." Yes, I'm off-kilter without my powers. This, however, is my element. Convincing people to do what I want is something I've always been especially gifted at.

Callie trails me with a doubtful furrow between her eyebrows. I want to smooth it away by hand, but I'll have to do it by deed instead. "Follow me," I say as breezily as Zephyr herself on a particularly westerly day.

"Gentlemen," I hail them. "Might we have a word? We have a favor we'd like to ask."

As we get closer, it's clear they are indeed a couple. They consult each other before folding their newspapers at the same time. The synchronization of a life together. One wears a polo and a mustache, the other a button-down and a sun hat. Their wedding bands are simple and matching. They make a nice pair.

"Do you like games?" I ask when we don't get a response.

"You're not planning to punk us, are you?" the mustached man asks. "We're just enjoying our Saturday."

"Of course not. *Your* plan looks idyllic from where we're standing. But we'd love to convince you to change it."

Callie hovers at my side again. I wish she wasn't so obviously anxious about my ability to pull this off.

"I like chess," the sun hat man says, relaxing at my words.

Wrinkles around his eyes hint at a surplus of smiles. But I get no hint of one. "You planning on asking us to play chess? Somehow I don't think so."

"Not exactly." I gesture to Callie. "Explain."

She launches into the whole Great Escape Good vs. Evil explanation. "It should be fun," she finishes brightly. Too brightly.

"And why can't you two do this simple, *fun* task?" the chess fan asks.

This is where I go in for the kill. I put my arm around Callie's shoulder and spin a lie that's close to the truth. "I had a big surprise date planned for this one—it's our one-month anniversary—but I screwed up because I didn't know about her work schedule."

The two exchange another look and I'm certain they'll say yes. Young love, who can resist?

"Sorry," mustache says. "Good luck."

"Are you sure?" I can't believe it. No one ever says no to me, not about things like this. Even Callie eventually agreed to work together the night we met.

"Absolutely certain," the chess fan adds.

I gape and watch as they fold up their newspaper sections, get up, and *walk away.*

Callie puts a sympathetic hand on my arm. "I'm sure it's just the power thing."

The power thing. Oh, so the *one* thing I know about myself—my infinite charm—is a demonic superpower.

"I'm still handsome, right?" I ask her. I don't like the advance in my heartbeat. I feel so . . . so . . . *human.*

"You're gorgeous and you know it," she says. "And I like your idea. Let's try again."

She heads farther into the park. "There," she says when we find the two skateboarders flipping their boards around in the air up and down a long set of steps. She approaches them.

Slowed by my failure and newfound crisis of confidence, I hang back. By the time I reach her, the boys are whipping off their T-shirts to don the ones from the shop. Callie's explaining that she'll be back later to pay them if they do a good job and stay off her mom's radar. She waits for a sec and then reaches into her pocket and pulls out two twenties. "An advance," she says.

Damn it all. I should've offered money. Except I don't have any. She must have used my powers to make it. She's learning fast.

"We're *the best* at fooling moms," the bone-skinny boy who's the clear leader of the two says. "Don't worry about anything."

Callie looks at me. "I am," she says under her breath. Then, "Don't try to fool *my* mom. Please don't screw this up."

One of them makes a sign of the cross. I see Callie stiffen, but I could've told her that doesn't hurt. Only going inside sacred spaces does.

She waves a good-bye to the teens. "We'll be back."

They smile at her as if she's enchanted them. I guess that confirms some of my charm *is* a superpower. Although, her smiles enchant me easily enough . . . She turns and we're leaving them behind.

"Where are we going now?" I hurry to keep up.

She beams at me like a self-satisfied sun. "I just thought to myself, *where's Sean Tattersall?* and I got this image and the knowledge popped into my head." She shakes her head at me in awe. "I am so jealous of you."

Back at you.

"Where is he?" I ask.

"You're not going to believe it."

"Back in Hell already?"

She looks skyward at the blue, the clouds, and above them, well, *Above.* "We wish. Kind of the opposite."

Not the actual opposite, surely. "You can't mean it."

"Oh, no. Not up there. He's in Vatican City, though."

I exhale in partial relief. "We're going to Italy?"

"It's not actually part of Italy. It's the smallest country in the world, inside Italy." She smiles. "I knew that one already."

"You would," I say.

"Where else would someone go from Hell but straight to the seat of the Vatican? Unbelievable. Can you travel again so soon?"

After failing with those dapper gents, I'm not about to disappoint her. I can't bear the idea of her thinking I'm weak. I've had enough of that from Father to last a lifetime. "With pleasure."

She grips my hands tightly and leans in to kiss me and her lips are something to savor as we disappear into the dark screaming journey.

We land on cobblestones again this time, smoother from age, and halfway around the world. They're warm from the day's sun, but not as hot as they would be at midday. I know because my fingertips touch them. I'm purposely in a crouch so I can regain my balance. This time the voyage hurt so badly I wasn't sure I'd survive.

The distance, of course. I remember explaining the same to Callie once.

Callie, who bends in front of me, waiting, clearly afraid.

"One moment," I grit out.

She does me the favor of standing and giving it to me.

Slowly, my fingers and the backs of my knees recede to tingles instead of thrashing pain and then I rise to take in our full surroundings. We're in the midst of a flock of tourists who don't seem to notice our arrival.

Callie says with pride, "I think I made them unable to notice us."

Yeah, she's definitely liking her new talents. Who could blame her? What happens when she loses them?

I take a slow spin to absorb this place I never expected to visit—the sprawling plaza of St. Peter's Square. Callie does the same. The sky above us is a deep cloudless blue. We're surrounded by tall monuments and grand stone buildings that look pale or golden in the light. It's majestic and packed with spiritual symbolism. There are crosses and statues of the pious everywhere. I suppose it's nice, if you like that sort of thing.

Callie does. She points at the ground below us. "These cobbles? They're *sampietrini*! It means *little Saint Peters*."

I raise a brow. "Little . . . Peters? I do like the dirty talk, but I can't help with the 'little' part."

"I bet." She smacks me lightly on the arm, then lets her hand linger. "They're named for the people who originally looked after the roads. Sometimes children. I *didn't* know that."

Her face is lit with energy and excitement, similar to how she gets after she has two of her favorite coffees—vanilla soy lattes, no one's perfect—in a row. "My brain just . . . supplied it. And it's six hours ahead here, so just after six o'clock. You can seriously just know all this stuff?" She puts her hand on her hip, incredulous.

"Only when I focus," I explain.

"I would never get anything done. I would sit around and call up fact after fact. Like—wait, did you know that Vatican City has the highest per capita wine consumption *in the world?*"

"Hardly surprising given all the priests and secret societies. Speaking of . . . while I love learning random tidbits about this grand destination from such an enchanting tutor . . ."

She makes a face at me.

"You said he's here? Tattersall?" I'm more determined by the minute to get this sordid task behind us. I want my charm and other abilities back, perhaps more than I want to save this man from eternal damnation. Not to mention, we need to find out what we're truly up against.

Callie takes on that distracted expression Rofocale—and me, I guess—get when we're using certain powers. "He was, and he's still nearby. This way," she says, and launches across the square toward St. Peter's Basilica.

Curved, columned walls with statues—saints, I presume, and wonder which is Peter—flank our approach. The front of the church has a sparse line of people outside at this hour. The column theme continues along its front, only these are taller, grander. Two large robed male statues stand on either side of the entrance. Above them is yet another row of disapproving statues, the church's massive dome behind them, a cross at its very top. *The church.*

I hope our quarry is not inside.

"You're all right out here, I take it?" I ask Callie as casually as possible.

This is a holy country, after all. I'd never worried about its possible effects on my kind since I had no inclination to visit.

"I guess so," Callie says, moving quickly across the cobbles, employing some of my magic so that the clusters of people part for us. A little girl with sunburnt cheeks almost drops a cone of pink gelato and Callie pauses to make sure she has it secure before we pass her family.

We stop at the black barriers blocking off the basilica. Its shadow falls over us, large and ominous. Callie is silent, until, "You asked that because I can't go inside here, can I? Not while I'm . . ."

Like me. Unholy. No. "Let's not test it," I say. "Is he in there? I can go in alone." *Not that I want to.*

She closes her eyes and concentrates. "No . . . but it was the most direct route. We can . . ."

I hear the spike in anxiety in her tone. She's thrown by the possibility she's in some way not good and it's slowing us down. Or maybe she's grappling with the idea that I'm not, despite her best efforts and beliefs. I hold out my hand, "Zap us there."

She hesitates. "You're sure?"

"Please. Let's do this."

Callie sighs. I presume acknowledging what I'm up to and knowing there's no better solution. She grips my hands in hers and we vanish.

The trip is far less painful and when we emerge this time we're indoors, in a simple, spotlessly clean hallway. "That wasn't so bad," I say, reassuringly.

"Good," Callie says, and lets go.

The tidy hallway is empty, aside from us. Regularly spaced doors dot the walls.

"Apartments," she says, keeping her voice down. "Everyone who lives here works for the Vatican. Mostly priests."

If that's true, the occupants must feel like they're engaged in a daily battle between good and evil. Not unlike the game we abandoned, and our task. That could prove troublesome. There's a sinister thrum under all this beauty I recognize from home.

"He's at the end of the hall," she says, but then she hesitates. "Do you think your father sent him here?"

"I can't imagine it. But who can say?"

"If he didn't, there's another reason this Sean might come here. Do you think he's trying to ask for forgiveness? Maybe he knows a priest here."

I consider. If this was going to be that easy, there's no way the guy would've been in the great down Below to begin with. Demons were toting him. I don't want to rain on Callie's optimistic parade though. "Only one way to see."

We slowly move forward past the line of doors until we reach a small welcome alcove paneled with dark wood and yet another door. Shrieks and moans leak out from behind it, chanting beneath them. The sinister thrum inside me gets louder too. Like a scream.

Hang on. That's *not* inside my head. That was an actual scream. I have a sudden suspicion of what we're about to discover inside.

I press Callie behind me and try the door. There's no lock and the hinges are so well-oiled, it doesn't make a sound as I open it.

Inside the room is a cleaned-up version of the broad-shouldered, dark-haired man Father so briefly introduced to us in Hell. He's handsome enough I have to admit he's in *my* league. Except now he's wearing an off-putting clerical collar.

Sean the handsome priest hefts a bottle of what must be holy water in one hand and places his other palm on the forehead of a woman with long black hair hiding most of her face as he chants at her in Roman-accented Latin. I only understand a word here and there. Immediate language translation, another talent I'm missing.

The woman being administered to on a small bed screams and moans and thrashes. A gray-haired woman and a thirty-something man stand nearby, in clear distress, but the older woman clutches the man's arm to keep him back.

"What in the world?" Callie whispers to me.

"An exorcism," I whisper back.

They don't even notice us.

Thing is . . . if Sean Tattersall was possessed by a demon then saving him wouldn't be difficult. We could exorcise it ourselves.

And I don't detect the smells that I normally would if a demon were about. No sulfur. No excruciatingly barbaric body odor sweating out the possessed's follicles. (Demons have contests to see who can cultivate the most disgusting eau de putrid.) Are these things not present or do I not sense them without my faculties? Callie's nose isn't wrinkling with a foul stench, so that must not be it.

What is going on here, then?

Sean continues in Italian-accented English that's missing the distinctly British flair he had Below. "Devil, leave this vessel," he says. "It is not for you. Mariana is a holy woman who will have this man with her for life once you depart." He turns to the other man. "You will marry this woman and protect her from such invasions? Offer her guidance?"

The woman—Mariana—twists with abandon on the bed.

The younger man—American, clearly—nods quickly. "Father Sean, I'll do anything to make it stop. It's all my fault."

Callie and I look at each other. So he's *running* the exorcism.

The woman moans as if she's in pain but I catch a momentary flicker of a smile on her face. Not a demonic grin. A satisfied human one.

Callie closes the door behind us with a firm click, so the trio finally realize they're not alone. "What do we have here?" she asks.

Sean looks over at us and rolls his eyes. "Bugger off. Busy."

Ah, there it is, the clipped British accent from before.

"That answers that. I'm pretty sure you're not a priest," Callie says. "Though you could give Hot Priest a run for his money, Fleabag."

Sean shrugs. Presumably he's not caught up on the past few years of television. I know Callie has eyes, but the smallest hint of dismay pounds in my chest at the fact she noticed how attractive he is.

"You're not a priest?" the American asks. "What's going on here?"

Mariana stops feigning possession and gives a heavy sigh. "You said you were good at this," she says, before sitting up and straightening her dress.

"What's going on here?" the man demands.

Callie stays focused on our quarry. "We've been sent here for you. From your previous home. You need to come with us."

"No thanks," Sean says. "I'm fine right where I am."

Maybe I'm not totally without use, even powerless. I've hatched enough devious plans to suss out the particulars when I happen upon one in action.

I examine the tableau in front of us. I find it obnoxiously clever.

"Let's see if I can explain what you're up to in one try," I say and walk over to the supposedly possessed woman. "Sean here approached you somewhere," I say to the man, who nods, "and he told you your girlfriend was possessed by a demon. Oh, and that he could cleanse her of this evil spirit. Said girlfriend—"

The girl nods, a disgruntled frown on her face.

"Mariana," I say, "has been after you to put a ring on it. Sean must've approached her with the solution to her prayers. He then brought you here to some unwitting priest's apartment and conducted this sham exorcism. How much did he charge you?" I ask the woman.

"A thousand euros." She holds up her phone at Sean. "Venmo it back."

"How can he have a Venmo account in the first place?" Callie asks, astonished.

That's the last thing troubling me. He couldn't have had that much of a head start on us, and this isn't a beginner scheme. Who exactly is this guy? Why has Father hidden so much about him?

"He stole someone's phone and created one. Am I right?" I ask him.

Sean shrugs those two ripped shoulders. Whoever was torturing him must've been into CrossFit—unfortunately, a lot of the types we get these days enjoy that.

"Pinched from a shop," he says, all chill, as if he hasn't been busted. "Couldn't believe one of my old accounts was still active, if a little light. Fixed that."

"You really should have known the Vatican doesn't charge for exorcisms," I tell the woman.

She shrugs.

"Where are you from?" Callie asks Sean, squinting hard.

The most basic details about him must still be concealed from her. "Really?" she adds. I guess she caught the changing accents too.

"I'm a citizen of the world"—he smiles that slow smile and I swear the woman who must be Mariana's mom *and* Mariana swoon—"and beyond." He turns his attention to those three. "I must be going now, I'm afraid. I try never to overstay my welcome."

He swings around, past us, and out the door. Callie and I hurry to follow him.

"Wait," I say. "We need to talk. You don't know what's going on. We have a proposition for you."

"I love a good proposition," he says with a wink to Callie.

Callie's hair is tucked behind her right ear and I watch as it flushes pink before my very eyes.

Metaphorical smoke emerges from my ears. Winking at Callie is my privilege.

I hate Sean Tattersall already. But not as much as I hate Father.

CHAPTER SEVEN

CALLIE

etting out of the building has the distinct air of fleeing a heist—which technically I suppose we are.
The only people we see are two actual priests up
the long hall before Sean Tattersall presses open the door to a
perfectly maintained spiral staircase and launches down it at
speed.

We're running then. *Great.*

Normally running isn't in the top hundred activities I prefer,
but it comes easily. More of Luke's magical powers. Though
without them, he's not huffing and puffing or anything. But
there is a distinctly grim set to his mouth. I wish we could have
a sidebar to discuss this situation.

Sean was conning people out of their money by pretending
to be a Vatican priest doing an exorcism. Who *is* this man?

We exit the ground floor and Sean slows once we're outside.
Tall trees surround the building behind us, groomed into cone-
shaped topiaries. A driveway has a few cars parked along it.

The best way to describe Sean Tattersall really is to imagine

a missing Hemsworth. He's at that level of sexypants. He has
the strong jaw, flinty eyes, muscled chest . . . and the rest of
him seems muscled as well. And he has a stunning ability to
switch accents in a nanosecond.

Thing is, he's even more striking when he steps into the
full sun and removes his priest's collar to reveal a glimpse of
neck beneath. He dangles the cloth in his fingers. I stop my
brain from filling in the image of the broad chest beneath the
black shirt . . .

"Like what you see, princess?" he asks. Still British.

These new senses are wonderful, except at this particular
moment. I swallow. Then and only then do I remember, oh,
yes, Luke, who I lo—wait, we still haven't said *that* to each
other—is watching this exchange.

Not that I think he's a gross possessive type. He knows I'm
my own woman. And he trusts me.

I hope.

Though it's also true that anyone could be forgiven for
thinking a missing Hemsworth-level sexypants could make a
woman—or almost anyone—forget their romantic priorities.

I check in to see how Luke's dealing with Sean's flirting
and find him frozen in a way that means he's considering a
number of options. All of them will escalate the situation. The
last thing I want is these two fighting in some misguided show
of macho prowess.

So I slip my hand firmly into Luke's. Beside me, he relaxes.
A little.

Sean smirks down at our hands and I swear his eyes actually sparkle with mischief.

"We should get a drink . . . or three," Sean says. "When in
Rome."

I try to convey my lack of amusement. "We're not in Rome."

"Details. We can be. I know just the spot. We will need a ride." Sean scans the driveway and it's fascinating. There's so much calculation in it. Two men in suits lean against the side of the building next to this one. "I'm sure they won't mind helping us out."

He does *not* think we're going sightseeing in Rome.

I go for stern. He's probably not used to stern.

"We're on a tight schedule," I say and the words vibrate in the air around us.

I'm also not used to my voice coming out in something like stereo. I jerk in surprise.

Sean tilts his head at the same curious angle Bosch the dog does at an odd noise. "Can't say I ever saw many demons like you. I might've stuck around. Come on."

"I'm—" I start to explain to Sean that I'm not truly demonic, that Luke is, and what we need from him, since Lucifer didn't bother to . . . *But* it's day one and I have the distinct impression the more information we give this guy to use against us, the worse off we'll be. We still need to make it back to Lexington in time to take over for those skater goofballs.

"Yes?" Sean asks.

We need to find out about him first. Then we can figure out how to redeem him. Hashtag thoughts and major prayers. "I'm happy to get you that drink," I say, changing tactics.

"You are?" Luke asks. But after a beat, he seems to catch on to where I'm going with this. "Yes, you are. We are."

"Great," Sean says. "Like I said, I've got just the spot."

He takes off toward the two men in suits. Does he intend to borrow a car from some Vatican officials? He must be dreaming.

"We're going along to get him to trust us?" Luke asks.

The question behind the question doesn't escape me. There's a note of insecurity. It'd be adorable if it wasn't so unlike Luke. Being human after having a universe of random facts and all sorts of other abilities I haven't even begun to discover at your fingertips can't be easy.

"Yes. And we're a team," I say. "Us *against* him." *For* his *ultimate benefit, but still.*

Luke drops a kiss on my cheek. He makes a noise and says, "Not good enough," and I angle my head for an actual kiss. A quick one. A reassuring one. That we're an us.

I resist the urge to sink into it. Which is good.

Because when we part, it's to Sean honking the horn of a small green sedan as it barrels toward us then screeches to a halt. The two men in suits have been joined by others. They hop in the other cars and floor the gas after him.

Men sporting the flamboyant red-, yellow-, and blue-striped floppy uniforms of the Swiss Guard stream from the building pointing guns at us and screaming in Italian. I understand a few of the words, another element of my newfound gift. "Stop! Thief!" and variations.

"Get in," Sean says through the window as it cracks. "Now."

"You could zap him," Luke offers, but he's already opening the car's back door.

"We're playing him, remember."

Against my better judgment, we jump in as the other cars' brakes shriek to avoid hitting Sean's stolen one. As soon as Luke shuts the door, Sean guns the engine and laughs while checking the rearview.

"You may want your seat belt, demon or no, love," he says.

There's a car gaining on us fast, a sleek black sedan nicer

than this one. I'm confused about many things in this situation, but it's the most random that comes to the front of my mind.

"Is this a Ford Focus?" I say. "My brother has one of these. I guess I figured the Vatican would only use Italian cars . . ."

Oh no.

We hit an intersection and the screaming of sirens and blue lights greet us. My brain supplies an inconvenient fact about *this* Ford Focus.

"You stole *the pope's* Ford Focus!" I shout.

"I did?" Sean sounds surprised and pleased.

"Why does the pope have a Ford Focus?" Luke asks. He's impressed despite himself, I can tell from his tone.

"Man of the people," I say. "Drives himself around in it sometimes too."

"He did before I took it," Sean says.

I kick the back of Sean's seat hard and he laughs harder and cuts a right like we're in a remake of *The Italian Job* and drives down a row of short steps, across cobblestones as people dive out of the way, and onto a street. Miraculously, perhaps literally I guess, the car makes it unscathed.

And he's *still laughing.*

"This is not funny!" I say.

"Don't worry, we'll leave it for him when we're done," Sean says. "Admit it, you're having a blast."

"I am not." A car chase is not something I ever wanted to be in. I don't even like movies with car chases (except the feminist epic of our time, *Mad Max: Fury Road*, obviously: *We are not things*).

But the truth is more complicated . . . Part of me wants to cackle gleefully. We are in a car chase with the Italian police and the Swiss Guard because we're in a stolen beater of a car that belongs *to the pope*.

"Okay," I say, lower, to Luke, as I'm thrown over into his lap by another wild turn. "I admit to you only, I'm having a little fun."

He wolf-grins and tightens his arm around me. "I am too, now."

"I heard that," Sean says. "You could do better than him, sweetheart."

I keep my focus on Luke. The seasick motion of the car hurtling through the streets and the blare of the sirens makes the connection I feel that much more intense.

But when I speak, it's to Sean: "Call me *sweetheart* again and you'll find yourself tied up in the pope's apartment."

I hear it the second I say it.

"Don't either one of you make a joke right now." The words vibrate again. Sean wisely keeps his mouth shut and drives on. Luke grins like he could eat me up.

"There's the smallest spot of trouble." Sean slows and the car stalls.

Ahead of us is a bridge that my mind tells me immediately was built by Hadrian, arched and lovely over the Tiber, pedestrian only now, closed to car traffic.

Meanwhile, the street directly in front of us is blocked by gendarmes and flashing lights and tourists snapping a thousand photos. Behind us, it's the same thing.

"That *was* fun," Sean says. "But I know when I'm beat. Go ahead and take me back."

He's giving up. I didn't expect that. Did he do this with that intention?

"Not yet," I say.

He does a double take at that. "Why not? That's what you're here for, isn't it?"

"Shh." I need to think.

Luke holds up his hand to silence Sean. Outside the car, men and women in police uniforms are creeping closer to us.

"What do we do?" An image passes through my mind and before either of them can answer, I decide it's worth a shot. "Hold on."

I close my eyes like I did when I had the Holy Lance briefly in my possession and I imagine my—well, Luke's—wings on the top of the car. Not in reality, but I visualize it lifting and I hear Luke gasp in surprise.

"Didn't see that coming," Luke says.

"Me neither," I say as I open my eyes.

We're flying across the Ponte Sant'Angelo, the bridge of angels, statues of different heavenly beings below us—along with gawking tourists. The green Tiber below, romantic in the startling warmth of the late sun as it begins to sink in the sky. Ahead is Rome.

Sean gapes at me, something I get the feeling he doesn't do often.

"You're not just anyone, are you?" he asks and he studies the two of us, the calculation from before back in evidence.

I don't want to be a demon. But part of me is joyous at the sheer audacity of what we're doing. At what the world below must think.

Focus, Callie.

I look at the streets below us and find one that seems deserted of people. Closing my eyes again, I envision the softest landing I can. The wheels skip on the ground once as we hit pavement.

We're still breathing and the car isn't smoking or anything. Soft enough.

"That was the best time I've had in years!" Sean says. "I like you."

I shake my head. "Now *I* need a drink. And we need to talk."

Luke's breath is warm against my ear. "I wasn't sure about bad Callie, but I like it."

I turn to face him. The way the words hit shows, because regret reflects back in his blue-ocean-sky-cornflower gaze. I could fall into it.

"You're still good," he says, low. "You could never be anything else. I . . ."

I'm worried about the fact he's moved to reassure me, but more at the implication he's bad. This isn't the time though. I hear sirens, not close enough for human ears but getting closer by the second.

"Everyone out, quickly," I say.

Neither Luke nor Sean protests. We hop out and head up the street toward what looks to be a busier avenue. Sean glances around and says, "You brought us to the perfect place."

He looks too happy. What can we do except follow? He leads us into an alley, then another. Soon we're walking along a more crowded avenue with a fountain and I'm about to tell him to knock it off and pick a place when a stone staircase covered in lounging Italians and tourists comes into view.

"Those are the Spanish Steps." There are times when this life still stops me in my tracks, and this is one of them. Maybe this date isn't a complete loss.

"Yes," Sean says over his shoulder, dodging around people lounging on them. "What'd you think? I was bringing you to any old pub? Just a bit farther."

When we reach the top, he's stopping to shrug into what has to be a couture jacket. That he's stolen on the way up.

"I'll bet he's quite the pickpocket too," Luke says. "I used to find that kind of thing amusing . . . until I grew up."

We both know if Luke wanted to pick someone's pocket he'd still do so with zero regrets.

"I've got *at least* ten years on you," Sean says, his grin wide. He's enjoying the challenge.

"There's no contest between us," Luke says.

Sean winks at me again.

"You can knock that off too," I say. "It's not helping your cause."

Then I remember *he's* our cause. *Think of Agnes, Callie.*

"You didn't use your demon voice," he says, cheery. "But I'll do my best."

He takes us a little farther and stops with a flourish. "And here we are."

Night has fallen around us. The white facade isn't ostentatious, barely lit with soft ambiance. A sign this is a truly fancy place. It doesn't need to announce anything.

A mustached doorman stands beside an arched entrance that leads into the building, a twinkling courtyard visible beyond. He gives Sean a long look.

"Mr. Sean! We haven't seen you in . . . it must be five years," he says. "I was afraid something had happened to you."

"Missed you too, old chap."

The doorman smiles with genuine sincerity. "It is good to have you back, sir."

"You know I always love it here." Sean lifts his hand and gives the tip of an imaginary hat to the guy, who nods like he's been paid the biggest compliment in the world.

As soon as we're past, I shake my head again.

"You brought us to a place where they know you?" I ask. "Why would you do that? Aren't you *dead?*"

"Only the best for you," he says. "That, back there—*up* there—was sensational."

More deflection. Luke's growl under his breath summarizes my feelings exactly. "Where are we?" he asks me.

I blink and know. "Hotel de Russie."

"And its secret garden," Sean supplies.

We walk into a terraced courtyard that's one of the most beautiful spots I've ever seen. He escorts us farther in and up a set of steps, nodding to a waiter in a crisp uniform. Trees surround the terrace and courtyard, luscious and green. Every scent comes at my nose and I can't bring myself to push them back.

Orange trees. Blossoms. The slightly chemical note of fountain water. The complicated bouquets of wine in the glasses of the people at the tables spread throughout the lower and upper levels. Fresh, buttery, oily pasta.

Sean slides into a seat at a table near the edge of the garden, where we have a view of the dimly lit tables around us and the courtyard below.

"Nice choice," Luke says.

"My table," Sean replies. "They hold it for me."

"They still hold it for you." I goggle. "But you were in Hell for five years, I take it?"

"More or less," he says. "Or a lifetime."

I've had it with the cute quips. We need answers.

The waiter bustles toward us with a tray holding three glasses and two bottles of wine. "White and red, your usual varietals," he says to Sean. "Excellent vintages."

"Leave them," I say.

The server waits for Sean's agreement and I consider demon-voicing it. The waiter discreetly vanishes before it comes to that.

"Here's how this is going to go," I say to Sean once he's gone. "You answer a question, we open a bottle of wine."

"Fine. Shoot."

"She wasn't finished," Luke says.

I'm touched that he knows me well enough to catch that. "You answer another question, we pour ourselves a drink. You answer a third, you get one. Understand?"

Sean shrugs a shoulder languidly. A night bird in the tree above us sings what might be a paean to his beauty. Funny, that's starting to wear on me already. Luke was a *lot* when I met him—cocky, beautiful, infuriating—but I never actually wanted to be rid of him.

I can't *wait* to get rid of this guy. A problem, since we have to redeem him. I'm beginning to understand exactly where Lucifer gets his reputation.

"You also have to answer truthfully," Luke adds. Then he looks at me. "You'll know."

Sean glances between us. "Interesting that she takes instruction from you."

"She doesn't, and it's none of your business," Luke says.

"Are you ready for your first question?" I ask to prevent the two of them from going full bicker-twins.

Sean leans back in his chair like he doesn't have a care in the world. "Shoot. Metaphorically speaking."

"What landed you in Hell?"

Sean considers. He leans forward and plucks the bottle of red up and across the table, a challenge. "I don't think we've got that kind of time, love."

I reach over and take the bottle back, returning it to our side of the table. "Can I make him talk?" I ask Luke.

His lips curl at the edges. "Your so-called 'demon voice' is also known as interrogation mode."

Sean frowns. "Can't I at least have wine with my torture?"

I shrug at Luke and he opens the bottle and pours a glass. But he keeps it on our side of the table.

"Why were you there?" I ask. "The short version."

"I did some bad things."

I don't use interrogation mode, not yet. "I bet. Did you choose to come to Vatican City?"

He nods. "I did."

"Why?" I don't believe he just had a massive craving to do a fake exorcism.

"Since you asked nicely . . ." He pauses and I'm pretty sure it's for drama.

"Go on," I prompt, a slight hint of interrogation vibration in it.

More casual than a stroll in the park, he says, "I'm a Grail seeker. I figured this was as good a spot to start looking as any, and better than most."

A Grail seeker. That's a term tied to a specific relic. The Holy Grail. Also known as the Holy Chalice.

It hurts me to think too much about the Grail at the moment and although I try to locate it without meaning to, the site is obscured from view. I can't tell where it is. Thankfully.

I don't have to use any special powers to supply the other details about it. This one's right in my occult knowledge wheelhouse.

The vessel Jesus used at the Last Supper, believed to be a cup or a serving platter or a bowl, depending upon the translation. Joseph of Arimathea used it to catch his blood at the crucifixion. In various traditions, the Grail is credited with the ability to grant immortality and provide healing, to offer up plenty and create peace. Supposedly a legend, but I learned with the Holy Lance that legends like this can be all too real. Why do I always seem to be in the path of people looking for them?

"Did you find it?" I'm fairly sure the answer is no, since I don't know where he'd be hiding it. But I've learned you can't be too careful where magical objects are concerned.

"Wasn't there," Sean says, and waves for the wine.

Shaken, I nod to Luke and he pushes the glass across the table.

"So not yet," Sean says. "But I will."

Sean picks up the wine stem with delicate fingers and drinks deep. I try to figure out what's the best thing to ask him next. And how we broach his potential redemption.

Unfortunately, that's when the shouting starts.

CHAPTER EIGHT

LUKE

I can't catch a break. The courtyard buzzes with intrigue as a veritable horde of Italian police in blue uniforms rushes in. They're not alone either. They do their best to keep a quartet of paparazzi clicking the shutters of long-zoom cameras from pushing in alongside them.

After a few moments, my fear is confirmed. They're definitely headed our way, pointing up at us as they weave through the tables toward the stairs to the upper level. The waiter who brought our wine is attempting to stall them by asking questions.

Why on Earth are they here for us?

Oh, wait, Callie did pull quite a showstopper back there. Technically, we're supposed to keep it more low-key on Earth— not go in with our demonic super-guns blazing, not so flamboyantly, not where the whole world will see the echoes of any event on smartphones. Not after stealing a car belonging to the Vatican.

I may only be human at the moment, but no way is Callie going to jail or, worse, becoming an Insta-celebrity who has to go into hiding for using my powers without the lifelong tutorials I've had. Whether I pay enough attention to them or not.

"On your feet." I stand and reach over to grab Sean by the back of his stolen jacket.

He's already up and sporting a self-satisfied smirk.

Callie has done the same math in her head that I did. "I shouldn't have made the car fly?" she asks with a wince.

I shrug. "I wouldn't say that. But it obviously got some attention."

Before I can protest that zappitying us out the back way would be ideal, my gleaming black wings extend from her shoulders. Around us, the flash of cameras and the volume of excitable Italian increase. We're far past what-in-unholy-hell-do-we-do-now territory.

"Sorry," she says in near-panic. "I didn't mean to."

"We should go," I say. "Now."

I turn and notice that Sean is gone. I search faces and exit points and consider darting into the trees that are the only place he could disappear without passing us. "We have a problem. Sean's not here anymore."

Callie absorbs this with a quiet nod. That distance in her gaze comes back, and then she flickers back to here, now. "He's in . . . Spain."

We exchange a wide-eyed look. That's a shocker.

Callie clocks the progress of our pursuers. The police and paparazzi with their flashing cameras are getting closer and closer, on the steps now, headed right for us. She raises her hand and points down, to where the doorman who greeted us—greeted *Mr. Sean*—is smiling with the satisfaction of a man who made this happen.

The waiter is still in front of the police and the paps when they hit the top of the stairs en masse. Callie scowls at him. "He had you make a distraction? The doorman called the cops?"

He blinks at her wings. "Yes, yes, we assist Mr. Sean when—"

Callie sighs as a gendarme pushes past him.

"Nothing to see here," Callie says in vibrato and it stops everyone in the courtyard in their tracks. The command will wipe every mind in this place clean, probably of this entire day. She likely has no idea.

"Might want to blank out the camera memories too," I suggest.

"Done." She nods and then extends one wing and folds it around me. "Hold on," she says, and I paste myself to her side as we rise.

We fly instead of zappitying, and I'm glad for my leather jacket as we travel up, up, and above the clouds, Rome reflecting the night sky in its lights and romantic buildings. I wish this *was* the evening for exchanging newfound commitments we had planned.

"We're headed to Spain?" I ask.

She hesitates. "Yes. But how did *he* make it so fast?"

The only answer is that he can travel in some fashion akin to ours. "Father only knows. Maybe he gave him the ability to make our lives harder."

"Seems like him." Callie bites her lip. "I don't want him to have too much of a head start. Luke, what happens if he finds the Holy Grail? Who *is* this guy?"

"I don't know," I say. "I wish I did."

"He has to be redeemable. Otherwise, your father is cheating, right?"

"I assume so." Who knows what Father is capable of?

"Anyone can be better. Can do good. They can change. I have to believe that."

I hope she's right about the existential stuff; I still don't know. "I never thought I had a soul, so I say trust your instincts."

She speeds our progress across the sky, and I can sense her frustration at the relatively slow pace of travel. "Do you mind if we . . . we *can* go this way, I like flying, and it almost feels like an actual date, but . . . we have a timetable and . . ."

What Callie is actually asking is if it's okay to drag me to another new country, traveling through the borders of Hell by zappitying, singeing me the entire way. "Do your worst."

I don't scream. I suppose I'm getting used to my human limitations.

We alight in an evening city with bustling sidewalks shadowed by the gothic edifice of a cathedral. There are more intimidating statues in robes—I'm beginning to wonder if they outnumber living people in this region—but this church features far more gargoyles and imposingly stiff flourishes. The kind of building meant to remind humans of their place.

My breath comes back much faster, so wherever we are in Spain must not be that far from Italy's Hotel de Russie and the blanked minds and cameras we left in our wake. Callie retracts her wings before they draw more attention.

"Where are we?" I ask. First things first.

"Valencia," she says. "Specifically, that's the Valencia Cathedral, which contains a little something called the Chapel of the Holy Grail and a supposedly legit relic to go with it."

"Ah," I say. "Why do you think he wants the Grail?"

Callie continues to stare at the cathedral. "I can't imagine for any good reason. He doesn't remind me of Solomon Elerion, exactly. But in some ways that's worse."

Worse than Solomon? Given the ways he threatened Callie, attempted to use the Holy Lance to bring about my father's kingdom on Earth, and almost wiped out us and most of existence in the process, I can't agree.

"Why?"

"Because with Solomon, his motives were painfully obvious. Sean's a mystery."

She has me there. "I guess this means the Grail is real?"

"It's hidden from me."

Definitely real then.

"Did Porsoth ever talk about it?" she asks.

I'm sure he did, but I remember none of it. "I think I skipped that day. What does your—my—magic brain say?"

"Lots of stuff I already know. Lore, legend." She gives a tight nod to the church. "Valencia's entrant into the possibly-the-Holy-Grail sweepstakes has been used by popes for Holy Mass. It's been dated to the time of Jesus. We have to assume he's here for it."

"What are we going to do?" I ask.

Callie looks at me. Her muddy, stormy eyes are wild with her current state and what it means. "I'm obviously not going in."

She does a fair job hiding how that must shake her. But I know. "I'm sorry," I say.

"Blame your father. I don't like the idea of just cooling our heels out here. You okay with going after him solo? We haven't even told him he has a chance to change."

I don't suppose I can say no. Although, matter of fact, the idea of crossing that threshold freaks me out entirely. The dangers inherent in trespassing on a sacred space are drilled into the heads of Hell's children early and often. One of our few true vulnerabilities, one not to be flouted.

The last thing I want is her contemplating the downsides of my demonic nature. "Why not?" I toss out.

She nods. Before I can change my mind, I dash up the steps and through the heavy wooden front doors.

I don't burst into flame or begin to writhe in ecstatic pain so those are positive signs.

The massive interior seems empty of people, but that must be an illusion if the doors are open. I suppose they have proper names, the various parts of the inside of a church. Not being able to physically enter houses of worship means demons aren't even *assigned* to learn the lingo.

The church itself is impressive. I assume it is, anyway. Tall paintings filled with suffering take up wall space. I spot what I recognize as art—one of the few subjects I did pay attention to—from Goya, a crouching demon over a body in the darkness. Some of the other pieces must be of saints proving their mettle: gut extractions and lying on metal bars over flame and so on. Another thing the godly and the hellacious have in common is a penchant for scenes of torture.

The ceiling is high and domed. I walk by long wooden rows of stiff-backed seats.

"Gah!" I jump gracelessly at the unexpected sight of an arm behind glass, dark and mummified. The plaque identifies it as Saint Vincent's left. Another relic. How rustic.

Suddenly I'm glad I've missed all this grotesque grandeur up to now. Home has plenty of severed arms, if fewer glass display cases.

The church's design steers me ahead into a second chapel,

as festooned with sinister finery as the first. Ahead, another relic sits, this one elevated on a platform inside yet another glass case. It's a reddish-brown stone cup with a tacky bejeweled gold base with curved handles.

Looks Holy Grail–ish to me.

Sean sits halfway between the back and the case in a row all by his lonesome.

He turns his head at my approach. "That didn't take long."

"I could say the same." I enter the row to take a seat beside him. "How are you traveling?"

"I have my ways. Less painful for humans than yours, I presume."

"I can't really know unless you tell me what they are." Is it part of being on the loose from Hell? Is he a ghost of sorts? I should pay more attention to Porsoth's lessons.

I drum my fingers on the wooden seat, which is even more uncomfortable than it looked. I won't pretend I'm not nervous being in here. Lingering.

But I should take advantage of this opportunity. "Want to tell me anything? We want to help you. Callie won't want me to explain without her, but . . . we're on your side." I remember her question about his motivation and create some wiggle room. "I think."

"For your own reasons," he says. "Reasons I'm curious about. I didn't expect you to be able to enter here."

"It's been a surprising day." *And I'm not quite myself.* "Why do you want the Grail?"

"It's a very shiny object." He holds up his far hand and brandishes what looks to be an identical copy of the cup in front of us.

I swing my head between it and the one on display. "Is that . . ."

"The chalice there, it's old, but it's not magic. If it had been, I was going to swap this for it—it was made by some jewelers I know here. The best copies available." He sighs. "But it turns out that's *only* a shiny object. Another to cross off the list."

I try to corroborate what he's saying sans powers, about the lack of anything supernatural. "I don't feel anything, true. We should head out. We have places to be."

He doesn't make any move to get up. "Sit back," he says. "Don't you feel *that?*"

I settle back, but my muscles are tense. I don't like being in here.

"I feel the readiness to get out of here."

"I used to feel that." He slants a smile at me. "I mean the calm. Don't you feel the calm?"

I humor him and give it a try. My eyes drift closed and I soak in the feel of the place. Until I peek out of one and find him watching me. "I imagine the calm will only last until some priest arrives and tells us to get out or tries to make us confess," I say, honestly.

"When's the last time you came to a church?" he asks.

"Haven't had the—pleasure—before." An overstatement, calling it a pleasure. "It's fine, but not for me."

"It scares you." He lifts one shoulder. "It scares me too."

That's enough male bonding and effort to draw him out by myself, I decide, and stand.

Callie rushes forward as we pass the doors, but catches herself and stays on the sidewalk to wait for us.

"Don't vanish again," she says to Sean.

Good luck getting him to agree.

That's when she spots the fake cup in his hand. "Did you

steal that? Is that it?" But as she squints at it, I can tell she feels the truth. "It's a fake," she says.

Sean sets it down on the ground by his feet. "Which you could determine by giving it a close look," he says. "I'd like to know exactly who you two are."

"Likewise," Callie says. She rushes on. "But for you. You'll have to wait though." She waves us forward and once we're on the sidewalk, she says, "Brace yourself. Sorry, Luke. But the time difference—we have to get back."

"Back where?" Sean asks. "Hell?"

She ignores him, waiting for my response. "Get it over with," I say.

Her wings—*my* wings—stretch around us and Sean curses and then we're traveling again and I fully suspect I may vomit when we stop . . .

. . . back on the cobblestones of the Lexington park we left from. Sean and I cough the envy of death rattles while an astonished crowd of onlookers admires Callie's widespread wings.

"Go with it," I manage to tell her.

Picking up on the advice, Callie struts. Preening, she makes her way over to the two skateboarders, who I can't believe actually stuck to their assignment. There are a few other people nearby in costumes. She almost blends in.

Except for the fact she's magnificent. That would be true even without the sheen of my powers and the shine of my wings. But the sky is only beginning to darken here and she radiates like the moon.

Callie speaks louder than she needs to, still playing to the Saturday night park crowd. "Pretty realistic, aren't they? These are the kind of effects you can expect at the Great Escape every day."

She walks close enough to let the assembled people *ooh*

and *ahh*, but steps back and snaps them behind her when a girl in a Taylor Swift T-shirt reaches out to touch her wings. Instinct kicking in.

I could tell her that's intrusive—unless it's someone you want an intrusion from. I only like it when Callie touches my wings. She has no idea how it feels, the intimacy of allowing it.

The memory of the sensation brings me back to my feet. I catch Sean by the elbow, in case he's contemplating taking off on us. Seems like his usual move.

Our task is made more complicated by this Holy Grail business and whatever abilities allow Sean leeway to travel freely. Father must be standing at the World Watcher and laughing with satisfaction at our dilemma. That thought makes me burn with the need to show him I'm more than he assumes.

I march Sean closer to Callie. "Where do we go now?"

"The Great Escape." Callie is hesitant because it's a terrible idea. "I have to show my face to Mom." She shoves cash as discreetly as you can shove a wad of bills to the two kids. "Good job. Put your number in my phone if you're up for the same tomorrow."

The bony boss kid does that and passes back her phone. Callie waves them away.

Sean puts his hands in his jacket pockets. "The Great Escape, hm? Sounds like my kind of place."

"It's not," Callie says. "When we get there, you'll behave or . . ."

"Or?" Sean lifts a brow in challenge.

I hate that the two of us have so many of the same go-to moves.

"Or you'll never escape from anywhere again."

I half expect an argument. It's a gamble and a challenge. Instead he nods, giving in with ease.

"Interesting," Callie says.

Callie must sense I can't withstand another quick trip so soon or maybe she wants to add a slight delay to seeing her mom. Whatever the case, we set off on foot.

"It's time we come clean with each other," Callie says to Sean.

"You first. I assumed you were both demons, but he came inside the church."

Callie checks cautiously over her shoulder and in front of us and disappears her wings. My wings.

Mine. Woman and wings both.

She wants this to work out. I have to make that happen.

"I'm Luke Astaroth Morningstar," I say and bow, even though technically it should be the other way around.

Sean absorbs this information. I suppose if he's been in Hell for five years, he might've heard of me.

"And she is?" He nods to Callie.

"May I present Callie Johnson, the most beautiful being I've ever met." I wink at her, and know her ears turn scarlet. Temporarily human or not, our chemistry remains.

Sean eyes us both. "I thought it was you," he says to me. "But then you came into the church."

I bow again.

"But I've never heard of her unless . . ." He snaps his fingers. "*You're* the one who ruined all the battle plans. They did *not* call you Callie or beautiful, not in my part of the pit."

Hearing that sends a spike of angry heat through me. "They will before long."

"Luke, it's okay," Callie says, with affection. "I'm not going to spend a lot of time worrying about what the gossiping Real Housewives of Hell call me."

Still, hearing demons are cursing your name can't be the easiest thing. Not when you're good. Demonkind might love those shows, but they would cringe at the nickname she just gave them. I feel the scales balance.

"Your powers," Sean says. "They're his. Not yours."

"Yes."

"I wondered," he says. To me, "I didn't think you were human."

He sounds apologetic about it. As if I'm likely to be offended. The person I esteem most in all the worlds is human.

Sean isn't done with his interrogation. We pass out of downtown, the sidewalk bordering stately residences and a wide, busy highway. "So, Lucifer has sent you after me, but you didn't take me back there, why?"

Callie and I exchange a glance. She says, "Lucifer has given us three days to prove you can be redeemed."

Sean scoffs.

Callie ignores him. "And if we manage it, then we get to give more people in Hell *who deserve it* second chances. Including an eleven-year-old girl we're—not fond of *exactly*, but that doesn't matter—she deserves a chance. You're the key to it."

He tilts his head at me, asking if there's more.

"That's about the size of it."

"Your old scratch handpicked me, I take it," Sean asks. "Wily bastard."

"You can say that again." I'm surprised to be agreeing with him, but oh well. Stranger things will probably happen before the three days elapse.

The light of the shopping center where the Great Escape is comes into view in the distance.

"*Why* did Father pick you?" I ask.

"I think we've established that." Sean keeps walking.

"That you're a pain in the ass, yes," I say. "But I'm assuming there are more specifics."

"Are you up for it?" Callie asks. "Letting us try to redeem you?"

She stops on the sidewalk and I do too. Sean has to come back, but he only takes one step in our direction.

"Here's the thing," he says, raising a hand to scrub his eight-o'clock shadow. "If you help me get the Grail, sure, maybe. I can't promise anything without that." Callie is going to argue, but he rushes on. "It has that power."

That's the most direct thing he's said so far.

Callie considers him. "There's another reason you want it. And I'm going to find out what it is."

Sean's lips quirk. "Spoken like a true demon."

"Oh, you have no idea." I grin. "She's way more dangerous than one of us."

Sean waits, forcing our full attention on him. He grins back. "I'd think so, since the inspiration for pursuing the Grail came from the both of you."

He hums as he strides ahead, leaving us to rush to catch up. It's turning into a familiar feeling that I could do without.

CHAPTER NINE

CALLIE

My head spins with possibilities and impossibilities of what Sean Tattersall could most likely mean in a dizzying Escher-esque array. Go—the devil only knows what he intends by saying such a thing.

And I couldn't even think the G word fully just now.

"Callie, there's steam coming out of your ears." Luke passes his fingers slowly in front of my face.

Ah, some of the Escher effect is actual smoke. It clouds the air around us, and Luke steps out of the cloud to avoid coughing. Sean continues walking ahead.

"My reactions are like a cartoon character . . ." I throw up my hands.

Luke attempts to soothe me. "A very brave cartoon character."

"You agree I'm a plucky cartoon character and I'm supposed to save him? How?" I gesture to Sean.

"That's not what I meant," Luke says.

"I know," I tell him. And I do. "The question stands. How on Earth am I going to save *him*?"

Sean does a half-turn. "No offense taken."

I continue to process this situation the best I can. I stalk forward. "What do you mean, we inspired you?"

"The story goes you found the Holy Lance and it almost worked," Sean says like it's plain. "I want the Holy Grail, and I'm good at getting what I want." An indefinable emotion crosses his face. "Usually."

"You want to live forever?" Luke asks. "How did you die?"

No, that's not it. I can tell by Sean's lack of reaction. He's still hiding something from us. But what? When I try to call up even basic facts about him, my mind goes blank. Lucifer's block.

"If we agree to help you, you'll behave?" Not that I'll believe him and I intend to figure out what he's up to, but better to keep him where we can see him.

"You have my word that I'll try," Sean says.

Luke gives a slight nod and so I say, "Good enough."

I realize we're within sight of the Great Escape's standalone building at the end of the complex. Giant halo and horn signs are hung on either side of the front sign with arrows, the symbols echoing the shirts. The shirts we're not wearing, because I forgot to get them back from the stand-in crew.

But I set that aside. It's such a small thing and Mom probably won't notice. (She notices everything. She's Holmes *and* Watson in one nerdy bibliophile package.)

From here, I can see Mag and Jared working at a table out front. They must be finishing up.

I want to see my friend. And my brother. To touch base with my real life.

But you want this *to be your real life,* I remind myself.

"Am I still smoking?" I don't think I am, but I consult Luke to be sure.

"Only in the metaphorical sense." He grins wickedly at me, and I'm pretty sure it's meant to comfort. It works.

"Why won't you tell us anything about yourself?" I ask Sean while we walk.

He shrugs and gives me that annoying smirk of his. I study him and if I'm not mistaken, he's doing his best to feign an innocent look. *Yeah, right.* "I think you just don't want to tell us because it'll make you look bad," I say.

He gestures from his face to his torso. "Darlin', nothing makes me look bad."

Luke and I both roll our eyes at him.

"Knock it off," I say. "And behave like you promised. Sort of. Follow our lead."

He gives a sarcastic twirl of his fingers in deference.

In addition to the shirts, I didn't get the folder from the guys. I don't know if I was supposed to bring it back or not. I envision the neatly labeled manila file and it materializes in my hands.

I have no idea if it's the same folder they had and it just disappeared from their hands or the trash or wherever or if I've created something identical. All I know is it's cheating.

Like knowing facts without learning them is cheating.

Like not telling my mother the truth is cheating.

Cheating that I have to do. There's no alternative in the time available. That's what I tell myself. Too bad that feels like cheating too.

I don't bother to magic the shirts onto our bodies, though I could. One less lie to feel crappy about.

"Callie?" Luke's hand is on my arm. This is what I wanted, the test case, a shot, but he must be able to sense my sudden case of the major doubts. I hired someone else to do my job and I'm going to let Mom believe I did it. What am I doing?

It's for the greater good. Of the not-all-bad. *Agnes is counting on you, whether she admits it or not.*

"I'm fine," I say and speed up, crossing onto the parking lot blacktop.

Mag calls out as we get closer. "The prodigal child returns!"

"The prodigal child is Jared," I point out.

Mag and Jared rise from the table when they realize we have a tagalong. "And you've brought the new James Bond with you, I see," Mag says. "Who's he?"

"Sean Tattersall, at your service," Sean introduces himself and gives Mag a bow.

They clap with delight and I expect Jared to glower. Luke goes over and claps him on the shoulder. "I understand, but don't worry about it."

"Yes," Mag says, "do not."

"I wasn't," Jared says. "This?" he gestures to himself. "This is a confident man who trusts his person one hundred percent."

Mag blows him a kiss. "Smooth," they say.

The two of them are so good together.

"How'd today go?" I ask to gauge what Mom's mood will be. "Everything okay?"

"Better than," Jared says, confused. "You must know."

I say nothing. Concern crosses Mag's face. "Yes," they say, "since you passed all those people through your checkpoint. So, *as you know*, we have ten teams still in, seventy-five people. Another thirty washed out. We broke a hundred participants. Way exceeding our goal. Of fifty."

The goal part I remembered. I try not to resent that I was clearly not needed, because I know how unfair that is. "Mom must be thrilled."

"Over the moon," they say. Then lower, "Why does this seem like news to you?"

I'm not sure how to answer.

Luke steps in. "Our date may have gone the slightest bit sideways. Nothing to worry about."

Sometimes having a boyfriend who lies as easily as he breathes comes in handy. "I'd better go check in with Mom."

"I'll stay out here," Luke says. "Unless you want me to come with?"

"Nah, that's okay." Luke will only remind Mom of all her issues with me. But I don't want to face her alone. "Mag, do *you* mind coming in with me?"

They give me a shrug and a "No problem."

We enter, but Mom's not up front. Bosch is though. I bend to give my dog a hug, one of her favorite things. When I stand, Mag is looking at me funny and then they open their arms and I step into the hug.

"Thank you," I say. "It's been a lot of day."

"Hey, I know you," Mag says. "Disappointing people is your kryptonite. Your mom will get past this. She's just worried about you."

My emotions threaten to flood me like an engine. Worse, to short-circuit my brain. My feelings are as intense as my senses, now that I have a moment and my best friend has nailed my emotional state.

I take a deep breath and push the feelings to arm's length, the same way Luke advised with his heightened senses. I flush with embarrassment as I back up. "Sorry," I say.

They hesitate. Then, "What's going on?"

"It's . . . Sean."

Mag frowns. "The new James Bond? What do you mean?"

"I see him more as a Hemsworth."

Mag tilts their head. "Good call."

Talking with them centers me. "You know our big idea?

The giving people second chances? He's the test case Lucifer forced on us."

"Not Agnes?"

"Not Agnes." I huff. "He also wants to find the Holy Grail. We've agreed to help him. For now."

Mag's eyes go wide.

I don't even bother with the part about my having Luke's powers. That's too much. And it would lead to admitting how I cheated today. I don't want Mag complicit in that.

Mom bustles in from the back then, humming the theme song for the *She-Ra* reboot. "Callisto! You're back!" Mom says. "We made enough to pay off the rest of the repairs." Turns out an act of God wasn't something we could claim on the place's insurance. Another disaster courtesy of my adventures.

"Amazing!" I chirp. "What time should we be here tomorrow?"

Mom puts one hand on her hip. "Where's your shirt?"

"Uh," I say, articulately.

She goes on. "And you're not coming home tonight—did you tell me that?"

Oh, good point. We have nowhere else to stay without going back to Hell—where we can't take Sean yet.

Mag jumps in. "She's staying with me. I think they stopped by home already?" they say and I nod with gratitude at their quick cover story. "I'm going to tell her Jared's and my big news."

Mom relaxes. "Ah. Okay, see you tomorrow. Be here by eleven." She pauses. "No, wait, ten thirty."

"Great." I don't risk another hug, especially not a Mom hug. "Do you mind if Bosch comes home with you?"

"Never," she says. "Honey, my house is home as long as and whenever you need it. I didn't mean *that* earlier. I just needed to say something."

"No, you're right," I say. "I'm working on it. I promise." *Not in a way you'll approve of, but we can't have everything* . . .

"I know, sweetie." Mom nods. "Love you."

I repeat it back and even at arm's length the emotion is a deep river.

As soon as we're outside, Mag asks, "Where *are* you going to go? You guys can stay with me."

Luke, Jared, and Sean stand awkwardly a few feet away, not talking.

Mag's one-bedroom studio will be a snug fit for this crowd, to say the least. We'll go to a hotel. I imagine with my powers I can (cheat and) get us a suite.

I'm not ready to give up on figuring out Sean. We need research. A plan.

"That's all right," I say. "We've got somewhere to go for the night." I remember Mag's cover story. "What's this news of yours?"

"Oh." They duck their head, a little shy. "We're moving in together. End of the month."

"That's great. I'm happy for you." If I let my feelings surge, they'd be a mix of happiness and envy. Their relationship looks so easy. I know it's because I'm on the outside of it, and that no relationship is easy. But they're from the same world. Home court advantage, to steal the kind of sport speak Jared might use.

"Congrats!" I call to Jared. And I add: "You better learn to squeeze the toothpaste tube from the bottom. Finally."

Jared laughs. "They already schooled me on that one."

Mag speaks just to me. "Jared hasn't told his landlord yet. You could take over his lease—think about it."

I have a little money saved and I have been thinking about moving. But it makes me uncomfortable they've been discussing me. *Poor Callie, let's help her.* This is my best friend though, who covered for me without asking. "Okay, I will," I say.

"All right then." Mag smiles. "See you tomorrow. Good luck." Mag goes over to kiss my brother and no doubt fill him in on what he's missed.

I decide that we deserve to stay somewhere nice and land on the fanciest hotel in our town. I should say the fanciest I know about. Or at least the hippest. It has a free art gallery Mag and I have spent many afternoons strolling through, loving and hating on bizarre and gorgeous contemporary art by turns. Also, a restaurant we've eaten at a couple times named Lockbox because the building used to be a bank.

Special occasions only, because it's spendy. But if this doesn't count as special I don't know what would. What a day. What a date.

"Time to go?" Luke asks.

"Beyond." Figuring out Sean's past, present, and, maybe, future is our next order of business.

Luke convinces me all I need is to apply some light suggestion to the clerk. Apparently his powers aren't limitless—not that he's disclosed the places they stop short.

And so inside an hour we've Lyfted—to give zappitying a break—and checked into the last suite available at the 21c Museum Hotel. That's how Luke and I find ourselves headed up a hotel hallway, keycards in hand. I'm feeling tired, superpowers or no, and I can tell Luke's dragging. But we have to get some answers to sleep on.

So much for the not-much-sleeping night I anticipated in Luke's apartments.

I find our room number along the hall and swipe. Luke and I enter first and Sean stays in the hall. The room is spacious with a private bedroom off a large lounge area with sleek furniture that I hope is more comfortable than it looks. A wide skylight shows a swath of stars and black night.

"Do I have to invite you in like a vampire?" I say to Sean.

It takes him a moment to respond. "My mind chose that moment to remind me where I was at this time yesterday."

"Well," I say, gently, "you won't have to go back there, if this works out. So, come on in. There'll be room service—something else Hell lacks."

"Not strictly true," Luke says.

"Even outside the palace?"

"Beings of pure evil still have to eat," he says, and flings his body onto a chaise so much more gracefully than I'd be able to, it hardly seems fair. "They work up quite the appetite."

"Subject change, please, before I lose mine," Sean says, and comes into the room. "What kind of food are we talking?"

I rummage through the tidy array of publications on the glass-topped desk until I find a menu and pass it to him. "Live it up. It's on your Venmo victim."

He doesn't protest. He opens the menu, and walks over to the hard-angled but generously sized couch and sinks onto it, eyes closed with a smile of complete happiness, as if he's seen a glimpse of the good place. "They have biscuits," he says.

His accent has mostly settled into the British I've begun to think of as its home turf. Their biscuits are cookies with tea, something I know from books. I haven't been many places, but the list is growing: Hell, Portugal, now Italy, Vatican City, and Spain. I should wish a passport into existence. I content myself with pursuing the biscuit lead.

"So you've traveled here?" I ask.

"Been almost everywhere," he says.

Doesn't sound like he found anything he wanted in all those places. Who *is* he?

We don't know the first thing about him, except what he's looking for. But soon we will. We have to.

I get our order sorted out and text Mag, Thanks for the hug. It helped. Then I ease down on the room's other couch beside Luke, who guides me to sit lightly between his thighs. Hotel room. Luke. His scent, masculine and clean and, best of all, familiar. I wish again that we were alone.

"Sorry you had to lie to your mom," he says as he leans forward, his chest against my back. It feels so good to have him behind me, body and, I think, soul.

"I could leave you the room and eat downstairs." Sean sounds amused. And a touch jealous.

"No," I say. Luke backs off a fraction. "Let's talk. We need to know more about you."

"But I'm so shy." He arranges his lips into a pout.

"Good luck with that. I'm used to this one here."

Luke settles a hand on my waist over my T-shirt. "She's got you there. If you don't want to be up with us all night, start talking."

Sean lies down on the couch so we can't see his face, legs stretched out long.

We may be about to provide free therapy. Why, yes, that is a twinge of sympathy for this pain in my ass. I've learned enough about Hell that I question whether anyone except the worst of the worst *can* deserve to be there. We don't all start out with the same head start on morality and ethics and caring. That difference in circumstance follows us like an invisible weight, making feather-light souls heavier, harder to carry, than they would be without it. I know Luke must feel it too, since he discovered he has one.

"Let's start big. Who is Sean Tattersall?" I lean back into Luke's chest.

Sean coughs a dry laugh, but then he answers.

"The greatest con man who ever lived," he says.

I wait for the punch line that doesn't come. Is he serious? Because the truth is, it tracks.

"What about Victor Lustig?" I ask. "He sold the Eiffel Tower twice, and ran a scam on Capone," I explain to Luke.

"An amateur compared to Sinner Sean," Sean says. "You don't know my name because there's more competition for newsprint than in Lustig's day."

That is certainly true.

The knowledge hits me that we haven't even done the most basic thing. We haven't googled Sean's name. If he's only been in Hell for five years, he must have a digital footprint.

The room service knocks—that was fast—and I sit up. "Can you get that?" I ask Luke.

I sneak my phone from my pocket and open the browser, tap in Sean's name. He sits up as the waiter bustles in to present us with half the menu in elegant domed dishes, setting out a spread worthy of a royal court. Burgers, truffle fries, biscuits, a Southern cheese plate, and fried chicken. Too much for three people, but probably nothing compared to what the waiter has seen before.

"Tip," I say and then think better of leaving the task to Luke or Sean—who knows what either of them understands about tipping—and pass the waiter a hundred.

The waiter leaves, and I turn to Luke. "Those aren't counterfeit, right? The bills I make."

Sean stands beside us and shakes his head at me. "What a lamb you are."

Luke says, "Money makes the world go round. Hell has an endless supply of it. It'll spend."

Satisfied, I hit enter on my search of Sean's name. Too many results come back.

Luke and Sean both dig in, but I stay with refining my search. Luke comes over with a burger and a plate of fries and peers over my shoulder. "Con artist, hmm?" he asks and feeds me a fry. Perfect crisp salty goodness. "Add theft," he says.

He's right. That's something most cons have in common. I enter the new term.

Bingo.

I scroll down the first page, and hit next, and then scroll down the next page. Sean has been a busy, naughty boy. I think we'll learn more about him by reading these than asking him more direct questions he can dodge. Will it be enough to get more truth from him? Enough to redeem him? That remains to be seen.

"You know what, we've had enough truth or dare for one day. Sean, take whatever food you want in there." I nod toward the suite's bedroom. "Luke and I will sleep out here on the couch. Don't get any ideas about taking off."

Luke has a frown. "It pulls out," I say. And then, "Neither of you make a joke."

"I would never," Luke lies and goes back to inhaling his burger.

Sean artfully balances the fried chicken and a plate he's loaded with biscuits and other things and nods to us as he disappears. "I hope there are earplugs in here."

"We're working," I say.

"Uh-huh," Sean says, and vanishes into the bedroom with a click of the door.

I flush as I remember what we'd be doing if today had gone as planned. Settling in for a romantic night. Crossing the intimacy Rubicon, which is how I've been thinking of our finally having sex.

Luke looks a question at me. "Why'd you banish him?"

"He *is* a con artist. We've got some reading to do."

"Ah." Luke nods and his eyes blink sleepily. He's already eaten the entire cheeseburger.

He's asleep before I've finished the first article about Sean. I let him rest.

I keep reading. My greatest gift, an attention span that will easily last way past my bedtime.

What I learn about Sean Tattersall gives me even more questions that he won't answer. It makes me triply curious about what he wants with the Holy Grail.

But it also makes me think we might be able to save him after all.

DAY TWO

TRUTH OR DATE

"Who are *you*?" said the Caterpillar.

. . .

Alice replied, rather shyly, "I—I hardly know, Sir, just at present—at least I know who I *was* when I got up this morning, but I think I must have been changed several times since then."

"What do you mean by that?" said the Caterpillar, sternly. "Explain yourself!"

"I can't explain *myself*, I'm afraid, sir," said Alice, "because I am not myself, you see."

ALICE'S ADVENTURES IN WONDERLAND, LEWIS CARROLL

Now shall the prince of this world be cast out.

JOHN 12:31

CHAPTER TEN

LUKE

I wake up in near darkness, almost immediately convinced I'm dreaming. Callie's scent wraps around me. The sweet weight of her head is on my chest, a leg twined between mine. She never stays overnight, or she hasn't yet, and I wouldn't lose track of such a significant event. So it can't be real.

Until where we are comes back to me. The fact it is both more comfortable—Callie nestled beside me—and less comfortable—a stiff couch in a hotel room on Earth—than my bed clues me back in. If yesterday had gone as planned . . .

Callie must've fallen asleep or decided to take a break or both. The skylight above us shows a hazy lightening blue. I do my best not to move, to let her sleep.

Her phone sits beside her hand, and I gently take it to check the time. Eight a.m. Yes, we can afford the time, even with a Holy Grail to find. Or pretend we're trying to find? I need to figure out what her motivations were when she agreed to help Sean locate it.

His door is still closed. There's no way I'll be able to get back to sleep with Callie's delicate scent in my nose, even with human senses (speaking of, their sense of taste turns out to be better than ours; that was the best cheeseburger of my life). I key in the passcode to her phone. She gave it to me; she won't mind. I decide to retrace her steps before she exhausted herself.

Who needs superpowers when the internet exists? The article that's up is about a robbery at a museum in Paris, where three paintings were taken. A trail of bread crumbs led to two and the thief—Sean Tattersall, alias Robin Hodrick, who later escaped from jail—had supplied a convincing explanation that the third painting vanished into the underground market. The grayed-out link shows that Callie clicked through the link about that painting. I follow *her* bread crumb trail. The image is of a meadow scene of children and a goat. She'd have loved the goat, even if it is white instead of Cupcake's black. The article describes a famous piece controversially kept by the museum after a claim by a Jewish family in Beaune, France, that it had belonged to an ancestor and was looted by Nazis. A great-granddaughter was quoted sternly criticizing the museum for not only keeping it, but losing it.

I go back and see Callie has left a bunch of stories open in other windows, and I choose another one.

The next involves the bankruptcy of, well, a banker. Almost as infamous as Sean himself. In this story, his colorful nickname is Slippery Sean. I refrain from making the ribald joke, even though Callie isn't awake to tell me not to. Sure enough, he managed to escape jail again in this case. Another story, another in a series of aliases. The schemes were always complicated and, it appears, successful. Which leads me to believe he gets caught because he wants to. I'd stake everything on it. But . . . why? Is it really to build a legend?

That hasn't been successful, not yet. Not if Callie knew about Victor Eiffel Tower Capone guy instead of Sean.

I look down at the elegant lines of her peaceful face. She stirs and I murmur, "Go back to sleep, love," stealing Sean's not-an-endearment. I do love her.

But I can't be the first to say it. Not this early in, no matter how certain I am. *Oh, how today—yesterday, now—was supposed to go.* Our bold audience and a daylong glow, her moved to say it first, us beginning a happily however long she'll stay with me.

I set down the phone, and, gently as a whisper, trace the edge of her jaw.

Her wings extend from her back in a sudden thrust and almost stir us off the couch. I manage to scoop her in closer and in the process touch one of the feathers. She moans low, pure pleasure. Her eyes pop open, pupils dilated to dark pools.

"Do that again," she says, a command. Not that I need one.

The sultry undercurrent of her voice sends a shiver through me. I lightly stroke two fingers down a single feather. Her eyes close and her face slackens.

She presses herself flush against me and her mouth finds mine. Open and hot. My hand traces down her side to cup her breast. She gasps.

The sensations she's experiencing will be what I normally feel. A new level of intensity.

"Callie, should we wai—"

"Shut up," she growls.

Fair.

We haven't progressed past giving each other mutual pleasure yet, though I believe we're on the cusp of it. I'm not about to pressure her. I will never be like Father and boasting, bilious demons. She'll have all the time she needs and I will die waiting if necessary.

She grinds her hips into mine in slow circles and I come close to praying it isn't necessary.

A knock sounds at the door. No "Housekeeping!" follows. Instead, there are three more tentative knocks.

We still, and then Callie sighs, with regret I think—hope— and sits up, straightening her clothes. "I bet Sean ordered breakfast." From her tone, he better wish for death, if he did.

"That wasn't a breakfast knock," I say. "Better stow the wings."

Before she can, the door is flung open. I leap to my feet as fast as humanity allows and then breathe easier as Porsoth rushes into the suite.

Although his arms and hands are aflutter. He's like a miniature scholarly demonic tornado. The sight is so charming and ridiculous, I nearly forgive him for interrupting.

"I apologize for the intrusion!" he cries. "But you must be warned, even if I've been forbidden I couldn't in good conscience allow—"

Loud thumps land above us on the skylight. *Thud thud thud* and then a *crash* as glass flies into fragments and shards. Callie tosses her body over mine and Porsoth's, my reflexes kicking in as she shields us from the shattering skylight with feathers strong as steel when they need to be.

A half-dozen warriors descend into our suite from the roof, wielding swords and axes and scythes and whatever the other bespoke shining weapons are called. They're all in white. Like the avenging angels they're meant to represent on Earth, under Michael's guidance.

Guardians. We're being invaded by guardians. Humans of certain bloodlines trained to be the long arm of Above's law on Earth.

The glass of the former skylight glitters on the floor around them in the morning sun.

I put myself between Callie and the woman in front, Saraya. Their leader, dark-skinned with a pile of reddish braids arranged above a murderous expression, she always manages to be at the head of her minions. She and Callie had a run-in during the almost-apocalypse we thwarted. I might have briefly convinced Callie she was a guardian, and Saraya laughed at her. And that was just the beginning.

I need to keep things as calm as possible. I have no idea what they're doing here.

"That's going to ruin our reputation at this hotel," I say, voice even, as I cross my arms and toss a glance toward the gaping hole above us.

The bedroom door swings open behind us and Sean appears, his mouth open to make some smart-ass comment—but he doesn't. He stares as if bewitched. Figures he'd be no help at a time like this. Guess he's never seen religious warriors in white leather before.

"You," Saraya says.

Callie awkwardly shuffles next to me, her wings impossible to miss.

"Uh, hi—I mean, greetings, Saraya the Rude." Callie softens her voice on the "the Rude." Callie referred to Saraya that way on the day the world nearly ended and, because she was holding the Holy Lance at the time, it, well, stuck. Yes, Callie gave Saraya, leader of Heaven's Earthly warriors, the permanent moniker Saraya the Rude. An understatement to say she isn't a fan of the name.

I fully expect Saraya to lob an insult back, then threaten to dissect us into tiny pieces.

"You know she didn't mean the name thing," I say and put as much charm into it as possible. It hurts to have to try so hard for no guaranteed effect. "It's lovely to see you all. And so soon. Why are you here again?"

"*You*," Saraya says again, and I notice she's staring behind us now. I turn to make sure. She's not speaking to Callie at all.

Saraya is focusing her pure burning hate completely on Sean Tattersall, the con man, the mystery.

"Lovely to see you, Sarry," Sean says, and swallows. Somehow the short form of her name lets him avoid having to add her new handle.

Saraya lifts her sword and levels it at him. "Get him," she commands.

"Oh dear," Porsoth says. "I'm too late."

"Wait!" Callie puts the vibration into it, flexing her demon wings.

The guardians are taken aback enough by Callie sporting powers and wings they know are mine that they hesitate. We won't have long, but it's an opportunity.

"We should go. Now," I say.

Sean moves past me, toward the guardians, like I didn't speak. Callie blocks him with a wing.

"As you can see, we have some unusual things going on," Callie says with a rustle of the wings. "I'd be grateful—I'd owe you—"

Oh no, never promise a favor to a guardian.

"—if you let us leave here without some big battle. I'm sorry about the flying popemobile. It was . . . well, not an accident, but the best I could come up with on the spot. Claim it was a movie stunt promo or something."

Oh, right. They must be here about the scene we caused, and the blank memories in central Rome.

"Yes," I add, smiling with what I hope comes across as innocence. If such a thing is possible for a wicked soul like mine. "It's funny if you think about it. We'll simply be on our way and take more care. Apologize to Michael on our behalf. So sorry to trouble you."

Saraya squints at us with her usual disdain. "I'm not here for you two," she says, as if we're idiots for assuming.

"Then what?" I ask, directing it to her and then glancing at Porsoth. Because I honestly can't supply another reason.

"Ha." She shakes her head with disgust. The light coming through the broken skylight gleams along the curve of her blade. "Your tutor must be the worst in all of Lucifer's kingdom."

"I am the foremost scholar in Hell," Porsoth says, wounded.

"His tutor is great," Callie protests and Porsoth's beak bobs up and down. "Luke's just not the best student." She looks at me. "Sorry."

"No need," I say, still working out how to de-escalate this. "It's true."

If I had to hazard a guess, I'd say that Saraya holds in a growl. "Then you should know that when a human—seemingly what you have in tow—leaves the bounds of Hell, it's our job to bring them back. Our alarm goes off every time you come and go, and we have to reset it. We thought that's what it was, or we'd have found you sooner."

Huh. I did not, in fact, know any of that. Father did. Another point to him.

Porsoth says, "I did not realize the usual rules would be in effect or I would have warned you, er, sooner."

"We need you not to touch him, not this time," Callie says, holding up a hand. "We need two more days. Can you . . . I don't know . . . drag your feet?"

"You can touch me," Sean says, and he still doesn't take his eyes off Saraya. "I don't mind."

"You stay quiet," Callie tells him.

Saraya's gaze slides to Sean. Hardens again. Then back to Callie. "We have a job. We're here to do it."

"So do we," Callie says. "Look, we need to save him. We have two days left—it's a deal with Lucifer. Just give us a little time."

Saraya lifts her weapon.

"I'm irredeemable," Sean says.

"And dead," Saraya says.

Sean ignores that and keeps going. "I'm the rottenest apple in the garden. Ask Sarry, she'll tell you." He stops and inclines the slightest bit forward. "I didn't know if you would come. Personally." He risks a sad grin. "I hoped. But then after last night stayed quiet . . ."

What in the world? "Last night was *not* quiet," I say.

"I came because of duty, not you," Saraya spits out.

The two obviously hold a past of some kind between them. Callie and I confer silently. "You know each other from . . . ?" I ask.

"None of your business," says Saraya. At the same time, Sean says, "Her story to tell."

Saraya scoffs. "You made a bad deal and we're taking him."

"I was afraid of that." Callie's shoulders dip, the picture of defeat.

Until Saraya begins to advance and then Callie spreads the grand black wings wide and folds them around Sean and me on either side of her, saying, "Brace," to me.

And we're zappitied out of Lexington's hippest hotel.

The spike of pain is shorter and I realize the reason: we haven't gone far. We're in the Great Escape's lobby. Not far enough to outrun the guardians for long.

Porsoth appears a heartbeat after us. "Oh, I feared this! What a terrible development!"

Callie straightens and fixes a stare on Sean. "Care to tell us what you did to piss off a guardian?"

"Not just a guardian, the head guardian," Porsoth says, and *tsks*.

"How long has she held the position?" Sean asks. "And what's the deal with the Saraya the Rude thing? She must hate that."

"She hates me," Callie says. "It's my fault. But it was an accident."

The back door opens and Mag's laugh reaches us. Jared's low reply is making them happy. They're here early. They sound so normal, it almost makes me wish for a normal life. But we will never have that, Callie and me. I have to hope that's not what she wants.

Porsoth rushes forward. "Mag the Magnificent!"

Mag's laugh dies and then they and Jared come into view. They smile with delight at Porsoth and it lasts until their eyes find Callie. Callie with my wings.

Jared says, "Holy shit."

"More like unholy," I put in.

"I guess you left out something last night," Mag says. There's hurt there.

Callie's response is pained. She gathers the wings in tighter behind her. "It's temporary," she says. "And complicated."

"I can see that part," Mag says.

"I meant too complicated to get into last night." Callie is apologetic.

I hate it when things are strained between Callie and Mag, and I know she hates it even more.

"We can't linger," I say. Saraya and her death squad will be throwing bones or telegramming Michael or whatever they do to find us.

Callie nods. "I know."

"You're supposed to be working today," Mag says, and sighs. "This is why you were all in your feelings last night. Luke, I want a word."

"You can talk to me," Callie says.

Sean says, "I feel like I should go."

"No," Callie and I say in chorus.

"We'll just be a minute," I say, curious. Callie must know my loyalty is hers.

Mag steers me through the antechamber and the open door into the restored version of the Chamber of Black Magic. A now-fake grimoire rests on the pedestal, the pentagram a reminder of a trap laid for Rofocale that caught me instead. The beginning of everything, and nearly the end. The symbolism of my almost being unmade by Father in this very spot isn't lost on me, though I suspect it's an unintentional choice on Mag's part.

They cross their arms and frown with concern. "Where do you think this is going to end up?"

"Hopefully with Sean having a shiny good-as-new soul." Not that I truly care about that, but Callie does. "Then Agnes." Who I do care about.

Mag is stiff. "I'm worried about my friend. I want her to be happy." They wave their hands. "I'm beginning to think her mother has a point."

I know I'm not worthy of Callie, but I don't want to hear it confirmed. "Things got out of hand. That's all. Father switched off my powers and gave them to her."

Mag is quiet for a long moment. "You love her?"

I am flayed alive, as vulnerable as if Callie herself was here. Well, maybe I don't feel *that* exposed. But close. "I never thought it was possible."

"Drama king." Mag rolls their eyes. "You should want what's best for her too then. That's all I wanted to say."

"She wants this." I hope. "She wants to make change."

"She's read too many books. And she wants you too."

My worry is that even if she does, it won't last. No way I'm saying that aloud. "She's a good person. She wants to live that."

Mag shakes their head. "I know. Why did I have to be cursed with the best friend who's willing to go to Hell and back as a commute?"

I want to ask if they think Callie loves me yet. If they think we truly have a chance or this is all temporary, like my wings on Callie's back.

More words I can't manage to say.

"You have how long left on this Sexpot Sean thing?" Mag asks.

Another nickname. He collects them.

"Two days."

"But what happens the next time?" Mag raises a hand. "Don't answer that. Just make it through this one. All right?"

"You couldn't say this to me, why?" Callie joins us, coming in the same way we did.

"Don't be that way. You don't listen. I thought Luke might."

"I was listening—at least to that last part—and what I'm hearing is that you don't trust me or think I can do this."

So she didn't hear the question about love. I hope.

Mag's lips are a line. "You're talking about changing the universe, Callie."

"And you don't think I can," Callie says.

"I'm not sure that you should. I believe in you, but I also want the best for you."

"Maybe Callie knows what's best for her, have you considered that?" I ask.

Callie gives me a grateful look. "I'm figuring it out."

Mag nods. "Okay. But . . . just don't hang on to bad ideas to be stubborn."

"Is that what you think I do?" Callie sounds hurt.

There's a clatter outside and so, on that anticlimactic, unsatisfying question, our confab is at an end. Mag swings into action toward the door, but I stop them and insist on going through first. Callie and Mag follow right behind me as we exit through what's usually the customer entrance to this room. Once we're in the walkway, I begin to worry. Then I see the lobby and beyond and it hits a fever pitch.

Porsoth has barred the door with iron—but it's not guardians out there. It's Callie's mother on the other side of it. Staring in at her daughter. Her currently winged daughter.

Bosch and Cupcake wriggle on the leashes she holds.

My wings retract, and Callie's appearance is again human.

But she waves a helpless hand at Porsoth. "There's no point. Let her in."

The bars disappear.

Callie's mother unlocks the front door and enters. Bosch scrambles over to Callie, Cupcake right behind her.

Her mother says nothing at first, taking everyone in. Me, Porsoth, Jared, Mag, and Sean, the unfamiliar face to her.

"At least I know this isn't the devil," she says, nodding to him. "Callie, are you here for work?"

None of us expected that particular question.

She continues. "Or are you here to tell me you have to skip work to go on another supernatural odyssey? We're only running the game to pay for the last one. That couldn't be avoided. I have a feeling you're choosing this time."

Callie wants to protest, I can see it in every fiber of her being. I also see it when her muscles lose that tension. The guardians could be here any minute.

"You're right. It's dangerous for me to be here."

She and her mother lock eyes. I can't help but feel this is my fault. That I created this mess and now stand here powerless to make it better.

"I won't make you do it," Callie says, at last. "You're all right that I'm trying to do this big, huge thing that I might not be capable of. And while you may not think it's possible, I believe it's worth a shot. But I can't do both. I can't be here and try to change Hell too. So you don't have to fire me. I quit."

Her mother hesitates and I'm not sure if she'll accept. My heart feels like it's being torn on each side by hungry demons, so I can only imagine the roil inside Callie.

"If that's what you think is best," she says, quiet but accepting.

Callie's nod is grim. "I'll text the guys who took over for me yesterday and have them come by here. That way you won't be shorthanded."

Even when she quits, she makes sure not to leave her mother in the lurch. But I'm not about to speak up and point that out.

"Oh, okay," her mom says, and it's clear she wants to say more. She doesn't.

Callie gives a farewell scratch to Bosch and Cupcake, then she steps toward me, pausing to hook her hand in Sean's shirt and drag him along. "Nice not to meet you," Sean says to Callie's mother and gives her one of those grins that's like a facial expression and a double entendre in one.

"Read the room," I say to him and take over towing him the rest of the way to the door.

Porsoth follows. "Hi, Mrs. Johnson," he says before leaving.

"Always good to see you, Porsoth," Callie's mom says. No one can stand being mean to Porsoth, who basks in the attention. Maybe I should take a page from his book. Heart on sleeve.

Except mine would be hidden by my leather jacket.

"Be careful," Callie's mom says, and the words tear out of her. "Check in later. Let me know you're . . ."

Alive remains unsaid.

"Okay," Callie fills in instead. "I will."

We leave a far more somber day-two brigade. I wish I could read Callie's thoughts.

But at least we're out of there before guardians show up to wreck the place.

CHAPTER ELEVEN

CALLIE

I hesitate on the sidewalk. We haven't made much progress on redeeming Sean. All his thefts strike me as attempts at good. But he's insistent on this Holy Grail thing *and* he's hated by guardians (and *knows* guardians). And, this is a *big* and, we have no idea what he did to end up in Hell in the first place.

Leaving aside that I just torched the bridge to gainful employment at the family business. Jared always used to say that the danger of a backup plan is lack of follow-through. We'll see.

Sure, I can imagine a circumstance in which my mom allows me to come back. I'm good at my job here. What I can't see in this moment is having to come grovel and ask for that job back. I need to show them that I know as much of what I'm doing as anyone ever can—that I can build the life I want. The only way out now is through.

If this is the path that gives my life meaning, the path I want, then I have to try.

Luke stands beneath the special sign for the weekend with its floating halo—he's giving me a second to gather my thoughts—and I realize that means I'm right beneath the matching horns. If we were a regular couple, this would be prime selfie time.

We're not.

As evidenced by our demon friend Porsoth looking Sean up and down. He *tsks* into Sean's handsome face. "I thought you'd be . . ."

"You're *not* going to say taller . . ." Sean says.

"No! I never heard how you died," Porsoth says with great care. Odd. That is not how Porsoth usually speaks. "I don't . . ." He pauses. "I was surprised to learn you were in our realms."

I glance back and forth between them. "You two know each other? You know Saraya the Rude *and* Porsoth? How?" I ask Sean.

"He doesn't know me," Porsoth says. Again, cagey for him. He's usually blurting out too much.

"Unimportant," Sean says. "Details."

Porsoth's owlish eyes have gone shifty, refusing to meet mine. I'm definitely missing important context here. "You're more than a con artist and thief who always seems to be playing Robin Hood."

Sean shrugs. "If you say so."

I understand Saraya's impulses to throttle him. "And the most maddening person I have ever met."

Luke steps forward and puts a hand on my arm. "Hey, I'll get offended. That's my title." Gently, he adds, "You all right? What happened in there . . ."

"Was the right thing to do." I frown at him.

He frowns back. "If you're sure."

I bristle, then do my best to smooth the feelings down. Press them away. It only barely works. "You don't agree with them, do you?"

"Of course not," Luke says. "I'm with you."

"I hate to interrupt your argum—discussion," Porsoth says, changing course when my eyebrows lift. "But the guardians will be here soon and I would hate for your mother to experience another financial setback."

"Right," I say. "That's all we need. We should go. Sean?"

In the absence of other good options, I decide to ask Sean where he intends to go next. I have a suspicion, after a little searching on the Grail last night. Though I'd expect him to have more research to narrow potential sites down, given his illustrious history. When he fixes on a goal, he doesn't stop until he gets it. There's no way he got caught on any of those jobs without *trying* to.

He's more of a riddle than ever. I still don't fully understand why Lucifer saddled us with him, but I'm guessing it has something to do with whatever past he and Saraya clearly have. My luck, Lucifer intends for Saraya to take me out, plucking the thorn from his side. Maybe we can pry some more information out of Sean when we get to possible Grail location three.

"Sean?" I ask again and yeah, he's no longer here. I poke my head back inside the business. "Did Sean come back?"

Mag shakes their head. "You need help?"

No way in my boyfriend's home I could ask for it now. "No, we have to go." Once I'm facing Luke and Porsoth again, I scowl.

"How does he do that? Travel so quickly?" This time I ask Porsoth.

"There are . . . ways," he says.

My hand rises to my hip. "I don't like it when you keep information from us. Friends share things."

Porsoth, horrified, places his wing to his chest. "Please forgive me, I would give anything to reveal—I have already risked so much . . ."

Now I feel mean.

"I'd better get back," Porsoth says, "before anyone realizes and misses me and I wouldn't want to—"

"It's fine, really," I tell him. "Go."

"Yes, go on, Porsoth. Thanks for the early warning," Luke says. The bone from his prince calms Porsoth a bit and he leaves in a burst of foul-smelling smoke.

"Where to?" Luke asks and extends his hand.

My family is inside the building behind me and leaving the business feels like parting from them somehow too. No going back from here. But what lies ahead?

I think back to this morning in the hotel room. I don't know that I'd have been able to stop. I didn't want to. But I also don't know for certain that Luke is as committed to this as I am. To us. And whether it matters if he is, or whether we're another impossible thing, like saving Sean.

I check and confirm Sean's where I assumed he'd head next.

"Genoa," I say.

Back to Italy so soon. If the guardians beat us, Saraya might take Sean straight back to Hell. We can't let that happen.

The Cathedral of San Lorenzo in Genoa is home to yet another relic that legend says might be the Grail. When we get there, it's bright and busy on the city street, and jarring coming from home where it was still early morning, depending on your usual bedtime. (Way-too-early morning for me . . . except with an ocean of coffee or at times like this, when there's no choice.)

The medieval cathedral has an unusual striped stone facade, and around the plaza in front of it are a variety of ordinary businesses. A pharmacy, a place to grab gelato. Luke and I are still holding hands and I lean forward and support him as he recovers from the journey.

Forehead to forehead. Steadying us both, I hope.

The amount of zappitying is getting ridiculous. We could be in one of those old movies, represented only by fake airplanes traveling via little dots all over the map and back again.

"I didn't think we'd be traveling this much on our date," I say.

"I'm getting better at it," he says, after a few long moments. "But next time, we're staying in."

I'm relieved that he's recovered. "Deal."

We grin at each other.

"He's here?" Luke asks.

"Inside again." I confirm, but don't pull away.

His breath whispers against my cheek. This thing between us has to be real. Being close to him wouldn't short-circuit my brain if it wasn't real. *How many people have thought that over the centuries?*

"You're sure you don't think Mag has a point?" I press, knowing it's the wrong thing to say and saying it anyway. I feel like I'm demon-possessed. I suppose, in a way, I am.

Luke's lips pull tight for a second before he answers. "They just want to make sure I'm making you happy. You heard most of it?"

"Only the end. I don't buy that."

"Okay, Detective Callie. Since we're asking each other questions . . . are you sure turning your back on your family was the right thing?"

Ice spreads from somewhere in the region of my heart throughout my body. My veins fill with crackling cold. "I would never turn my back on them. But I need to do this too."

That's when he pushes back and gets a better look at my expression. "Got it. You want me to go in again?"

I nod, incapable of speaking. I'm only staying quiet by using every part of my brain that knows this is stray emotions spilling over. Things aren't going well and so we're taking aim at each other. I push my unruly feelings to arm's length as hard as I can.

"Back soon," he says, the words clipped. I want to tell him to wait, but we're in a hurry. I need to get better control of myself.

I raised my hand and volunteered for this. I made these choices.

I *would* call him back and apologize, but, after a brief hesitation at the door, he vanishes inside the cathedral.

Somewhere inside sits the *Sacro Catino*, a hexagon-shaped bowl made of Egyptian green glass that people in ye olden times thought was fashioned from a single emerald and magically powerful because of that. Napoleon stole it, and then it got returned broken into pieces. One missing. A few people consider it a candidate for the Holy Chalice.

The thing that surprises me is that . . . I can practically see it. I sense its presence so strongly that I could go straight to it. If it wasn't inside a church.

That almost certainly means it's not the real thing.

A relief. We still don't know enough about what Sean's playing at.

I wait, and wait longer, and then I wish I'd used my hyper-acute senses to check the time on my phone before Luke went in. It could've been an extremely long minute or a relatively fast ten minutes. Twenty tops. I don't think it's been any longer than that.

Truth is I've aged a decade waiting out here for him to emerge with Sean. Maybe more. I'm an ancient now, the kind of long-lived being who knows exactly where the Holy Grail is.

I wish. Then I could hide it from Sean.

I'm stuck on the question of why he wants it, another puzzle we don't have any pieces to.

I age another year—at least—when Saraya strolls around the corner. She doesn't have a weapon drawn, which I suppose is something. Her cheekbones are sharp as the blades undoubtedly tucked in handy locations all over her outfit.

She'd probably punch me for calling her bad-ass leather gear an "outfit," even in my head.

"You aren't going to say hello?" she asks and climbs the steps to the entrance. She must know I shouldn't risk getting any closer to the cathedral, not in my current demon-powered state.

She turns to face me and leans against one of the cathedral's front columns in what is still a lethal stance.

"Hello," I say. "Fancy meeting you here."

We stare at each other. This situation doesn't compute. Why is Saraya out here and not barreling in there? And . . . why is she alone? I've never seen her without her whole squad.

"Did you send your minions in to get him from the back or something?" I resist panicking at what a squad of guardians might do to a human Luke, purely as collateral damage. Or for fun. I have no way to alert him of the danger.

Saraya doesn't seem to be in any hurry. "I decided to give myself the pleasure of bringing him in."

Again, doesn't compute. "And you're not in a rush to do it?"

"May as well wait. He'd only enjoy it if I went in figurative guns blazing."

So here we are. Me and Saraya, waiting in what might pass for a companionable peace to an onlooker, for Luke to return with Sean. She's acknowledged their past. I need to convince her to talk to me. Tell me how she knows him. We can't let her take him.

You also have no way to stop her.

Even as I contemplate using Luke's powers, I put that thought aside. This is a deadly warrior. I am . . . not.

But I am good at asking questions and finding answers. I think.

"I spent last night reading up on our mutual friend in there—Sean's—criminal exploits, Saraya *the Rude*," I say. "Impressive résumé."

She sniffs. "You *would* think so."

"You don't? It seems like he only goes after people who deserve it. Why is that?"

Saraya's lips harden. "I know what you're doing. Trying to get me to talk. Your little deadline approaches."

The clock is ticking. True. I go for a reaction.

"He's on a quest for the Holy Grail," I say. "That's why we're here."

Her lips now part in surprise. She collects herself. This is the closest to bothered I've seen the unflappable Saraya—since she saw Sean earlier. "No way. He's playing you."

I watch her with extreme care and all the benefit of Luke's senses. "I don't think he is. What's your past together?"

Once I spotted the pattern to Sean's actions, all I could see was an effort to atone. But for what? And how *did* he end up in Hell? Porsoth seemed to find it surprising he had been there.

"We knew each other a long time ago" is all she says.

"You didn't know he was dead?" I ask.

"I knew he hadn't popped up on the radar in a while, so I assumed his bad habits caught up to him."

I remember what she said earlier, dismissing my read on him. "You don't believe he was doing good work?"

"He was committing crimes. Showing off. Enjoying himself."

"Are those things mutually exclusive?"

I flinch when Saraya spins, pulling a knife from a thigh sheath and throwing it through a gap in the foot traffic and into a sign for a movie on scaffolding across the street. The blade lodges right in some poor actor's left eye socket. She stalks over, then leaps up and retrieves it in one smooth motion.

I'm blinking when she comes back. "What was that?"

"I don't like talking about this."

"You mean you don't like me." Why am I provoking her? Is this part of Luke's powers? (I know it's not, but he is good at it. Why isn't he back yet?)

It's like she reads my worry.

"Since he must be in there . . . You aren't concerned about your boyfriend bursting into flame?" Saraya asks idly. "Did you find the dog on the facade yet?" She tilts her head to indicate the cathedral behind her.

How she's able to look so composed and cool standing on a sidewalk, a knife in a sheath on her thigh, wearing white leather, I'll never understand. Even with Luke's powers, I'm starting to sweat in the sticky summer heat. I can feel my hair starting to frizz, strand by strand.

"He's human for now," I say. "He'll be fine."

Saraya's eyes widen. "You trust Lucifer an awful lot. Wasn't he about to unmake him last month?"

These are not helpful thoughts. Because I can't do a damned thing about it if Luke is in trouble. I'm stuck out here.

"I really don't," I say. A thought occurs to me. "But . . . are you trying to be helpful?"

I'm honestly not sure. I need a Saraya decoder ring. An encyclopedia about the ways of guardians.

"Not particularly." She stands there, cool as can be. "So, did you? Find the dog?"

I bite. "What *dog*?"

"I thought you were considered well-read," she says.

Fighting words. "I am."

"The story you don't know goes that a workman on the cathedral back in the fourteenth century had a very good dog."

"They're all good dogs," I put in, because, well, Saraya may not be aware.

"His dog died, and so he put a small sculpture into the facade, a memorial." She stops and I'd call it a frown if I'd ever seen her smile. Laugh at me? Yes. Smile, no. "Legend goes if you see the dog, then you're destined for true love. If not, no such . . . love." Now she smiles, but it's not happy. She lifts her hand and points. "There, I'll even help you."

I would never have guessed that oblong blob is supposed to be a dog, but check. One sight of Genoa seen. "Why would you help me and Luke?"

The cruel grin widens. "You'll end up making each other miserable. That's what love does, true and otherwise."

"Ouch," I say.

"Spoken like someone who's never known real pain."

I'm not going to say it, but: *double* ouch.

The gash where the eye of the billboard actor across the street should be stares like a warning. I want Luke to come out sooner rather than later, but I have absolutely no idea what's going to happen when he does.

My fake money is on nothing good.

CHAPTER TWELVE

LUKE

want to turn and saunter right back outside, and not only
because I've walked into another church. I long to finish
our conversation. I sense that's the only way to make sure
Callie and I are all right. The unit, not us as separate beings. I
can't stand the idea that *we* might not be.

This is a new emotion and I'm not going to be shy about
saying I loathe it. I'd rather only have access to the boiling oil
variety of bubble bath than to feel this way. (What? Men aren't
supposed to have nice baths? Check your toxic masculinity at
the washroom door.)

I'm sure this relationship unrest is *exactly* what Father had
in mind when he came up with his abominable plan.

The entryway inside is quiet and I reach out for the calm
Sean claims these monstrous buildings provide . . . Nothing.
But there is a sign advertising the MUSEO DEL TESORO—
Museum of Treasures—off to the right. There's no one at the
desk, and past it, a set of steps goes down. I'm not surprised
about the lack of staff. The place isn't busy, not a peak church

time I guess. Servants of the Above keep different days and hours than we do Below, and I've never had cause to learn them.

But for a second time, I've entered a church and haven't burst into flame. I'm feeling smug on that score when I take the steps going down and down and then exit them at a creepy mausoleum of an underground museum. The stone walls keep it cool and dry, which means the air has a clammy, haunted feel. I find a light switch and flip it, and the weak spotlights trained on the museum's holdings come to life. They show off cases filled with the oldest, most antique, overly gilded . . . junk.

I pass by the cases while navigating the twisting warren of rooms, and spot *another* limb encased in glass. An arm and hand. There must be holy ghosts ranging all over the Above with a torso here, and a head there, missing the rest.

I imagine how much Callie would hate this, if she'd had to come inside instead of me. She's terrified of feeling trapped beneath structures, of being in enclosed spaces under anything. Yes, it's funny that she fell for a prince of Hell.

Is she out there right now thinking about how mismatched we are? How we should break up? How our worlds are too different? How *we* are? If she quit her job, anything is possible . . .

No, I can't think that way. After I'm out of here, I'll tell her all about this underground horror show, how Father did us a favor switching our powers. She'll soften. We'll apologize by moving on, no need to say the words. This is one fairy tale I hope to be true.

There are more museum cases with golden objects in them, and I pause to read the plaque in front of one for an anecdote for Callie. It's a story I'm familiar with, for once. Salome—one of Father's—asked for John the Baptist's head at King Herod's wedding celebration. The platter in the museum supposedly held it as it was presented. Ghastly.

There must be something pretending to be the Holy Grail around here somewhere. And our quarry looking for it.

"Sean?" I call.

The sound echoes in the museum.

Then I spot it. Ahead there's a case lined with red velvet and lights illuminating a green glass hexagon that is apparently nothing of real note. The glass around it is broken—Sean, I assume—but the dish sits where it should and that means he determined it's magic-free. I can find him and get out of here.

I have to retrace my steps. The museum being closed means the exit isn't open, and forcing my way out might put me outside the church. I want to speak with Callie, but not until I have Sean in tow. A story *and* the MIA soul we need to save. Gifts to seek forgiveness for questioning her actions.

I should have explained instead of asking. She and her mother are so close. Her mother plainly loves her. I can't imagine *not* doing anything a person like that asks.

But I am well aware that I can't understand their relationship. I've never known anything like it. My soul is new and I don't even know what it means. There's no way I could have explained any of that without sounding like the saddest boy in sad town. And I'm not.

At least as long as we're good.

This time, I enter the cathedral proper. I catch myself thinking it's more to my taste than the other one before I correct: there are no churches to my taste. That said, if there *were*, then this might be one, with its striped arches and stately gray columns.

Same uncomfortable wood benches, if fewer of them. Sean's

about halfway along again, sitting in the middle of a row. I make sure my footfalls are audible so as not to startle him.

"Made a bit of a mess downstairs," I say and slide in next to him.

"I was in a hurry." He pauses. "What took you so long?"

"Mad it's me and not your girlfriend? I can't imagine dating a guardian." I shudder without meaning to.

"She wasn't my girlfriend. And I'm sure it's mutual." I see a glint that some might call deadly in his eye. We study flash cards of human expressions, body language, the various glimmers in the eye as young demonlings. The better to spot opportunities for corruption.

"You care about her as if she was." I may as well say he's breathing. Which . . . *is* he breathing? Without my powers, I can't tell. I can't listen for the beat of his heart. Is he technically dead or alive?

He doesn't deny it either. "I thought she hated me."

It seems like she does? I keep my own counsel on that.

"Sucks to be proven right," he goes on.

I can relate. "Sorry." I have a sudden thought. "The Grail business—does it have something to do with her?"

That certainly seems like the kind of thing feelings for a woman could inspire someone to do, embark upon a quest to gain a magical object all these cathedrals claim to have and no one can locate.

Sean closes his eyes and sighs, slumps down in his seat. Enough of an answer for me.

He must know guardians can't be wooed. So far as I've heard. "She'll come after you," I say.

"I know. I wish I knew where it was, so I could obtain it first."

I think of what Callie would do. "You should let us help you. Callie's great at solving puzzles."

"You shouldn't," he says.

"Why not?"

He places his hands on the back of the bench in front of us. His knuckles flex as he grips it. "The Grail holds an immense amount of power. I told you that you were the inspiration for me deciding to steal it—the Order of Elerion wanted to create Hell on Earth. But the Grail can do the opposite. It can bring paradise into existence."

I still. What would it mean—Heaven on Earth? An actual utopia? It might put Hell out of business, but wouldn't it put Above out too? What would guardians *do*?

"I don't think she'd want that," I say, carefully, leaving aside the rest. "Saraya the Rude seems to quite like her job."

His response is grim. "A warrior needs a war."

I can't argue that. "This is above our pay grade, my friend. What you're talking about . . . it's . . ."

"I'm aware," he says. "I thought you might understand, given all this second-chance business. I like a grand gesture. She's never noticed the others."

Without asking, I'm certain he means the litany of high-profile thefts. I do understand.

"Maybe we could back up a few steps and you could tell me *why* she hates you and you're willing to find the Grail to create some version of paradise for her *without her asking*."

And then I'll figure out how to redirect you. Callie must achieve her goal.

Sean looks at me. A long searching look, and he's seriously considering it. Maybe he's about to trust me, ask me for help, and I can walk out of here with a *real* gift for Callie. Or . . .

A squad of guardians rushes in through whatever the front of the church is called and fans out to flank us with their weapons on full display. Yes, that's the scenario that happens.

They cry to each other in Latin and other tongues my current state prevents me from interpreting. Their arms gleam a metallic threat, picking up the light from the cathedral windows. Holy weapons.

Sean and I gain our feet in seconds.

"She's not with them," he says.

He means Saraya. We exchange a look. The squadron sans leader is closing in on us, but I check behind us and see him do the same. They've made one crucial mistake.

They left us an exit through the front of the cathedral. Saraya is likely waiting there, but we don't have another option. If she's out there, so is Callie.

"Run for it?" I suggest.

"After you," he says.

We bolt unceremoniously from the end of the row and back toward the entrance. An arrow pierces a wood bench inches in front of me and the sounds of pursuit follow us but I force my legs to keep pumping. I don't have to ask if they're shooting to kill or wound. They certainly would be happy with each option.

Neither of us—fugitive from Hell or its prince—is anyone they would stoop to protect from their deadly aim.

Sean puts on a burst of speed and reaches the door first, slamming it open. We're panting with the exertion as we reach the steps out front and I turn to try to bar the door. "Callie, can you lock it up?"

But it's too late, the guardians inside push against it, moments from forcing their way out. "Some help here," I say and glance over my shoulder to find Callie or Sean.

Callie stands in front of Sean, defending him, wings extended wide. Saraya has a blade leveled at her neck, the point nearly touching the skin.

Passersby give us a wide berth, a few on phones probably summoning the authorities.

I take a few steps away from the door and toward Callie without thinking. The guardians behind me rush out and surround all of us in what is probably a semicircle formation they've practiced a hundred times. My powers will protect Callie from almost anything. But from a guardian's blade? Doubtful. There's a reason we avoid them, besides their bad taste in fashion.

"Just let her take me," Sean says.

"I can't," Callie says, and the words come out as a whisper. A scared whisper. "You know that."

I scream at Father with every fiber of my being. I vow revenge. I threaten the entire world with destruction should anything happen to her.

I stand right where I am and try desperately to summon a way to help.

"This is tedious," Saraya says. "You have no chance against us and you know it. Our orders are to return him, as with any escapee from Hell."

Saraya doesn't want to hurt Callie, I realize. Because of her association with me? Or is it something more? Is there a real person under that snobby, off-puttingly sanctimonious, weapon-toting armor?

There is for Sean.

Put in a position to do anything to please Saraya or let Callie die, I fear he'd go with door number one. I fear it, because it's what I'd do if the positions were reversed.

I'd do it without hesitation—or I would have if I'd never

met Callie. But if I'd never met Callie I wouldn't know what it means to care about someone deeply enough that you'd remake the world for them. I get what Sean's about all too well.

This situation must be dealt with first.

"Come on," Saraya says. "This is taking too long. You're ruining our retrieval time average."

"So sorry," Callie says, and the motion of speaking allows the knife to prick her throat. A red bead blooms on her neck.

Saraya doesn't press the advantage, but this is headed nowhere good. All I can see is Callie's neck, bleeding. My mind supplies a full-on tableau of the worst-case scenario—Callie prone on the ground with far more blood pooling around her. *Stop it, stop it, I have to stop it.*

There is one person who *could* put a stop to this situation.

I close my eyes and shout for him, not that the volume will matter if he decides to ignore the call: "Michael! Arch! Angel! Michael! I, Luke Astaroth Morningstar! Call! Upon! You!"

Saraya snarls. "He won't come."

But there's a change in the air around us. It grows heavy, dense, charged from one breath to the next.

He *is* coming.

Saraya gazes at the sky and then assumes a devout stance, dropping her sword to her side, bowing her head. The rest of the guardians follow her lead.

Callie is able to turn her head with the blade gone and our eyes find each other. I go stand at her side as the dust on the streets lifts into a swirling cloud that will cloak us from anyone who isn't among our party. Anyone whose eyes might disintegrate at the sight of an archangel on Earth.

I reach out and gently wipe away the small tear of blood on Callie's neck. *That's better.*

Sean blinks at the glow descending toward us. "What did you do?"

"He saved you. Again," Callie supplies. She nods to me. "And me. You're a genius. Let me talk to him—I have an idea."

"You always do."

She smiles at me with the warmth I'm used to and I imagine our apologies contained within it like I dreamed.

Michael descends into the maelstrom of us and the dust storm he's conjured. His pale wings glimmer with their own light, his skin smooth and hard. He radiates power, just as the first time we met him. His energy is also . . . different than when he helped us stop the apocalypse. Not that he was cuddly that day. But right now he scowls in a way that says he's actively peeved, like we interrupted his nap. It takes effort to look at him.

Even with my powers, Callie is squinting. Her wings ruffle, no doubt sharpening, a reflex in reaction to the presence of an angel. Simply being here, he's a threat.

I hope my gamble pays off, and he's currently a lesser problem than Saraya and her history with Sean.

"Why did you summon me, child of Satan?" he asks.

Callie starts to answer, then must remember one of the first rules of protocol Porsoth shared with her. We always address one of higher rank only after being addressed.

She's never been that good at following it.

"I require a stay of execution," I say, "of your orders."

"My orders?"

Michael is like Father, if Father went for the distant alien air. He's like what Father would be if he stayed up Above, far from mortal concerns. Which means unlike Father, he can't be baited. I have no idea what Michael *wants*.

Callie needs to talk, to present her idea. I make her an opening.

"Callie?" I say.

She jumps in gratefully. "Your guardians are here to capture Sean Tattersall and return him to Hell."

I notice for the first time that Sean's head is bowed too. None of the guardians have changed their posture yet.

"He was set loose from the bounds of Hell," Callie says. Though certainly Michael could have read the details in the fabric of reality for himself in a nanosecond. "Luke and I have . . . We have less than two days left to show he can be redeemed. It's a bargain with Lucifer—to prove that people can change . . . Can deserve second chances . . ."

She's losing steam in the face of Michael's inscrutable lack of serenity. The dust in the clouds around us spins with renewed fervor.

"Is it a bargain or a game?" Michael asks.

Callie looks to me with a helpless expression.

"Father considers everything a game," I say. "But for us, it's serious."

Callie nods. *Good answer.*

Michael goes silent for an amount of time that I'd remark on for any other being in the universe. *Dust storm got your tongue?* I can taste the words.

I wait as we all do, silently.

His first move isn't to speak, it's an actual movement. He glides toward Sean. I can see that Callie wants to do what she did earlier and block the path, keep our quarry safe.

"*Look at me,*" Michael says, low.

Sean raises his head. He doesn't flinch or disintegrate.

After a long moment, Michael faces Saraya. "This will

continue, my loyal servant, Saraya the Rude," he says, "for the length of their terms with the damned one. You are not to prevent their activities."

"*Thank you*," Callie says, a gloating note in it that I appreciate but Saraya of the sour-lemon face does not.

He glances over at her and my wings. The dust swirls harder. He speaks to Saraya again. "You are to give them any assistance they require."

Saraya's face ticks up and I admit to grudging admiration that she doesn't hide her complete outrage from Michael.

To us, he says, "Good luck."

Like he was eavesdropping earlier in Father's throne room, joining the echo of everyone else. So far our luck hasn't been.

The dust swoops in around us and I shut my eyes, only opening them when the sensation of being stung by a million tiny pinpricks ends. Michael is gone, and here we are.

With our new allies.

CHAPTER THIRTEEN

CALLIE

The aftermath of Michael's departure is filled at first by the roar of the sandstorm that follows him up and up and up, then an unsettling quiet. Finally, when the sounds of the street return to us, and whatever bubble Michael extended is completely gone, Saraya breaks it.

"If you thought I hated you before . . ." Saraya says through gritted teeth.

I'm not sure who she's talking to. Sean isn't either. "Do you mean me?" he asks.

"No," she says.

I'm it then. "Sorry?" I offer. "I really am. But maybe this is for the best."

Saraya works her jaw in a way that fully communicates what words never could. One of her minions, a lean man with a scar down his left cheek and a hint of beard, tries. "In what possible way?" he asks.

"Go," Saraya tells him, and by extension the rest of the squad. She jerks her head.

"What?" the man asks. A woman in leathers behind him says, "We're with you."

The loyalty is touching . . .

"Go home," Saraya says. "That's an order. I'll babysit."

But only touching to me, apparently.

Sean is watching the guardians' exchange with an intensity that borders on creepy. His handsome face splits into a genuine grin.

He leans forward the slightest bit to me and says into my ear, "She volunteered."

"Calm down," I murmur. I can't believe Luke summoned Michael. And it worked. Sort of.

"You have to help us," I say to Saraya.

"Now who's pushing it," Luke says, in my other ear.

Saraya sighs and then levels her chin at Sean. "You're going back where you belong at the end of this. I'll just be conveniently nearby."

This will be the longest three days ever only to fail. So we won't.

Sean's face, there's only one word to describe it—besides gorgeous—and that's yearning. He's pining and then some. What's their story? I want to know so badly I can hardly stand it.

Saraya's squad shows no signs of leaving. She gestures for them to surround her, huddling several feet away from us. While they're busy I take the chance to speak to Luke.

"You were in there a long time," I say to Luke. He opens his mouth, to argue or protest. I don't want that. "I was worried."

"You were?" he asks with a hopeful tilt of his head. It somehow manages to remind me of Bosch when I produce a tennis ball from my pocket and also makes me want to jump Luke right here, right now.

"I was."

"You won't believe what I had to do in there—it has a subterranean museum." He preens.

"Please save it for my nightmares."

He grins. "Right?" He's serious again in a blink. "I never want to see you . . ." he searches, "Hurt. I never want to see you hurt."

He means the cut on my neck. I would be perfectly happy never to get poked in the throat by a holy sword again too. The concern in his eyes does something to my insides, twists them around and puts them back together again.

"Luke . . ." I hesitate, my brain rushing ahead and back to our current dilemma. "Why do you think Michael was so helpful?"

"I have no idea."

I asked the question because it seems important. Sean has been uncharacteristically quiet during all this, mooning in the direction of the guardians. Of Saraya, probably not the others. Though they occasionally take turns shooting the look equivalent of daggers at him, no doubt wishing they were actual knives.

Grudgingly, the huddle breaks up enough to let Saraya step out of it. The others lean in, heads touching. The guardians are truly the jocks of the Good vs. Evil world. They chant together a phrase I can't decode even with Luke's powers. Then all but Saraya disappear en masse.

"Was that angelic tongue? So, it's real!" I know I sound like a huge nerd, but as a fan of everything occult even before I got involved in any of it directly . . . *The language of the angels exists?!*

"You should never have witnessed it," Saraya says.

"You're staying," Sean says to her. "You could've left, but you didn't."

Saraya could be talking to the sky. "I regret it already."

During our confab with Michael, the street has grown busier. There's more foot traffic. People going about their days, with no clue what has been happening here. I used to be one of them, assuming the stories of good and evil and supernatural forces were things humans came up with to avoid boredom. My family and my best friend seem to think I still should be. They don't believe it's my place to change the universe.

"What do we do next?" I ask.

How do we give Sean Tattersall a chance at redemption? We're no closer that I can tell. We don't even know how he ended up in Hell. And he's not toting the Grail beneath his arm.

Luke opens his mouth then closes it and fidgets. I interpret this as him having an idea he suspects I won't like. Better than the nothing I've got.

"Spit it out," I say.

"I don't want to fight," he says.

"Me neither." I wave. "Bring it on."

"I want to fight," Saraya says as if she's remarking upon the weather. She tosses her braids over her shoulder. "To kill. To maim. To defeat. To conquer."

We all look at her, Sean included, with a "you do know you just said that out loud" reaction.

"For the glory of the Heavenly Host," she adds.

"Obviously," I say with raised brows. I turn to Luke. "What is it?"

"We're helping Sean, correct?"

Luke's senses surge back to me now that I'm not pushing them away and his beauty stuns me all over again. His hair a golden halo in the sunlight, eyes clear as unspoiled oceans.

Luke ticks his head toward Saraya. Is Luke saying that we have to help Sean with *her*? I think we have a better chance of finding the Grail.

"He's seeking another trophy," Saraya says. "He'll never find it. Why bother?"

"I'll find it just to prove you wrong," Sean says.

That logic does appeal to me. We don't have any other grand leads and Luke must have his reasons for thinking this might soften her attitude toward Sean eventually. Assuming I'm reading his suggestion right. I trust him. I do.

"Okay," I say, "so we're helping Sean find the Grail. What's your plan, Sean?"

Because if there's one thing I learned from researching him, it's that he's a meticulous criminal.

Sean grins. Saraya sighs.

"Oh," I say when he doesn't answer. We've just been bouncing between reputed sites where it might be. "You've been making it up as you go along, haven't you?"

"Now you're starting to get me," Sean says.

I frown. *No, I don't think so.* He's behaving out of pattern. It could be the time in Hell or it could be something else.

Saraya pulls her favorite thigh knife and without looking manages to avoid hitting anyone or thing besides the *other* eye of the actor on the billboard across the street. She strides across the busy street, successfully dodging people without a hitch in her step, leaps up to retrieve her weapon, then returns to us. The whole journey takes less time than I've spent putting a book on hold on my library's app.

Saraya stops beside us. "I want to remind everyone here that I was willing to take him off your hands and deliver him back to Hell where he belongs."

"Noted," I say and think next moves. Sean said we inspired his quest, and given the timing, that may be true. Meaning we've created our own problems, in every possible sense.

I choose to believe that means we can also solve them. And then an even easier one presents itself. Luke's stomach growls.

An easy call, then. The time may be six hours later here, but as far as our bodies are concerned it's morning. "Breakfast planning session."

"I am starved nigh unto death," Luke says in happy agreement.

Sean claps his hands together. "I know just the place."

Saraya looks at me and I'll allow her the *told you so* on this one.

"No," I say. "I'm picking. We will not be stealing any more cars." From whatever religious leaders happen to be around.

"You used to be so much more fun . . . yesterday," Sean says.

Luke kicks his shoe. We set off a discontent foursome on the hunt for food.

If we make it through the meal intact, I deserve a trophy for keeping them from brawling in the street.

And so we find ourselves crammed into a table at a ridiculously cute café with the best pastries I've ever eaten and tiny espresso cups of nearly undrinkably strong coffee. Or Luke, Saraya, and me have espresso; Sean ordered an *aperitivo*, a fizzy cocktail that arrived in a tall glass. Italians saunter in and

out, few of them lingering at what for them is midafternoon.
And those few are clearly sticking around for the scenery.

Luke and Sean together cause a sensation. I catch three
different women and one man snapping photos with their
phones from nearby tables. Presumably they are also thinking:
missing Hemsworths.

Saraya could be the personal trainer for whatever movie
they're here to film. Their extremely serious personal trainer.
Who ordered three espressos.

"Is this how you do things?" she asks casually, after down-
ing the third. She kicks her feet out in front of her and crosses
them at the ankle. "Lazily? No wonder you're constantly given
deadlines. Otherwise you'd never get anything done."

"We can't all be as driven as you," Sean says, and what pos-
sesses him to smile around his bite of a custardy tart I couldn't
explain.

Saraya lifts her leg and kicks over his chair.

The two scarlet-haired young women nearby leap to help,
but Sean rights himself with a laugh. He winks at Saraya.

"So," I say to him, "you have a death wish."

And it occurs to me we still haven't answered a basic question about Sean.

"I've been wondering about that," Luke says beside me at
the table, polishing off his own espresso and then setting it
down. "Is he dead?"

Luke is looking at me with expectation.

"How should I know?" I ask.

He scoots his chair closer. He puts a hand on mine and I
lean into the touch. I don't bother checking to see what I assume is Saraya's expression of disgust.

"Close your eyes," he says.

I do.

"And now listen, cast out the sense. Listen and search for his heartbeat."

"I could just slice into him for you," Saraya says, sounding disappointed we won't go for it. "It would answer the question."

"Shh," Luke says. Then to me, "Can you hear it?"

I block out everything except the feeling of his touch on my arm. Then I get rid of the stray café sounds. No more clinking cups. No more frothing machines. No more low Italian chatter, pings of texts, scrape of chairs. I zero in on where Sean sits and listen. His breath, even, in and out. And yes, there it is. The steady thump of his heart. Pumping regularly to go with each inhale and exhale.

I open my eyes. "He's alive."

"I thought so." Luke doesn't look pleased about it.

"He's alive?" Saraya says, and straightens up. "How?"

"You never did give me enough credit." Sean gets up and busses the table, taking our items to a bewildered but grateful kitchen worker.

"Why is this a big deal?" I ask to distract from how freaky it is that I was able to listen to his heart from across the table. Something else occurs to me. "You don't do this to me, do you? Listen to my heart?" I ask Luke.

Luke, to my surprise, coughs with what might be embarrassment.

"You do?"

He shrugs a shoulder. "Sometimes."

"Why?"

His cheeks go a touch pink. "I like the sound of it. It centers me. Like a rhythm under the universe."

Swoon.

Saraya snorts. She is such a buzzkill. I frown at her as Sean returns. "Sean . . . You being alive, why is this weird?" I answer it for myself. "You were in Hell."

We all look to him. He gives us an innocent smile.

"Yes," Luke says. "That's not suspicious at all. We don't usually admit people for punishment who aren't deceased. It's known as the afterlife for a reason."

"Porsoth was surprised he was there," I say. "And now so am I. Sean, why *were* you?"

"He belongs there," Saraya says. "Why question it?"

But there's something almost like concern in her voice. Like she's afraid to know the answer. Like she's as thrown by this fact as anyone.

"I let myself in," Sean says.

As if it's simple.

"Most people don't do that," Luke says.

"You've probably noticed I have a talent for getting in and out of places."

"So, he let himself into Hell, but he still counts as a fugitive to you when Lucifer lets him leave? I will never understand how your rules work." I throw up my hands at Luke.

"They're not my rules," Luke says.

"Correct," Saraya says. "Though Sean has never followed anyone's rules but his own."

"Why, Saraya," Sean says, and then grimaces as he adds "the Rude" without a choice. "Apologies," he says, for the name. Then, "I'd almost think you care whether I'm alive or dead."

Saraya stands. "I'll be waiting outside."

She leaves before anyone can stop her. Sean watches until the door closes behind her. "Now that we've had breakfast," he says, "I'll just be going."

"No," I say and put a command in it. The espresso cups in the café rattle. "You will behave. At least a little. We're helping you. I'd ask where to next, but I'm beginning to think I probably know more Grail lore than you do."

"The Knights Templar stuff is all titwaffle," Luke says. "Made-up."

"What about the other knights?" I've been thinking along different lines. "The ones who had a big round table."

"You mean King Arthur?" Sean says, and puts his elbows on the table. "I didn't start there, because it seems like it must be pure poppycoddle."

Look at the two of them, using formal research terms. "I'd think so too, but it also has a certain resonance. The Holy Grail ending up near the legendary Avalon. It's old. Joseph of Arimathea supposedly took it there, after collecting it and bringing it on his travels. There are some natural signs and portents in Glastonbury, England. And a whole literary history of Grail quests within Arthurian legend. It's as good a lead as any of the other places you've hit."

Plus, I have a feeling about it. I try to look there and part of it is fuzzy at the edges. Not concealed, but not entirely visible either. The opposite of what I felt outside the cathedral here.

"If you think it's worth a look," Sean says, "by all means."

"What do you want it for?" I ask.

Luke joins the conversation. "He wants to impress a girl."

That means I did read Luke's silent suggestion correctly.

"A woman," Sean corrects.

"You're right. Sorry," Luke says. "A woman."

I can hear my *own* heartbeat. There's nothing sexier than a man showing respect to women—except a man who shows respect to women *and* people of every other gender.

"I don't think she wants the Grail, so what is it really for?"
I ask.

"Does it matter?" Sean asks.

"It does if that's your answer."

Luke touches my arm again. "A word?"

"I'll wait outside, I promise," Sean says.

He gets up and I say, "Tell Saraya I said she has permission
to break your kneecaps if you try to run."

He gives me a small salute and leaves.

"Go with this," Luke says. "She's his one weakness. What
are the odds we'll even find it?"

"Why are you suddenly Team Sean?" I ask.

"I'm not," Luke says. "But we need to keep him around in
order to meet Father's goal, correct?"

"This isn't even his second chance," I say. "If he let himself
into Hell, then he's still on his first one, right?"

"It must not matter." Luke taps his fingers on the table. "I
just . . . I think he does care about her."

"Under that hot exterior, I know you're a big mushy softie."

He raises his brows. "I am not."

Uh-huh. "But is that the only reason you want to help him,
Prince Softie?"

Luke hesitates.

A crash in the direction of the street interrupts, followed by
a loud crack against the window of the shop. I produce a bundle
of cash I hope is good in Italy and slide it over the counter for
any damage as we dash outside.

Sean is rubbing his jaw on the sidewalk across from Saraya.
Glass fragments dot the street around him.

"We probably ought to get going," Sean says.

It's easy to fill in what happened. Saraya threw him at the
window. I can't blame her.

There goes my imaginary no-brawling trophy. I'm not sure which is the longer shot—getting Saraya to stop hating Sean or fixing his soul. Good thing that doesn't matter for our next move.

"Camelot, here we come," I say.

CHAPTER FOURTEEN

LUKE

Everyone has their own vision of Camelot, saintly King Arthur's famous castle. There've been enough movies, some of them—Trash King Arthur is my favorite—were even part of our pop culture touchstones, aka what I got to watch when Rofocale was too annoyed to deal with me. These were considered quasi-historical for us Below, given our realm's involvement in the real events.

Even in the grimmest, grittiest fictional versions, there's a majestic quality to Camelot.

But Callie sets down Sean and me on a perfectly normal high street. Once we can breathe, it's time for a look around. Saraya shows up just in time, traveling via her own method and landing in a warrior's stance.

"Doesn't strike me as magical," Sean says. "Just your average town."

This is an unnecessary comment. We all have eyes.

"Give it time. We should hit Glastonbury Abbey first," Callie says. "The ruins of it, at least. This is the place that supposedly connects King Arthur and his knights to the Holy Grail."

She's in her element, bubbling over with history and legend, as we head off to the abbey. "Now most people think the bodies buried where we're going aren't really Arthur and Guinevere. The monks were basically genius tourism promoters. The historical evidence for any of this is thin—still, there must be some reason why this place became connected to the legends. And the tor outside town is considered a candidate for Avalon. Tor just means big hill, by the way. But it used to be an island." Callie takes a breath, then surges ahead. "Joseph of Arimathea was a rich man, an unofficial disciple who took custody of Jesus's body and buried him, after collecting his blood in the dish while he was on the cross. It's probably not a cup. And there are stories about Joseph coming here, founding the church we're going to see the ruins of. Apocryphal, and probably BS, but . . ."

That's when we reach the edge of the abbey property.

Sean hops a small stone fence, and we're forced to follow suit. No tickets and lines for us. I concentrate on making us harder to notice, then remember Callie has that power now.

"Do you have anything to add?" Callie asks Saraya. "You must know how much of it is true. Do you know if the Grail is here?"

"No," Saraya says.

I take back my earlier doubts based on the town. The sweep of green lawn with the ruins in the distance is about as an idyllic setting as my mind can supply. As far from Hell as it is possible to get on Earth. I don't say that maybe *that's* the reason this land became known as Camelot. Not to mention, Camelot legends aren't all fun and games.

"You should ask Porsoth about Arthur, Morgan the Fay, and Merlin."

"It's Morgan le Fay," Callie says.

"In your version it is. In ours, she's a demon queen. Porsoth trained Merlin. He was one of ours back then. Retired now."

Callie blinks at me. "You're kidding!"

"Nope. Porsoth had a real thing for the fay back in the day. They're a nasty variety of lesser demon, in truth."

"The more you know," Callie says, and I see her eyes glaze as she presumably accesses some of this information herself.

Sean is far ahead of us. Saraya has sped up out of earshot, but within range of him.

I slow. I should've told Callie Sean's plan back in the café, was about to, but then we got interrupted by Saraya perfecting her Sean-tossing. All I know is I don't want Callie to find out before I convince her that we can change his mind. I figure if we can find the Grail, he's fixed. Saved, right? And then Agnes will be.

But there's another reason I'm pulling for him too.

"What are you over there thinking about telling me?" Callie asks.

Of course, she's ahead of me, reading me like a book. This is Callie we're talking about.

We're far enough away to have privacy from the tourists busy taking photos in the shadows of the ancient stones. Fragments of what must have been a massive building, as big as the cathedrals we've visited. There's something more calm, as Sean might say, about these stone walls and solemn towers, space around them and sky above. Definitely less tacky and no stray limbs on display.

"Come on, what is it?" she prompts.

"I think Sean intends to use the Grail to bring about utopia, Heaven on Earth," I say and keep my voice as light and flip as possible.

"What? How do you know this?"

I scrub a hand along my cheek. "He told me. In the church. It's all about Saraya the Rude, and that's why I think we should still help him."

"But . . . Luke . . ." Callie's brain is working overtime.

"The other upside is it'll enrage Father if he succeeds."

That's not the real reason I support him, I admit with a sentimental pang. He won me over because I can imagine too easily being where he is. How much would it take for Callie's affection for me to turn to dislike, even hate? I want to believe it's possible to fix it, should that happen. I have more riding on this excursion than I thought.

"What would it mean?" she asks.

"It would end life as we know it, but maybe that wouldn't be so bad." I give it my nicest spin. "I'm sure we can talk him out of it."

"Yeah. I'm all for change, but . . . that's too much." Callie's jaw is set. "We need to talk to him. Now I finally know what interrogation mode is good for." She starts after him. "Saraya the Rude, Sean, wait up!"

Sean being Sean, he's busy climbing onto the ruins. He vaults from a not-so-high level of stone to one that's considerably taller. Saraya's tight, disapproving posture is visible from here.

Callie reaches the ruins and takes a step up onto the stone, waving for Sean to come down. He ignores her and she jumps across to the next stone, going higher.

A series of memories of her doing precarious things runs through my head. She has my powers, but I don't like her scrambling over the ruins after Sean, who climbs as gracefully as one of Hell's mountain monsters.

"Bloody Hell," I mutter Below's favorite curse and jog across the green toward them. I stop beside Saraya. "Can't you make him come down?"

"Stop making a scene," Saraya calls up, irritated.

"Yes," Callie adds, halfway between Sean and the ground. "I need to talk to you."

"He told you what I plan, I gather. I'd rather not," Sean calls back.

Tourists have gathered to gawk at the scene and a security guard shows up.

"Sean, get down here," I shout. Then, "Callie, you too. You could fall!"

She gives me an arch look over her shoulder and I realize I've practically dared her to continue. The sun glints on her brown hair and I want to remind her that she has wings. But there are too many people around and at least two of them have started filming this scene.

"Oh Grail," Sean sings out, "Holy holy holy! Where are you?"

Has he lost his mind? Callie finds a handhold and maneuvers her foot onto a slimmer ledge.

"Can't you get him? Please?" I ask Saraya.

"Can't you?" she counters.

"You're supposed to be helping us."

She shrugs. "I'm not actively impeding you . . . which is close enough."

Fine. I predict Sean's trajectory—he's going for the tallest tower at the edge of the ruined wall. I'll head him off. I circle around to that side and a security guard asks what I'm doing. I long for my powers.

Instead I have to move fast. I leap up, barely making it to the first ledge by the skin of my fingers. It hurts to hang onto the stone, but I do it anyway and haul myself up and then step out of reach of the guard. "I'm going to get that man down from there."

The security guard looks like he doesn't know whether to thank me or Tase me. *That's the kind of day I'm having too*, I want to say.

I shimmy along the wall, and then begin the slow process of climbing the tower. I find a handhold, then drag myself up. Again, and again. Thankfully, it turns out some of my grace is natural. The obstacle courses across smoking, ruined plains Rofocale delighted in putting me through when I was younger were good for something after all.

I'd never describe myself as someone who doesn't quit. Some things are worth quitting—like listening to authority figures. But I'm stubborn and I continue to climb, focusing only on getting where I intend to go.

I reach the top of the tower at the same moment as Sean. He does a double take. "Wondered where you'd gotten to," he says. "You couldn't have kept my plans to yourself a bit longer?"

"No," I say and look past him. Callie is still halfway along the wall. She wouldn't die if she fell, not with my powers. But it wouldn't feel nice and she might be injured.

I never want to see you hurt. I remember the words I spoke to her an hour earlier. I don't want them to be put to the test again so soon.

"Go on back down, I've got him," I call to her.

"I'm almost there," she volleys back.

When will I learn? She keeps coming.

Saraya, meanwhile, is apparently done standing by and watching. Things have escalated too much on the ground, with another security guard arriving. She's produced a bow and arrow from . . . somewhere . . . magically, I assume. There's a rope line attached.

"We need to get out of here," she shouts to us.

We're violating all sorts of protocols with the visual feast for the tourists, although no one is doing anything that's not precisely human. So what's the harm? Other than imminent arrests, and Callie can simply disappear us from the authorities' grasp. The Grail clearly isn't up here. I have no idea what Sean is even angling for.

Oh. Wait.

I get it.

He thinks Saraya will fear for his safety.

"Last warning," Saraya says.

"Come down," Callie puts in.

"You go down, we'll follow!" I yell to her. "Can we please stop this now?" I ask Sean.

"Not yet," he says. "I want her to admit she feels something."

I was right. I guess it takes all kinds. "You did see her throw that knife into the eye socket of that billboard, right?"

"That wasn't the kind of feeling I mean."

"Beggars can't be—"

"I've never begged for anything in my life," Sean says with sudden heat.

"Maybe you should start."

He glowers at me. I've made him angry. "Maybe you should mind your own godda—" He hesitates and I glimpse Saraya's holy arrow approaching and grab his arm. He pushes me and I lose whatever grace I have.

It departs in an instant.

And I go with it sailing to sky, to ground, and away.

My heart is pierced with who I am and what I am and then I am nothing. My eyes close on this world.

CHAPTER FIFTEEN

CALLIE

People talk about how time slows down in emergencies, but researchers say that isn't true. There was one experiment where people were harnessed in and dropped from great heights to see if their brains sped up, if the experience seemed to happen more slowly. But that wasn't it. The truth turns out to be that when we experience deep, bone-chilling fear the amygdala lays down an extra set of memories. It captures everything.

Or at least we feel like it does.

Luke grabs Sean—presumably to push him out of the way of the arrow—but Sean misreads his intention and shoves him back. By the time Sean looks over his shoulder to dodge the arrow, it's too late. It hits Luke.

Luke, who stands on one foot, nearly balancing. So graceful. But the arrow tips his weight. It hits him on the side of his thigh . . . or does it? I'm not sure, I can't see the detail well enough because of the blazing sun. I do know it doesn't sink into the flesh, but keeps going. Maybe it only brushed him?

That doesn't matter, though, because either way he's falling.

His arms straighten in the air like they're seeking his wings and I wish them to him but it's too slow. Everything is too slow, and so very fast.

He keeps falling until he's hidden by the wall in front of me.

My borrowed senses sharpen, my emotions intensifying to something approaching the heat death of the sun. I hear molecules expanding and contracting, the universe gasping its slow final breaths, beyond it the screams of the damned.

Everything narrows and slows, from the grandest vista of all life to what's in front of me limned in painful detail. The fabric of creation twists around me tight as a starving boa constrictor, and I feel Luke's power forced from my body. My heart gets a sucker punch. In the wake of becoming human again, there's only pain.

Eventually, I become aware of my feet on the narrow stone ledge and my heart speeds up, my breathing shallow. How will I ever get down? And Luke. *Where is Luke?*

Did he get his powers back in time to save him? His wings? He must have.

"Jump!" Saraya yells to me, standing below.

She holds her arms wide.

I don't hesitate—I'll marvel at that later, probably—but I do as she says. I careen through the air with screaming lungs, tourists around us shouting in startled cries and I want to tell them, *You have no idea what you're actually witnessing.*

I plow into Saraya, but she takes my weight easily. She's braced and lets out a gentle *Oof.* I scramble to my feet, and then I run. She trots along beside me—she must be going slower than she would normally on my account. That makes me more afraid than anything so far.

"I'm sure he's uninjured," she says, and I hear the uncertainty.

We reach the other end of the ruined abbey. The other side of the wall . . . the place where Luke fell.

A teenage girl wearing cargo shorts gapes at the ground.

"Luke," I say, and then I scream it. "Luke!"

But he's nowhere.

"He disappeared," the girl says. "The body disappeared."

I march toward her. "What do you mean, the body?"

"You saw him. He fell," she says. "That arrow hit him. That guy shoved him. The security guy left to get the police. But . . . he disappeared."

The body. *The body.* She means Luke fell and he lay there like he was dead. He didn't suddenly have wings that broke his fall. He didn't rise into the air and fly away. He lay there and then he vanished.

Understanding sends me to my knees. "He was human when it happened," I say.

Our powers switched back when he hit. Not before. It could mean . . . It could mean that . . .

I look up and Sean is standing on the tower, but the light hits him differently from this side. I can see how shocked he is. I can see his regret when I say, "You killed him," including both Saraya and Sean in the accusation. "You killed him."

My head swims and everything after is a blur.

Saraya gets us out of there. Somehow. I come back to myself on the street. I can't say if I've been unconscious or if my brain simply shut down, unwilling to supply even one random fact, unable to think of anything except Luke absent. Gone. Maybe forever.

"I have to get to Hell. I have to know." I get up from my seat on the sidewalk by a not-so-busy road. "Oh no. I don't have my handkerchief. I gave it to Luke."

I spin to find Sean. "You could take me."

Saraya says quietly, "Then you'd forfeit, wouldn't you?"

"I don't care!" But I do. I'm nothing except care. I stop and throw my head back and scream for Porsoth. "Porsoth!"

He doesn't come. That's not how reality works, a woman calls for a demon and the demon comes. But it seemed worth a shot.

Porsoth will be mourning too. He might even blame me.

I want Luke. I want Mag and my mom and Jared. *Oh god.* I can think the word again, but it's no comfort. I'm trapped here, at Saraya's or Sean's mercy to get anywhere, even home. When I was busy zappitying us all over the world, hurting Luke along the way, I never stopped to consider being stuck.

And there's another sneaky terrible thought. *If* he's alive, he'd have come to me by now, wouldn't he? He would've popped back to Earth to make sure I knew. To see that I was okay.

But I can't believe he's gone either. I can't, not until I see the evidence. The body, like the girl said. I've seen enough movies and TV shows. Except for that terrible last season of *Veronica Mars,* no one's officially dead unless you see the body.

"Callie?" Saraya asks.

"I need an entrance to the underworld." An answer hits me. "The tor. Glastonbury Tor."

The hill outside town is a magnet for eau de incense types, but it was also a pagan site, a Christian temple, and, when the Celts ruled this land: an entrance to the underworld. And to Faerie. Didn't Luke just confirm that the fay are varieties of demons? I think of the demons and beasts and sorcerers of Arthurian legend and I'm certain we are close to where the Grail once was, even if it's no longer here.

And I don't care. Not about that.

I'm nodding. "I can go from the tor to Lilith's."

Sean speaks, at last. "That might work."

I point at Sean. "Why did you push him?"

Sean has a helpless air, for the first time. He lifts his hands, rakes one through his hair. "I thought he was about to push me. I didn't mean to . . ."

"And you." I turn to Saraya. "*You* shot him with an arrow. Do you know if it hit him?" What will that mean, if so? Guardians' weapons can't be the everyday variety.

"It did," Saraya says carefully. "Though I don't believe it created a mortal wound."

"Except it seems like you're probably wrong, Saraya the Rude." I hurl the words at her.

Enough of this. I set off on foot on the sidewalk and, to my surprise, the two of them follow. I guess it's for the best, although right now everything seems meaningless. Life as I wanted to know it may well be over. I'll have to apologize to Agnes for getting her hopes up.

"You are mortal again, correct?" Saraya asks.

"Yes." I continue along the street. Signs helpfully guide us through town and toward the tor. I dodge the other people on the sidewalk. I imagine I look haunted and hunted, the messy outside reflecting the messier inside.

"That means he likely regained his nature. He might survive." Saraya pauses. "Surely Lucifer would not allow his progeny to come to real harm."

Lucifer. He engineered this.

Sean snorts with disbelief. "Lucifer would definitely kill his own child if it suited him," he says.

I scowl at him. I'll take whatever straws I can grasp at and so he needs to shut up. I can voice doubt and blame; he can't. He's not allowed.

"I have to know . . . one way or the other." If he's okay, he'd have come to me. He hasn't. Saraya doesn't understand.

Lilith will take me to the Gray Keep. She will help me find the truth. That's as far ahead as I can think at the moment. My feet manage to keep going, one in front of the other in front of the other as we leave town and find the path up the sweeping hill.

It's a romantic fantasy landscape. There's magic in the vibrant green, so alive, alive as if it's land that breathes with power and has for thousands of years. If I wanted, it might even have the power to heal my heart. I won't give up yet.

The remains of the stone tower at the top of the hill are my destination, but I don't know how to find whatever entrance is here. I force myself to focus, but flashes of Luke intrude. Me almost telling him how I feel about him, but chickening out. Us together, and me saying good night before going home, regretting every step. I don't have that trite thought, the thing about how *Oh no, our last words were midconversation*. What I have is a clearer view of how that conversation should resolve. Luke was willing to roll the dice on Sean's plan. I wasn't. It was almost an argument. And arguments can be just another way to express love.

Love.

Yes.

I love him. I'd tell him that.

And so I march up and up the path. There are tourists here too, and I wish for Luke's powers to make this private. It doesn't feel fair to grieve for him where anyone can see me, not until I truly *know.*

We finally reach the hilltop, the tower directly in front of us. Saraya and Sean are watching me like I'm a time bomb. "Any thoughts?" I ask.

"To be able to go through, you have to see the entrance yourself," Sean says. "You can find it."

"Once you find it, just go," Saraya tells me. "I will keep watch over Sean. I will take him home, to Guardian City. You will join us there when you are able."

Sean's mouth opens in shock, but he says nothing. In fact, instead of the smile I'd expect, he goes grim again.

Interesting, but not enough to distract me from my task.

I return to the rhythm that brought me through town and up the hill. Walking steadily, slowly, I search this place and my mind. Entrances to the underworld, in particular ones associated with the fay—beautiful demons who can't lie except by telling curious versions of the truth—are often said in myth to live under the hill. Underhill.

Instead of looking around, out, up, I look down. I walk, one foot in front of the other over grass trampled by tourists, and at last the view changes. The ground beneath my feet turns to black pebbles, then sharp shards of glass, and finally, when I do look up, there it is before me: Lilith's back garden. I'll owe some tithe for my passage. At some point, I'll have to pay it to leave Hell.

I don't bother with it now. I don't shout for Lilith, and part of me worries that in the delay of getting here, she's already left. Maybe even Lilith has some sort of maternal alarm that goes off when her child experiences great harm. Or a spell that tells her if he's alive.

I cross into the garden without seeing her, and the plants sway to let me know they're aware I'm here and aren't making a fuss. They know me from previous visits. The back door is more of a challenge.

I can't let myself into Lilith's house. Not without risking death from some poisonous booby trap.

I knock.

Nothing.

But I hear singing, coming from somewhere besides the house.

Here's the thing.

This is not ethereal and beautiful singing. It is not the haunting ghostly voice of beauty in the deep woods beside the witch's house.

No, Lilith is singing Guns N' Roses' "Welcome to the Jungle," enthusiastically, if not well.

I shake my head. This is awkward. Even in pain and desperate for news of Luke, I know this is a tricky situation. If I interrupt, she'll know I've heard her.

She must be aware that she's a terrible singer. But Lilith is not the kind of person one insults. Or insults by lying to.

Luke would have the perfect hand wave distraction to handle this situation.

He's not here. I am.

I shouldn't know the lyrics to this song. It is so not my jam. But I actually *do* know most of it. Because it was a favorite of Jared's when we played living room karaoke. How I didn't realize he and Mag had chemistry back then, when we were thirteen and he was fifteen, I'll never know. In retrospect, the two of them duetting with Mag pretending to be the bass player with the giant hair should've tipped me off.

I circle around the house toward the singing and when I get closer to it, in the woods as I suspected, I . . . I . . .

Well, I join in.

Lilith's voice hitches for a second then she belts louder. I find her in moments and then I understand I've created an even weirder situation. The song finishes and she grins wide and says, "Another?"

I have been standing here singing with the mother of my possibly deceased boyfriend. Not just boyfriend. The love of my life. My heart.

She takes a closer look at my face, reaching out and putting my chin into her hand. She turns it this way and that.

"We'll leave immediately," she says.

"What?"

"Something's happened to Luke. It's written all over you." She bustles past me, dark-lined eyes and wild hair and flowing black skirts and all I can do is breathe the words: "Thank you."

"Of course, darling." She hurries us into the house and she pauses at a burning fire in the hearth. There's a pot dangling above it—a witch's cauldron. She stands over it for a moment, humming darkly to herself, tossing out a stray harsh word here or there.

"We'd best go," she says. "I can't tell. He doesn't answer me."

"Does that mean he . . . he's . . ."

"It means we'd better go," she says.

She crosses to a closet and throws me a velvet traveling cloak. We're traveling by witch again, like the last time I went on a mission to save Luke. This feels different. She whistles as she opens the door and a moth with large, delicate black wings emerges from the forest and lands inside Lilith's palm.

I wonder what she's going to do with it, but she simply presses it inside the cloak. "Ready," she says, and doesn't wait for my answer.

I've never been so glad to have someone else take charge in my life.

Hold on, Luke, please hold on. I'm coming.

CHAPTER SIXTEEN

LUKE

fell—the family business, falling—and I'm still on my way down. I might not be a body at all anymore, just a soul screaming in pain, falling down

d o w n
D
E
E
P

down.

Brought here by the poison arrow of a knight errant's beloved. While my own watched. *Callie, I fell . . .*

Porsoth catches me, so I am somewhere even if only in mist and shadows. He weeps. "Oh, my boy, no, hold on. You must hold on."

But I have nothing to hold on with, I try to say but whatever plane of existence this is, I have no voice in it.

"We must try," Porsoth says. "Summon the healers."

No, not them. The monstrous demon lords and their

attendants, who spend their time fixing the broken damned so the hideous horde can break them all over again.

I haven't hit bottom yet.

Callie, I fell and I'm still falling.

I don't wake up, not precisely. My consciousness comes slowly, nearly back. But I'm not fully awake yet. Not myself.

My upper left thigh throbs, and time creeps in the pettiest possible pace as I confirm I am present. In one piece. In existence.

"I told you it would work," Father says, and he's gloating.

I move my hand to the burning, aching spot on my thigh and find it wrapped tightly in a cloth bandage. Easing an eye open, I sit upright.

I'm in Hell. My own chambers, at least. Rofocale and my father are here, lingering at my bedside. There's no immediate sign of Porsoth.

"Where's Callie?" I ask.

At the question, the three remaining tusk-faced healers scuttle from the bedroom to leave us alone. Father didn't even have to lift a finger to shoo them.

"Callie?" I ask again and manage to lift my voice the smallest bit.

"Oh, is it working?" Rofocale asks.

"Leave us," Father says to him.

Sitting up has given me the distinct sensation of recently being hit by a truck. But, no. I fell.

I remember being on top of the tower wall and Callie climbing up toward me and Saraya taking aim with that arrow and Sean pushing me—and then intense pain and I was falling through the air and . . . That's it until a few moments ago.

Once my head settles, I push to my feet and search for my clothing, then shrug. I'll just get fresh from the closet. "How long have I been here?"

Father strides over and touches my shoulder. I stop where I am and look at his fingers there. When was the last time he lay a hand on me motivated by any feeling? When I was a small child, surely.

I don't like it or trust it and I want to remove his fingers. I feel, quite literally, under his thumb in the here and now. But I behave that way too. I look at him, eyebrows raised.

"Rest," he says. "You got nicked by a holy weapon. Give yourself time to recover."

"Saraya the Rude's," I say and despite not wanting to, I turn back to bed. "I really should go to Callie or get word to her . . ."

"No need," Father says.

I can't interpret this. Does it mean she felt relief when I careened and disappeared? Does it mean she's waiting outside? "Did she take a holy arrow too?"

"She lives," Father says, grumpy, as if irritated he has to give me that small parcel of information. "And she's well. Now rest."

A fount of facts, this man. I let my body sink back to a seat on the edge of the bed.

"So," Father says, and stands looking down at me. His wings are gathered in tightly behind him, in a position that's nearly defensive. He's doing his best "good father" and I haven't seen it in so long it's almost become a foreign act.

"So?" I volley back. "What's going on here? We didn't lose the three days, did we?"

"No," Father says with a wisp of a smile. "Clock is running. Is that still what you want?"

I scoot back, putting my legs on the bed. I don't want to be closer to him than I must.

"You know what I want."

"Her," he says. "But you must set your sights higher. You could have the kingdom."

That's not higher, I want to say, it's *lower*.

The wound in my thigh continues to voice its dull complaint. I almost ask for pain medicine, then remember I have my senses back. I push at it, forcing it to the back of my mind. The throb grows fainter.

There.

"I want her," I say. "I want a life with light in it."

"I much prefer being a rebel than dealing with one." Father considers me for a long moment, and then he commands me: "Sleep." The vibration is more effective than any rocking cradle or palliative draught. I'm knocked out, my eyes slipping closed immediately.

"You need rest first," I hear him say and I want to know what this rest is before. What it's *for*. But I don't get to know that, not until Father decides to tell me.

I have dreams of Callie and she's walking away. She's running. She's climbing the wall of a crumbling castle and I'm stuck beneath her. She's turning her back. I can't see her face.

No matter how hard I try, it's hidden.

CHAPTER SEVENTEEN

CALLIE

'm too upset to marvel over riding the winds high and sharp across the suffering plains of Hell this time. I pretend it's the foul air that makes me cry every few minutes, but it's a thin lie. Lilith sets a determined pace, and trusts me to keep up with her in my borrowed black witch cloak.

When we reach the banks of Styx, river and goddess-dragon-who-hates-me, the waters are roiling and black. There's a chorus of moans rising out of it that makes every hair on my arms prickle with sheer uncanniness. The stench of sulfur and sweat and blood.

Styx bursts from the filthy water, dripping, and I dread whatever task I'll have to face to earn my passage—even with Lilith here, there will be some toll. Instead Styx cries out to us, her talons beckoning us closer.

"Porsoth must be beside himself about the young sire," she says, her long face mournful at the end of a two-story neck. "He's called in Buer and Glasya, which means this is beyond his own skill."

Lilith clucks in sympathy and I can see the worry line on her forehead deepen. It hasn't left her face since we departed from her house on our way to the Gray Keep.

She's his mother. I tell myself that's only normal.

None of this is.

I recognize the names Styx used from the demonology text Ars Goetia. Glasya-Labolas commands thirty-six legions of Hell's soldiers, knows all art and science, and is a specialist in slaughter and bloodshed. And he's a good (very bad) boy—a dog with eagle wings. Buer has the head of a lion and five goat legs that surround it, allowing him to walk in any direction and making him look like a weird furry wheel. In charge of fifty legions, knowledgeable about herbs, and supposedly in charge of the best familiars.

"You will be in a hurry to get to him, your prince," Styx says, and shakes her head at the end of her scaled neck. "Consider your toll a single tear."

For Styx, this is sentimental in the extreme. Whatever of my own worry eased after I reached Lilith kicks back into high gear. As a person with anxiety? That's off the charts.

The tear won't be a problem, I mean to say, since we've been traveling through the wind and I've been crying silently on and off the whole time. I reach up to stripe a hand down my cheek to offer one. I'm sure there's many to choose from.

Before I can manage it, Styx's taloned fingers reach out and—gentler than I'd have thought possible—she scrapes the back of a nail across my cheek, almost as if she's drying my tears.

"Hurry to his side," she says. "Tell Porsoth I cursed my banks that I could not leave them."

"Thank you, Mother Styx," Lilith says, and inclines her

head. The dragon disappears with a giant splash, collapsing into the water, the moaning chorus rising in her wake.

Lilith swirls her cloak, about to conjure the winds so we can continue our travel, but she pauses. "I'm surprised you still had to pay a toll."

"What?" There's no time for questions, but I've asked one and she gives me a fierce look. Judging something.

Me. Judging me. I feel a chill. "What?" Now I'm asking in truth.

"You are on the path to becoming one such as I. Soon enough, you'll be able to travel unencumbered." Lilith strokes her lip thoughtfully. "Which means you are not fully mortal. Even if he had your weaknesses, he might survive." Her cloak cracks at her back. "We mustn't delay."

And so when she launches into the sky, I grip my cloak and follow suit, letting the winds carry me. I'm not fully mortal anymore? What does that *mean?*

There's no way to know, so I cling to the possibility Luke survived, that maybe *I* helped him survive.

We reach the Keep in record time that still feels like an eternity, descending onto an upper stone landing that forms one reaching branch of the tree-shaped castle. No demonic guards rush to greet us. No torches burn on the outside of the Keep. A pockmarked moon, mottled black and gray, rises in the gray sky above. I've never seen a moon here before.

Lilith takes it in. "A portent. Of change."

"Good or bad?" I ask.

"Change is never all one or the other," she says.

I hate that this is the one thing stories definitely nail about magical beings: they love to speak in lyrical riddles. "I was looking for more of a yes or no."

Lilith hesitates, gazing at the moon.

"Let's go," I say. "He's in there somewhere."

"Wait," she says. "It'll be but a moment."

See what I mean? I have to hold in a growl. If I knew the castle well enough to navigate it from this random branch, I'd leave her standing out here trying to wake the moon and go find Luke.

It's the first time my worry truly becomes fear since we noticed his body missing, since I realized he hadn't come to me and there must be a reason. If he's gone, if he's—thinking the word is like a knife—dead . . . what will I do? I don't mean it in some way like an angsty heroine on the moors ripping my nightdress dramatically. *Oh, I'm manless, I can't go on.* Not that.

Though my life at present is a puzzle, a riddle I haven't found the answer for *yet*, Luke is part of the solution. There are some people that, even if they're absent, change your life forever, the same way their presence did. Yes, I'll go on. I'll be fine as far as breathing in and out goes. Maybe get my job back at the Great Escape and work there for fifty years and take over for Mom when she retires. Maybe get my PhD and become a fierce historian bringing all the haters to the yard with my rad occult theories. Maybe become a librarian and spend my days helping people (because that's what librarians do, they don't sit around reading).

I don't know how the not-being-fully-mortal-anymore part will fit in, but I'm not truly part of this world. No matter how much I want to be. So I return to my own and I mourn and maybe I meet someone and I sad-jokingly tell them my most serious relationship was with the prince of Hell. They laugh and eventually I realize it won't work out between me and this random nice person because I still. Love. Luke.

With my whole heart.

His damn secret-keeping, and his also-secret vulnerability, the way he can't quite stand up to his father yet but I know he has it in him, the way he admires my brain, and let's be real, my perfectly normal body, and the way we get each other into terrible situations and then back out again.

Please, back out again.

"I'm done waiting," I say.

"Someone's coming." Lilith holds up a hand. "I promise."

"Is this someone a snail demon?" I ask, getting cranky. I have to know. I have to find Luke. See him.

"You have an impatient streak," Lilith says. "I like it."

Doors clatter open in the distance behind us, closer to the main trunk structure of the Keep. She raises an eyebrow, so that must be where Luke gets that specific talent from. *See, why ever doubt me?* all in a brow arch.

Porsoth walks to us, his scholar's robe floating around him like he's an apparition. I can't stand how slowly he moves. One slow step, then another.

I want to run to meet him, but I'm afraid to. My Great Escape/historian/librarian futures flash before my eyes. The moon hangs above, taunting. *Bad change*, it seems to say, *if you're so desperate for an answer.*

The second Porsoth is close enough for me to see his face, I ask. "Luke?"

He spreads his wings wide. "We have employed all the darkest arts available. Now we must see if he wakes . . . You realize he was wounded by a holy weapon."

He sounds tired. Exhausted. It's taken me hours to get here, so he would be.

"But he's alive?" I seize on that.

Lilith latches onto the injury. "How badly?"

"On the surface, not so deep, my lady," Porsoth says. "But such wounds can be tricky, as you know. The weapons are designed to nullify our magic. We do not understand their mechanisms."

She tosses the hood of her cloak back, revealing her hair wild beneath it. "I want to see him."

Porsoth fidgets. His usual way. Foot to foot. There's a somber quality I'm not used to. "You can't."

"The hell I can't." I start to stride past him, but he extends a surprisingly firm wing. It holds me back.

"You can't." The words sound like a lesson. "Lucifer is with him. We'll have to wait. All of us."

"You must be joking?" I look to Lilith for support. This can't stand. She won't let it.

She nods. "I don't like this moon, 'Soth."

He crooks his feathered neck to examine it. "I don't either, my lady."

I can't believe this, but Porsoth still hasn't lowered his wing. He's blocking me from going to Luke. He doesn't move it until I take a step back, relenting.

"Porsoth," I say, "we're friends. Please."

"Some duties go beyond friendship," he says, noble owl's beak lifted.

I don't know what's worse, the sentiment or the fact he's broken out the lyrical pronouncements too.

Obviously, I only pretend to have given up and that I'm waiting semi-patiently for us to be allowed in, for Lucifer to arrive with an update. Once it becomes clear that may be a while, I start to scheme. It's what Luke would do.

He wouldn't sit out here cooling his hot heels under a cursed moon, not if it was me in there. I have as much right to see him as Lucifer. More, if love is a factor. (Because Lucifer loving anyone but himself? Doubtful.)

I'm surprised Lucifer even cares that he's wounded, honestly. He practically set us up for some catastrophe like this . . . I snag on that thought.

He probably *did* set us up for something *exactly* like this. No way am I waiting out here. For all I know, he's decided to murder his son. Once you've read enough books, the patterns are disturbing. And, with Lucifer, *anything* is possible.

When in doubt, I decide, go simple, not big. At least in this situation.

"Porsoth," I say, "I hate to ask, but I have to pee. Can we go inside?"

First step, get in there. I don't know where Luke's chambers are from here, but I might be able to find them. There's a chance that's where he is. I can't imagine a prince getting stuck in Hell's medical bay. "Does Hell have an emergency room?" I ask, before I can stop myself.

"It does not," Porsoth says. "Is this a ploy? My dear lady, you can't disobey, not this time."

"No, the question just occurred to me." I feel a hint of guilt as I twist the knife. "For you to shame me for asking for information . . . our love of knowledge is part of our bond." *It's for Luke.*

Behind his spectacles, Porsoth's eyes slide down. He's chastened. "I apologize. Yes, we can wait inside as well as out. I'll know when we can return."

But not to a medical area. *Hmm.*

Lilith studies me like she suspects I'm up to something, but true to form keeps it to herself. I don't think she'll mind, and might even be disappointed if I'm not. She won't violate the order herself apparently, for mysterious reasons, but I don't have her hang-ups where Lucifer is concerned.

Porsoth turns and we head across the stone limb to the doors. I pause to remove my cloak and drape it over my arm, because there's a distinct possibility I'll get tangled in it or catch it on a burning candle inside otherwise. Lilith wears hers like a queen, as darkly elegant as a sentence to Hell is long. It's difficult for me to believe we share even a hint of something in common, like non-mortalness.

Except for Luke. *Hang on, I'm coming.*

The wooden doors have two of the grotesque soldiers who frequent the castle posted inside. "We were coming to fetch you, sir," the one with horns like a skeletal deer says to Porsoth, and then adds a leering, "ladies."

Lilith's eyes go heavy-lidded and for a second I think she might flirt, but then she flicks her wrist at him. "May your fingers turn to ice and fall off," she says.

And . . . they do. The demon shrieks, but at a spear nudge from the other blue-skinned frog-like demon, quiets himself. The frog demon steps over his compatriot's frozen fingers and gestures. "Here he is now."

The demon Glasya-Labolas trots up the hall and it's nearly impossible not to react to him like a dog at first. His face truly *is* the ultimate slobbery, happy dog face (Bosch is a lady, not a slobberer), though the rest of his shaggy body and the thick claws ruin the effect. Not to mention the eagle wings.

"Lilith," he says with a voice like a deep bark, "Porsoth."

He doesn't even react to the frozen fingers on the stone and the antlered soldier standing with icy arms attempting to be as quiet and meek as possible.

"Report," Porsoth says.

"We were asked to leave by . . ." he begins and keeps talking. Doctors here, just like in the regular world, not letting anyone else get a word in edgewise.

Lilith and Porsoth are intent upon the strange dog demon's medical report and, while I'd like to hear what he has to say, I'd rather see for myself.

I make it two, then three steps away. A familiar head peeks out of a door up the hall and waves to me before disappearing again. Agnes.

The horned demon guard with the frozen, handless limbs raises one and says, "Excuse . . ."

Lilith shoots him a quelling glance that offers to freeze more of his appendages and he quiets. I shrug at him, and try to gauge when I should run.

Something tells me Glasya will be quick on those four paws of his. I look back and see Lilith waiting for me to catch her eye. She flicks her wrist again, behind Porsoth's back. And then she asks Glasya a question. Porsoth nods and listens.

I go as quickly and quietly as I can toward Agnes's position. She grabs my arm and drags me up the hall. Once we reach the end of it and round the corner, we're out of sight.

"Where is he?" I ask her.

"His apartments, I believe," she says. "I . . . I wanted to tell you that if it's a choice between Luke living and me staying here . . . I'll stay. You tried your best."

"It's not. Agnes, it's not. But I have to see him. Which way is it?"

Agnes shrugs, pained. "I'm not sure. I only have access to common areas and the library."

I take a beat. I visualize a mental image of where we were outside, and then where Luke and I have seen other people come and go from before. I *think* I'm on the back end of where I usually come in with Luke.

If I'm right, that means his apartments are somewhere on this side of the massive castle.

The corridors are empty, and the entire place has a feeling of holding its breath. Hell's big on omens (Heaven too—I can think it again). I imagine that ominous moon has forked tongues wagging. Along with whatever rumors are spreading about Luke's fortunes, and mine.

Something flutters against my face and I startle and nearly scream, but manage to swallow it. The moth from Lilith's forest hovers in front of me on wide black wings and does a little Lassie the dog maneuver, back and forth. It must think I'm a moron.

"I get it," I say. "Agnes, go now, back to wherever you're supposed to be. I don't want you in hot water." Here, it might be *literally* boiling.

She looks like she might say something else, but she only nods.

When the moth takes off down the hall, bobbing and weaving on its lacy wings, I follow and Agnes heads in the opposite direction. Twice, the moth and I pause. There are distant shouts behind us and possibly the scrabbling of demon-dog paws.

But I begin to recognize the corridors and then there's one final stairwell. The moth and I hide within it, one floor up, as tusked attendants in black leave. The moth circles the door.

I carefully tiptoe down the stairs and ease the door open to see what's beyond.

Luke's chambers.

The moth buzzes in my face once, then darts back the way we came, no doubt returning to Lilith.

The moment of truth. I prepare for whatever I find in these rooms.

And go through the door. There's an attendant working in the small kitchen and I breeze past, raising my hand to dismiss protests that never come, not looking at them. I get past unseen.

I have to find Luke before I get hauled out of here. Lilith helped me for a reason.

The rest of the place is empty, so I head for his bed chamber. I hear voices within. One voice is dominating—Lucifer's—but he's in a conversation. If he's talking to someone, it must be Luke.

If Luke's talking, he must be alive. Right? I'm shaking with relief and joy and—

The smart thing would probably be to wait out here for Lucifer to leave.

I do the only thing I can: I barge in.

Let the devil take the . . . devil. I'm here for my man.

CHAPTER EIGHTEEN

LUKE

I wake up filled with lightning. As if my body reached some regeneration point and exploded past it. The ache in my thigh is distant, barely there. I get out of bed in a hurry, ready to leave. This is the only part of the Keep I actively like, though even its extravagant silky textures and brocade goth vibe have started to wear on me.

But it's been my sanctuary. No longer, it seems.

Father is still here, sitting in the velvet corner chair. That shouldn't stop me; it does. I sink back down.

"You're awake," Father says, a more obvious opening salvo than his usual.

"After you knocked me out," I say. "I apologize, Father, but I have to get going. How long do we have left?"

He doesn't move. "Long enough, perhaps. It's still the second day."

So I haven't lost that much time, haven't abandoned Callie for too long.

"Good." I stand and head for my walk-in closet across the

room. The bandage wrapped around my thigh is the only stitch I have on. Good thing I've never been shy about bodies. No one in Hell is.

The sweet, hot way Callie flushes when either of us is missing articles of clothing and I look at her, just *look*, flashes through my head and I have to banish it. I may not be shy about bodies, but knowing Father is here is enough to chill any amorous longings. She must be furious with me for vanishing and not sending word. Maybe Porsoth managed to communicate with her. I can hope.

I hope she cares. That she didn't feel secret relief when I tumbled out of her world. I should have told her—how I felt, what I wanted—and damn any shame in confessing to such weakness. I trust her. More than I trust myself. It's time to come as clean as someone with a heart as dirty as mine can.

My favorite leather jacket hangs in its place of pride, the lone item on its rack. I asked Mother to enchant it to always return home. I pick a black T-shirt from a row of freshly laundered ones in the same shade.

Father clears his throat. "I need a word."

I don't turn around, but riffle for some pants. "And I need to get back out there."

"Sit," Father says.

I don't know if there's a hidden command in it. I tell myself there is to prevent a surge of shame as I walk back to the bed and do so.

"Only one of you can be my heir," he says, peering down his long nose at me. His eyes are a cold burn, measuring.

I shake my head, intending to clear it. Not a thing I've ever wanted or needed to do.

"I'm aware that I'm the heir." Is that what all this is? Being punished for not being happy to do my duty in this dark place, for wanting the light Callie brings? It's so hypocritical. "It's not as if Mother wasn't a human, at least starting out. I know what I am."

His head tilts. "No," he says. "I don't think you do."

I'm impatient and irritated enough that I snap. "As much as I'd love to sit here and pretend to be impressed by your verbal traps, if you could get to the point, it'd be wonderful."

"Your brother tried to kill you, didn't he?" Lucifer asks.

I still. My brother.

"A guardian hit me with an arrow—" Although Sean pushed me off the wall.

My brain avoids circling back to the word as long as it can. The implication.

Which isn't long enough.

Brother. Father is saying Sean is my brother. I have a brother.

"Half-brother, I should say." Father squints and I admit he's the most engaged I've seen him in ages. He's enjoying this. "He didn't tell you."

Sean is my half-brother and he *knows*.

"He didn't tell me much of anything, except that I'm an inspiration to him." Me and Callie. Father can't know what he means to do with the Grail.

I want to confess it. Anything to wipe that smug look off his face.

Something stops me. "*That's* why you set up this whole farce."

"I set it up to remind you where you belong. You are meant to be the heir, and you must put that above all."

No thanks. "You're in good health, at the height of your powers . . ."

Father rises, tall and immovable. "Beside the point. I desire time away, and I require your commitment."

Of course he does. And what Father wants, he gets.

"I'm going to pretend this is a hallucination." I climb to my feet, the insistent beat of my heart in time with the dull throb returning in my thigh. "And go back to what I'm doing. None of this is about you."

"Everything is about me." Father brings his hands together with a thunderclap boom. "For as long as I say it is."

I imagine myself as Callie in my dreams, walking, running, turning my back. But I'm not as brave as Callie.

"What more do you want from me?" I extend my hands, as if I'm pleading for an answer.

Attention, seemingly. Father relaxes a hair and strolls around my suite. "Did you know he snuck in here? Wanted to see what he'd been missing, I suppose. He'd known who he was for years. We met once, when he was seventeen, and I told him what I expected of him. I hadn't seen him since. But he came here, and let himself be tortured. He pretended to be one of them, a human. I only found out he was here by happenstance." Father lifts his hands out in a mimicry of mine, but he's asking a grand question, *Can you believe it?*

"That must've stung," I say.

"Yes. That my other son—the good son—abandoned the original task he'd been given and then allowed himself to be demeaned. Like he was in control of his destiny."

I wonder what task Father gave him, but I'm not about to ask. "And not you."

"And not me." Father thinks I'm agreeing with him. He thinks I'm similarly disgusted by Sean's rejecting him.

I burn with an envy of such intensity it surprises me.

"It can't stand," Father continues. "Others will find out he exists and that he's out of control. I don't understand him. He's too unpredictable. I am restless and want to travel. It is time for you to get serious about your position. One day you can find yourself a nice human or ten—or better yet, a harem of demons who'll suit without complaints."

He wants me to run Hell. To be fully committed to being his standard-bearer. Simply because he wants to take a vacation and Sean has done a better job than me of communicating the level of "don't care to." *I'm* supposed to be the rebellious son. I'm supposed to be the only son.

"You understand what I'm offering you," Father says. "Control. Power."

Those have never been things that attracted me. "And Callie?"

"You must know she's too *good* for you . . . This business of saving damned souls is the antithesis of who you're meant to be."

He's right. I *do* know all that. But I don't care, though I should. Or, rather, I care only as far as it might chase her away.

"You'll never be powerful with her shackling you to humanity. Now is the time to grow up. To assume your birthright. You will bring Sean back, humiliating him, and then he will not be an issue any longer. I will be well pleased," Father says. "You have always been my favorite, son."

There's a first time for everything, I want to say. *No*, I want to say.

I say nothing. Nothing at all. Not one word.

Something inside me wants to bask in being his favorite, in him saying it, even if it's a lie.

He must take my lack of response as an obedient silence. He grins at me. A smile to make angels weep, and that has. It's my sorrow he wants. My acceptance.

I have a brother.

His hand lands on my shoulder again.

That's when Callie shoves through the door to my bed chamber and takes me in, naked on the side of the bed but for the bandage, and my father beside me with his hand on me. She's a furious mess in motion, her hair a tangle of waves. She tosses a thick cloak onto the floor as she advances on us.

"If you're not healing him or something, get out," she says to Father.

My heart seems to swell to an ungainly size. I expect it to be visible from every corner of the universe. I couldn't like or love her more.

Father does his best sinister menace. "I'm considered more of a virus than a cure."

Callie should shrink under that tone and his gaze. She should turn and leave. I'm suddenly afraid she will. But she inserts herself between us, knocking his hand off my shoulder in the process. She gives me a searching look.

"You're okay," she says. "You're okay."

"Mostly . . ." I like being fussed over.

"I wasn't finished," Father says.

"Yes, you were, you were just leaving," Callie says, her field-green eyes only for me. She strokes a tentative hand down my cheek and I lean into the touch.

Beside us, Father hesitates and, then, to my great disbelief, he does what she says. "Remember what I told you. Remember who you are," he says, but after that he leaves us, a click of the doors shutting behind him.

Callie seemingly needs to make sure I'm truly whole. Her hand leaves my cheek and joins the other on my chest, skimming over my body. My breathing quickens. There's so much to tell her.

I open my mouth. She starts talking before I get a word out.

"You should have sent word. Somehow. We've been here for ages and Porsoth wouldn't let us come in, but I snuck away and your mother helped—"

Her hands are still tracing over my torso and I wonder how she got to Lilith and *here* and I know it must be an ingenious story, because this is my Callie. I have so many things to say to her—mainly that I have a half-brother and it's Sean. That my father has set us against one another and expects this to motivate me to assume my full rank. But there's something far more urgent than any of that.

"I love you," I say before I can think better of it.

She stops talking.

I might as well be not only naked, but transparent. My heart sits on a scale while I wait to see if it weighs enough.

Callie stares at me.

I regret saying the words. A moment of weakness. "It's all right—"

"Don't," she says. "Don't take it back. Luke, I thought you might be . . . When you disappeared and then I was mortal again. I thought you would send word if you were okay, but you didn't."

"I wanted to—"

She presses a finger to my lips. "Shh, I'm not finished. I

feel like I lived a whole life without you, just getting here. Not knowing what I'd find. If you were . . . If you'd been . . . I've never been that scared. I never want to feel that way again."

She lifts her other hand and cradles my face, gazing at me like I'm a miracle. "You can't know how good it is to see you. That you're here in front of me. You can't know how much it would have broken me if you were . . ."

"I'm fine." I put my hands over hers. "I promise. I'm sorry I worried you. About what I—"

"I have another idea," she says.

The words should make me quake at this point, but they don't. Purely due to the heat in her eyes as she says them.

"Don't keep me in suspense. Please."

She pushes her hair behind an ear with one hand and I note that it's bright red. "I've been thinking about how we were sort of arguing before and while I definitely think you need to start telling me things—" I don't stop her to point out that I just told her a pretty enormous, life-changing thing. "—I want to cross the intimacy Rubicon. I'm ready."

"The intimacy Rubicon?" I echo, not sure what that means.

"You know," she says, flushing, "sex."

"Oh. Ohhh." I'm definitely down for that. "Why are your ears red?"

"Because I grew up in a Puritanical society? Probably? Shut up. The Rubicon is a river in Italy—when Julius Caesar crossed it, that was a point of no return. It started a war, but I don't mean war here, I mean . . ."

Shut up is not close to *I love you*. But she's babbling and that means she's nervous. And she clearly went through a great deal to get here. Her relief that I'm all right is palpable, and that's a good sign. I force myself to forget the pang of disappointment and warm up to the intimacy Rubicon idea. It doesn't take long once I remember what she means.

Callie is giving me a hint of a frown now, as if I've rejected her, so I get as close as possible to her and my body responds as it always does to the reality of her. I breathe against her neck, the floral hint of her shampoo and the vanilla note in the perfume she dabs onto her pulse point. Vanilla is anything but boring when it combines with Callie Johnson's chemistry.

I press my lips there and feel blood rush to all the places it should rush to. I hardly feel the ache in my thigh. She releases a breathy sigh.

"This river we're crossing, what's on the other side?" I raise my head and murmur it against her lips. Not my best warm-up talk, but I'm on board the boat now.

Callie presses her palm to my bare chest and my heart and skin ache at the pressure. "I didn't say it." She rolls her eyes and I'm lost. I have no idea what's happening, except that I belong to her.

"I started talking and I forgot to say it. Luke . . ."

I go still.

"I love you too," she says. "Obviously."

My heart cracks open. It parts like a sea or this Italian river she's so fond of and encloses us both.

Callie loves me too. Obviously.

I feel fully awake. Alive. "You do?"

"Yes, I love you. I was going to tell you on our date. All this was supposed to happen on our date."

"Our date," I say with a cough. "The date that will live in infamy."

Callie tilts her heads to one side. "I like where it's going at the moment."

"Me too." She loves me. Is it truly possible? Does she know what it means? So many things have happened. I start, "I need to tell you something—"

"Later." She plasters herself against me and brings her lips to mine. Our kiss is a fever and we are on fire together. I'll banish anyone who opens that bedroom door to the most painful circle of Hell immediately.

We collapse together back on the bed with her on top, and I find the bottom of Callie's T-shirt. Our lips part and she raises her arms to let me pull it over her head. She doesn't get shy or climb under the covers or place a hand to hide from me. She lets me glory in the sight of her trust.

"Damn me forever," I say.

She grins at me and I can tell she likes this. She preens a bit, head at an angle, and I would drink the Rubicon daily if this is what it gets me. Her absolute pleasure in being seen is the sexiest thing I can imagine.

I raise a hand and skim my way to her breast and rub a thumb softly over her nipple. She moans and rocks her hips against me.

My sharp intake of breath sends her bolt upright. "Your thigh," she says. "You're wounded. Should we wait?"

I don't care if I lose the use of every limb but one, I want to say. "I'm feeling better by the second," I say instead and before she can protest I cradle her waist with my hands and flip her over so she's beneath me.

I feast on her perfect hand-sized breasts and when she squirms beneath me, ready, as I'm ready, I lower to feast on the warm heat of her.

"Luke . . ." she says, and moans again. "You should let me . . ."

"No," I say with a smile and see her looking down to meet my eyes. I love making her moan and scream in this way. She tastes like Callie. And if she touches me right now, we're not going to make it across the river.

Once she finishes, I kiss my way back up her body and it's her turn to toss me over—which I don't protest. She climbs back on top of me and opens her mouth and I can see a slight hesitation. She's about to ask something. Anticipating her request, I materialize a condom in my fingers and she plucks it from my hand.

"You read my mind," she says. "Metaphorically."

"All my best moves are metaphorical," I say.

"What does that mean?" She gives an amused tiny fake frown and for some people maybe this would be a disruption of our lovemaking—we are *in love*—but for me it is a reminder of what we're like, of the intimacy we already share.

"I'll show you," I say and give her a filthy grin I know she loves.

She tears open the condom packet and I die as she smooths it over my cock and then I die again and am reborn when she sinks slowly onto me. The slow doesn't last long. In agreement, we speed things up, the sweaty slide of skin and our panting breaths and noises that can only be made when you forget yourself and anything but the moment.

I love you I love you is the rhythm of my thrusts and it's not cheesy at all when she says, "Now, Luke, now," and I come harder than any person ever before in creation.

We breathe in the aftermath, nestled together, and my heart beats stronger on the other side of the Rubicon. No matter how different our worlds, no matter the obstacles we face, no matter what Father wants: *We belong together.*

I will never own this woman. Callie is not mine. I'm hers.

And I will do anything it takes to keep it that way, even help my brother find the Holy Grail and put my father's kingdom out of business.

CHAPTER NINETEEN

CALLIE

We did it. We crossed the intimacy Rubicon. There's something to this metaphor business, because I don't feel the least self-conscious. I'd be perfectly content to stay here in Luke's arms and bed without a stitch of clothing on.

We can't do that. We have to get going. It'll be a genuine miracle if Saraya hasn't murdered Sean or come up with an elaborate plan for the guardian version of torture. (Is there a guardian version of torture?) And I still want to know if Sean shoved Luke on purpose or if it *was* an accident. Luke is even more precious to me now that I know what it would feel like to lose him. I will not let Sean hurt him.

Luke has his arm around me, but I crook my neck to look at him. His ridiculously gorgeous face gazes back at me. He's warm and breathing and that is everything I need in this moment.

"I know," he says. "We can't take our time."

I like that he feels the same regret I do about that. "Yeah. Alas, alack, as they say."

Not the faintest hint of a smile in response. My nerves pick back up. Maybe the intimacy level has changed for me, but not for Luke? Is that possible? Even though we said we loved each other? My other relationships have never felt like this, serious and meaningful, and so sex never felt like that big of a step. Half the time with those two guys, it felt more like an awkward box I needed to check off. My body enjoyed it, but not like this. My heart beat harder due to exertion, but it wasn't involved in the outcome. I usually got dressed afterward as fast as I could without seeming rude.

I'm trying to figure out how to ask Luke if we're okay without just blurting out the words when he speaks.

"Father told me something," he says.

It's not us, then. That's a relief.

He's plainly troubled by whatever it is. I can see it in the furrow of his brow. He also lifts the arm that's not supporting me and strokes the bandage on his leg, making me think whatever wound it hides *does* hurt.

"You're sure you're feeling all right?" I ask. "That demon dog medic looked pretty serious."

"I was out for a good bit," Luke says. "The cut is from Saraya the Rude's arrow. It didn't kill me, so I assume it'll make me stronger. Did it work . . ." he lifts a single eyebrow, "in bed?"

"Are you really trying to do sexy fortune cookie talk to distract me from the fact you're hurt?"

He oozes heat in my general direction. I'm not immune, but it confirms he's trying to distract me. Like that's possible. I sit up and hesitate. I want to remove the bandage and check the wound, but Luke says, "Don't worry about it. That's not the problem."

"What is?" Because I'm still worried about the injury.

Luke breathes out a sigh. "The thing Father said to me is that . . . Sean's my brother."

I blink and do a double take. Whatever I expected, this wasn't on the table. His brother? Luke's *brother* is Sean? *Sean* is Luke's brother? "What?"

"My thoughts exactly." Luke says this in a way that doesn't reveal his actual feelings on the subject. I bet they're more complex.

I don't know how to take this revelation, but then I remember how Luke has grown up—isolated with tutors, one good and one terrible that I know of—and with a mother and father who treat him like a chess piece—an important one, but nonetheless—in their games. When we met, one of the words I'd have used to describe him would be lonely.

"But this is good, right?" I ask carefully. "You have a brother! Another family member." For all I know, Lucifer spreads it around. I've never gotten that impression, though. "Wait. You don't have any other brothers, do you? Or sisters?"

"I don't think so." Luke searches the air like there's an answer to be found there. "But Callie, Father called Sean 'the good son.'"

"Maybe it was ironic?" I pause. "No, your father doesn't do irony."

"No, he doesn't." Luke's brain is working so hard, I can practically hear it.

This changes everything. I want to get back to Sean to confront him and get his perspective on this. It might make him easier to work with. "We'd better get cleaned up and go. We need to tell him."

"He knows."

"He does?" I don't get Lucifer's play here. Or Sean's, keeping this to himself. He could've told me after Luke was injured. This must also explain his ability to travel with ease. I pry myself out of the sheets. "We should hurry."

"Now, now. Back to this cleanliness business." Luke gives me a wolf's smile, relaxed on the bed like an invitation. "I mean, we could leave now and everyone we see will know exactly what we just did . . ."

I don't blush. Though I am thinking about it. "To see your mother probably and your dad definitely. No thanks."

"Well then, we'd best get into the shower." His fingers drum on his bare stomach and it's a mouthwatering sight.

I pretend it's not and put my hand on my hip. "You never take a shower. You're a bath guy."

"I'll make an exception, in the interest of you and time."

I envision what he means. Yes, we're in a hurry. But this is a stolen moment. We can stay here on the other side of the Rubicon's banks a little longer, hidden from our troubles and whatever it is about having Sean as a brother that is making Luke's mind work overtime.

"Can you make it so no one interrupts?" I ask.

"Jeannie blink," he says, and I catch the reference to *I Dream of Jeannie*—one of my mom's TV Land favorites—and marvel once again at the wide range of learning down here in Hell.

He lunges forward out of bed and he must think he hides his wince from me. He doesn't.

"Come here," he says, and I extend my hand because he'll hate it and overexert himself if I ask if he's up to this. He kisses me, open-mouthed and hot, and I'm ready for this shower adventure in seconds, worry be quite literally damned.

When Luke presses back from my lips, he leads me forward into his ridiculously large and luxurious bathing chamber. The obsidian shower with the rainfall fixture overhead in what's probably a ridiculously valuable metal.

"It still seems weird to me that demons have bathrooms," I say.

"It's a choice. Is there anything better than a steamy shower after a day in a sulfurous hellscape? Or a nice hot bath to wash away the sweaty fruits of labor in be . . ."

"Don't say it."

I might not be embarrassed around Luke, but I'm not as comfortable where this stuff is concerned. I'm working on it.

"Your wish is my command." He waves a hand and the rainfall showerhead comes on and we are doing something of a dance to get into the water and it feels so nice for a second. I lean against the wall.

Which is a wall. A hard, rock wall.

I search for a better spot as Luke kisses my neck and I capture his mouth and things get steamier—by which I mean actual steam surrounds us.

The problem is, there's really no comfortable place on this wall. And being damp in addition to, well, wet is just making me feel like I've entered a naked figure skating competition. The obsidian floor is slick under my feet and Luke catches me against him when I almost fall.

I clutch his shoulders and laugh. "I don't think I'm a shower sex type of girl," I manage to get out.

Luke looks dismayed for a moment, but then our eyes meet through my laughter and he loses it too. "One of those things that seems like a better idea in theory than in practice," he says. "Got it."

I have another idea. My heart is fully engaged here. Body too.

"I've got an alternative," I say.

"Bed?" he asks.

I've got the prince of Hell all to myself for a little while longer. I thought I'd lost him and I'm not done yet, I want to say. But I say, "Not yet."

"I'm intrigued." He raises his eyebrows.

I lean forward and press a kiss to his pec, which jumps at my touch. I place my palm there. I do the same with the other. "Turn off the water," I say.

He does, and I push him back into the shower, slowly, guiding him against the wall that made me awkward. By contrast, he seems completely at ease.

"Towel?" I ask.

He frowns with curiosity, but produces a fluffy black towel from the air. I shimmy to dry off and then I ball it up and he watches me place it on the floor of the shower in front of him and lower to my knees.

He watches me like he couldn't look away if the apocalypse came. Again.

I reach out to stroke him and say one more word. "Wings."

They stretch out from his shoulders in seconds. I miss that they're not mine anymore, but I love knowing how it will feel when I reach up and caress one of the feathers.

Luke's wounded leg bends at the knee, but he moans in absolute pleasure. "Callie . . ."

Yes, I do like it here on the other side of the intimacy Rubicon.

After another, faster, more frenzied round of—ahem—sexytimes, I take a quick shower and leave my hair wet. Despite the fact whatever we're about to face is not going to be fun—a Lilith who's been kept from her son, angry med demons, and Lucifer (snarl), the rest of it—I feel infinity better walking out of here *together.*

I'm not sure what all of this means exactly.

And I haven't mentioned the whole not-really-entirely-human business either. Luke's dealing with enough. He'll have some guilt about it, until I can prove that this means I fit here. I'll tell him when the time is right.

What a pair we are.

I leave the bathing chamber and find Luke waiting patiently, dressed and ready to go.

"Fresh as a daisy, or a bundle of cloth daisies," Luke says, and gestures to the neatly folded stack of my jeans and GREAT ESCAPE game T-shirt on the corner of the bed. "What does that mean, I wonder, the daisy business?"

I cross over and drop the towel I'm wearing to change. I pull on my underwear and jeans, trying to remember what I read in a book on idioms. "In Old English daisy was something like *day's eye*," I say and pull my shirt on, "because it opens and closes with daylight. And it looks like the sun. Or it might be something else. It's one of those tricky ones."

I glance over to find Luke shaking his head and beaming at me like I'm up in the sky burning at 28 million degrees, give or take.

"You would know that," he says.

"I would," I agree. "We're still trying to save Sean's soul?"

"I suppose so."

"Lucifer thought, what, you'd kill each other?" I ask.

"I wish I knew," he says. Evasively. I don't like it. "I'm dropping the Jeannie blink," he says. "Say your prayers."

He's still distracting me, but I play along for now. Having an unknown sibling and being embroiled in your father's game with them—that "good son" business—is heavy. And I don't know if he means that final part literally. Probably best not to pray too loudly here, so I lift my hand and cross my fingers.

Luke snaps his.

The doors to the bed chamber fly open immediately and Lilith is in the lead with Porsoth right on her heels, black robe like a sail behind him. The moth that led me to Luke flutters in the air excitedly.

"I would never have helped you if I'd known how selfish you would be," Lilith says. "It reminds me of myself, and that is not a compliment. And you, son, to dally when your mother needs to ensure you are whole and healthful."

Luke gives me an amused look and then rises. He lifts his hands and spreads them out. "As you can see, I'm fine."

Lilith's eyes narrow and she rakes over him. He's dressed in his usual uniform of black, leather jacket and all. There are tired smudges that don't usually exist in the hollows under his own eyes. But otherwise he looks normal.

Which is to say gorgeous and untouchable and I love him all the more knowing he may have powers but he's *not* invulnerable. Not to me. I want to protect him. I'm his, and he's mine.

I'm disappointed Lucifer isn't with them. I'd like to get a glimpse into the gears turning in his clockwork heart. I'll settle for Porsoth's insights.

"Can I speak to you privately?" I ask him, my voice low.

Porsoth's beak inclines.

"Be right back," I say to Luke, who's trying to hold off a rare charm offensive from his mother.

Luke says, "Callie, don't leave me. Please tell Mother that I'm fine, that I proved it already in—"

"No," I say. "I will not be saying whatever comes next and neither will you."

"I'm still furious with you," Lilith says, though she sounds somewhat eased by seeing that Luke is more or less his same self and not dying. "Both."

I tug Porsoth's arm and tow him out to the antechamber. Three ghoulish tusked demons wait in the corner, but Porsoth flaps a wing and says, "You may go."

"Did you know?" I ask. "About Sean?"

Porsoth reaches up to fuss with his collar. "I do apologize, but I was prevented from saying anything. I didn't put it together until I saw the two of them side by side in Lexington. I knew there had been . . . an experiment earlier. I did not know Sean had been in Hell. I still can't find any record of his death."

"He wasn't dead. He snuck in."

"Oh." Porsoth flaps his wings. "The master will not have liked that. I feel somewhat responsible—I, I was the one who suggested Sean's mission be revealed to him on his seventeenth birthday. He . . . didn't take it well. Our lives are so long, and then Luke came under my tutelage and . . . I forgot about him."

I frown. There's no way the Porsoth I know has ever forgotten anything *or* anyone so important. "Or you were made to forget," I suggest.

Porsoth's beak opens and closes, opens and closes. He doesn't say anything, which is confirmation and agreement. Lucifer didn't want Luke finding out from anyone but him. Why?

"Lucifer will fear the strength they might have together. One must be the heir," Porsoth says.

"What is this, *Succession*? What are you saying?"

"That this deadline is serious. I don't know what he means to do at the end, but I fear for our prince. He has already been at death's door. My lady—"

"Callie," I correct automatically.

"Callie, I would not be a good friend if I did not warn you that Lucifer is against your match. He is focused on Luke . . . But I fear part of his aim is to split the two of you apart."

"Nothing I didn't already know." Lilith being angry at me too is not a comforting fact. Speaking of . . . "Lilith told me that I'm becoming immortal? You knew that too, didn't you? You said I was stronger than we knew when Lucifer gave me Luke's powers."

"Again, I am sorry, but we thought it would be better for you both to discover in your own time. It's similar to what happened with Lilith herself. Crossing the boundary between your world and Hell so frequently, it has an effect."

"We?"

"Rofocale and I."

I can't believe this. "I guess Agnes knows too. You're as bad about keeping secrets as Luke can be. Knock it off. It's not helpful."

Porsoth is quiet, chastened. I don't feel bad this time. It needed saying.

"I should get back in there," I say.

Porsoth raises a wing. "One more thing . . ."

"Yes?"

"Try to keep him safe."

My throat tightens with emotion. I'm back to my usual skill set, which is mostly summoning random facts and thinking my way out of problems. Coming from Porsoth, what he's asked is an honor.

"I promise I'll do everything I can."

We return to Luke's bed chamber. I cross to stand by Lilith's side, where Luke is waiting patiently and being fussed over. He smiles at me.

"I'm sorry I didn't come get you," I tell Lilith. "Thanks for the moth help."

The moth bobs and weaves around us.

"Apologies are so pedestrian," she says. "There'll be a time to repay me."

I exchange a look with Luke. "We'd better get going," he says. Then, he adds, "Where *are* we going?"

Porsoth and Lilith wait with expectation.

Luke picks up on my hesitation. "Now I'm intrigued. Where?" he asks.

"Guardian City," I say.

Luke's smile fades. Lilith gasps. Porsoth's wings draw tight circles of panic, the hands at the ends of them wobbling. He collapses onto the floor in a heap of wings and scholar's robes.

That went over well.

CHAPTER TWENTY

LUKE

e make a quiet, pensive party on our walk through the halls of the Gray Keep. Mother insists there's something I should see outside before we go.

Even with me awake, Porsoth isn't his usual self. He's not talking in circles over us leaving or making a fidgeting to-do over me. Not the way I expect after he collapsed when Callie revealed our destination.

Not that my own knees don't feel weak about that.

I suppose it's good that Father wasn't there to hear where we're going.

If what might happen to a demon who saunters into the wrong church, which is, yes, any church, is a cautionary tale drilled into young denizens of Hell, well, then Guardian City is . . .

I suppose it's like how everyone not from here thinks about traveling to Hell. We grow up on stories about the home of the good and pure, where there's singing in melodious chorus all day, and the plants are delicious, deadly, or medicinal, and the weapons practice is constant from childhood on, and the residents live in eternal readiness to slay our kind with speed and joy. Not that it's a place any of our kind would go. Willingly.

Until now. Until me. And Sean, I suppose. He's beat me to it.

"Prince," Porsoth says, speaking at last, "I . . . be careful with your wound."

"I'll make sure he is." Callie nods to Porsoth and I can't help wondering what they discussed privately.

My mother is gnawing her lip. Unlike Father, her concern seems real and I'm touched. She stops us and rests her hand on my cheek, light and affectionate. "My son," she says, "try to survive. I will be forced to curse at least part of the world if you don't return. I am not sure what your father is up to, but I don't like it." She hesitates. I told her about Sean—I was afraid not to. "I do not know the woman Lucifer consorted with to create this brother. I don't blame her and I presume we would be allies. But you should know that if Sean Tattersall harms you again, I will destroy him."

"Technically he just gave me a little push." Into a guardian's arrow or away from it, I'm not sure. "How about we not escalate things?"

"You are going to Guardian City." My mother's lips purse. She looks at Callie. "*You* are likely safe there. You better keep Luke safe as well. Your track record concerns me. I never let a man get hurt on my watch, not unless I wanted him to."

"Mother," I say with an affectionate eye roll, "you and Callie are nothing alike."

Neither responds, which I count as a victory.

An antlered demon missing his fingers is posted with another guard at the outer door. They bow low. "Prince, Lilith," he says.

"Better," my mother says.

The other demon opens the door for us. We step out onto the wide stone walkway of one of the branches of the castle. "What am I looking for . . ."

That's when I see it. A black-and-gray moon, low and huge in the sky. A moon that isn't usually there. "Oh."

"It's changing color," Callie says.

"What?" I ask.

"It was black and white earlier."

Mother frowns. "An omen," she says. "This is why you must be careful."

"I'm sure it has nothing to do with me. Father probably stuck it up there for drama."

Neither Mother nor Porsoth agrees.

"If you must go"—Porsoth wrings his wings—"it should be now."

"We must," Callie says.

I hold my hand out to her. "Ready?"

"You know where it is?" She slips her hand into mine. "They didn't tell me."

I close my eyes and reach out. Even with the low throb of my thigh wound, I am much more comfortable with full access to my powers back. And my wings . . . I think of Callie's gift in the shower, of how magnificent she is.

"Luke, can we get there?" she asks.

Oh, right. I'm supposed to be looking for Guardian City. I sense its direction and enough of its shape as a place to head toward it. The feeling belongs to nowhere I've ever traveled to.

"Not exactly, and I suspect it won't let me remember. But I can feel that it will let us find it."

I take Callie's other hand. She squeezes mine back.

"We still have a day," she says. "We got this. For Agnes."

"For Agnes."

Callie's still focused on our original plan. I can't throw an entirely new goal on top of it—I need to prove I can do it myself. To me *and* to her. I intend to join Sean on making *his* plan a reality, doing away with Father's kingdom. Surely that favor is the least a newly revealed brother could do.

I lean forward and press my lips to hers.

We're from two different worlds, and it's up to me to make them the same. That way, I'll know this can last.

I'm flying blind, but at least it doesn't make my soul scream with pain. We transition from Hell to Earth, but where we end up on the globe I couldn't say. Guardian City is hidden. It could be right beside anyplace, a secret beauty that's invisible to all but those allowed to see it.

We land on a dirt road surrounded by well-used fields laden with crops. Ahead are green walls of trees and vines knotted together, stretching high up to a cloudless sunset sky in nature's answer to psychedelic hues. We've lost an entire day to my sickbed—not that I regret the bed part.

The only place I can think this reminds me of is my mother's garden. On a much, much grander scale. Admittedly, part of me expected the initial view of Guardian City to have demon heads on spikes. For it to radiate a nauseating aura of light. This is more like a verdant oasis and living fortress in one. Is it the mythical Eden? Possibly.

Callie has her hands on her knees, recovering from the travel, and eventually straightens. She blinks at what lies ahead of us.

The dirt road we're on leads to an open gate. A cluster of white-garbed warriors appears in it and waits there. We're too far away to make out their mood.

"Should we go closer?" Callie asks.

My thigh continues to throb. "You're positive they're here?"

"Yes," she says. "Saraya—the Rude—was different. It really is a pain to have to say the full thing every time. Anyway, she promised she'd look after him. She told me to come here."

"And you trust her?" That surprises me.

Callie raises her shoulders. "No? Yes? I think so, for now. On this. Michael told her to help us."

"They're not coming to us, so I guess here we go." I produce my wings without a thought. No reason to assume a meek posture, and every second will count if this is a trick and we need to depart with haste.

Callie sighs. "I miss being able to fly."

"You can fly with me anytime, baby," I say and wink at her. She rolls her eyes at me. "In bed?"

"Don't fortune-cookie sweet-talk me," I return.

She loves me. Knowing someone does is a strange sensation—one I've never had before. And knowing it's Callie is even better.

We walk, not slow or fast. Steady.

"I don't really miss other things about your powers though. I'm not used to hearing heartbeats."

I listen to hers, a steady, comforting thump.

"And even though knowing stuff instantly was cool at first, it felt like cheating."

Ah, sweet, honest Callie. "That's because it is cheating. We're big on cheating Below."

A flock of pale birds soars out of the high green walls en masse, heading for us. I'm ready to fold my wings over Callie, but instead of attacking the milky doves swoop and swing through the air around us. An escort.

"I should tell you that *The Birds* is my least favorite Hitchcock movie," she says. "My mom loves it, but it scares me to death."

"You think we're about to be doved to death?" I say it as a joke to reassure her.

"What a way to go."

"At least we'd be together," I say.

Callie catches my eye, and I can't imagine the effort it takes for her not to watch the birds. I enjoy looking at her—truly looking with my full senses—the dying sun shining on her face, her pupils dilated small, ringed in stormy green.

"I love you," she says. Then, "Okay, *that* made it awkward."

"Never," I say. "I love you too."

Callie closes her eyes and scrunches up her face and I regret the loss of that green until she opens them. "Oh no, we're turning into that couple."

"What couple is that?"

"The schmoopy kind."

I put a hand to my chest. "Excuse me. It's not possible for me to be schmoopy."

Callie laughs. "Are you sure, Prince Softie?"

"Quite," I say, channeling my best Porsoth. "And no more Prince Softie. I have a reputation to maintain. It makes me sound like a creepy ice cream truck."

"We should come up with something else we say for every

day," Callie says. "A coded message that only we know means *I love you.*"

That's such a piece of Callie logic I can't say no. "You've already thought of something, haven't you? What is it?"

"Maybe." She wrinkles her nose at me. "It might be silly."

How we can be having this conversation amid the crying and careening doves is a wonderful mystery. "Let me have it."

"I don't know why, but this is the first thing that popped into my head."

"Now I'm dead curious."

"Don't even joke about being dead," she says. Then, "You've got something on your face."

I reach up to my cheek before I realize that's the code she's suggesting. I respond in kind, making the words gentle as a caress. "No, you've got something on *your* face."

She claps her hands together, pleased. My heart swells.

The birds increase their activity in a clear message of *Keep it moving,* and we start toward the gate again. Soon enough, we're close enough that the shadows of the high, leafy walls fall over us, the shadows of twilight joining them. The birds' flight paths seem choreographed, and we both gape as they set down on either side of the dirt road in front of us. We can make out the faces of the guardians, tense and waiting.

"Where is she?" Callie asks.

That's when Saraya finally appears. She strides through the cluster of guardians, but stops a dozen feet away and waves for us to approach her.

When we're standing right across from her, she says, "Protocol."

"Always protocol," I say. Hell is the same way, with its endless rules and ruthless politesse.

"What do we do?" Callie asks.

"Answer truthfully," Saraya says.

Callie nods.

Saraya unsheathes her sword, the blade gleaming though it shouldn't in the present light conditions, and holds it level in front of her. Her hand doesn't bleed where it grips the metal.

"Please place your hands upon the sword," she says.

I do not want to. I've felt what a guardian's weapon can do. But Callie does it instantly, and so I can't protest. With a measure of fear I'd never admit to, I follow suit.

The wound in my leg stabs with a sharp pain as if the sword is a tuning fork. The feeling fades to a dull awareness.

"Do you promise no harm to those inside these walls?" Saraya asks.

"Yes," Callie says.

"Sure." I wait for another stab of pain, but none comes.

"Do you promise to hold the secrets you may learn inside these walls quiet, so long as you draw breath?"

"Yes."

"Sure."

"Do you recognize the authority of the archangel Michael within the walls of Guardian City?"

This one's tougher. But the way it's worded gives me enough leeway to say, "Sure."

Callie lets out a breath, because she must not have been positive I could do that one either. "Yes."

Saraya whips the sword down with her right hand and touches the ground in front of our feet. "Welcome to Guardian City, travelers." She sheaths the sword once more.

The guardians at the gate all but growl at our approach. "Warm welcome," I say.

"They weren't exactly thrilled about Michael's edict either," Saraya says.

Callie asks the question of the hour. "Where's Sean?"

"Oh." Saraya smiles and it's terrifying. "He's helping the children train."

"Really?" I try to picture Sean surrounded by small guardians, allowing them to crawl all over him. I can't manage it.

"I never lie." Saraya's tone is a dare to challenge the claim. "You'll see for yourself. They should just be finishing up."

Callie raises her eyebrows and, by mutual silent agreement, we let it pass. For all I know, it's true.

The living walls of the city were impressive, but what waits within them is like nothing I've ever seen before. The structures in the city are shaped from trees and plants, living spires and domes, broad-trunked trees hollowed out into domiciles and shops that seem to mostly sell weapons. The long knobby shadows the trees cast on stone walkways reach everywhere in front of us. Bowls of flame light the paths and streets.

There's foot traffic, stony-faced guardians in white robes or combat leathers. Everyone seems to wear weapons, even though they're undoubtedly safe here. We pass a combat ring made of smooth wood where two muscle-bound guardians fight while receiving instruction from a man with a long white beard.

"Isn't it getting late for all this practice?" Callie asks.

"The evening feast will begin soon," Saraya says. "We fight until it is time for peace, every day."

Every resident of Guardian City examines us as if we're curious pariahs. I suppose we are. The looks aren't that different than what the demons used to give me when I was a boy and Father took me to tour the kingdom. *You're not so much*, they seem to say. *You don't belong here.*

And now Father wants me to prepare to rule them? For once, I'm glad he doesn't understand me, doesn't know me at all. He truly believed that making me spend a day as a human would have me viewing Callie as lesser. If anything, it made me appreciate her more.

Saraya guides us up a set of stairs carved into the trunk of a tree. We pause at a bridge made of knotted ropes. There's a sound of delighted screeches coming from across it, and the periodic enthusiastic cheers of schoolchildren.

"The training academy," Saraya says, and launches onto the rope bridge. It's not so tall, only twenty feet or so high. But there are no hand guides.

Callie gives me a panicked look. "Might be my turn to fall," she says.

"You'll be fine," Saraya says. "The children make it."

Callie's eyes are wide. I say, "Hold on," and pick her up. Wings do come in handy. She clings to me and says, "For the record, I've proven I'm fine with heights, but I'd rather not break a leg today."

I fly us above Saraya, who snorts her disapproval and puts on speed so she beats us to the landing on the other side.

"You have a real competitive streak, don't you?" I ask.

"How else would I become leader of the fiercest warriors on Earth?" Saraya shrugs.

"And so modest too," Callie says dryly.

"You could have made it," Saraya says.

I expect Callie to argue or be embarrassed, but she doesn't say anything. She casts a look back at the bridge, maybe considering it. "Where's Sean, again?" she asks.

"Right this way," Saraya says, and I swear another smile appears that makes me worry for my brother's health. I wonder if I'll ever get used to the words *my brother*.

She leads us toward the shrieks and claps and we round a bend and see exactly what sort of training is happening.

Sean is tied to the broad trunk of a tree. He's surrounded by knives and throwing stars and anything else pointy enough to stick in the wood. The children are taking turns using him for target practice. Or not-target practice. They're apparently trying *not* to hit him.

A stone-faced matron is observing the exercise, a sturdy table dotted with a surplus of weapons for the children to choose from beside her. Sean himself is pale, but stoic. He manages not to wince as a boy who can't be more than seven gives a feral cry and launches a dagger that pierces the wood between his thighs.

I glance over and catch genuine glee on Saraya's face. Callie is doing her best to hide a grin of her own.

"Hey there," I say and stride into the fray. "I hate to interrupt your fun, but we need to borrow your practice dummy."

"Oh, he's *not* a dummy," a little girl says. "That's what makes it fun."

"You're alive," Sean says to me. I detect not a little relief. Interesting.

"I am. And I'd like a word."

He closes his eyes briefly, then nods. "I imagine so."

"Aren't you a little young to be playing with knives?" Callie asks the children.

They shriek offense. The matron gives one stern shake of her head.

Saraya explains. "Our parents place our first blades in our hands fresh from the womb."

"Interesting parenting strategy," Callie manages. "Could you untie him?"

"Children, can you cut his bindings?" Saraya asks and the

children—twelve of them—rush toward him with sharp tools in hand.

"Luke," Callie says.

"Fine." I lift a finger and free him before we get to watch the children do it with their assorted blades.

Sean shakes loose with extreme care not to nick himself on any of the pointy items around him. Once free, he circles wide around the disappointed herd of kids.

"Thank you," he says.

"No problem," I say, "brother."

CHAPTER TWENTY-ONE

CALLIE

Luke is still unpredictable—even to me—and so I'm surprised that he put the word out there this quickly. I expected him to hold it close.

Sean is quiet for a long moment. Considering Luke freed him from target practice, the fact he looks more troubled now is saying something.

"He told you," Sean says.

"Yes." Luke crosses his arms. "Did you try to kill me?"

"Of course not," Sean says. "It was an accident."

Saraya is frowning between them. "What am I missing?"

"Is there somewhere we can go?" I ask. "More private—so this is not in front of the children?"

The children who stand around us in rapt amazement, like we've brought the best soap opera on Earth with us. "Demon!" one boy yells and points at Luke. "Kill!"

"Maybe put your wings away," I say to Luke.

He shrugs, but when his shoulders go back down they vanish.

"Kill the demon!" More children join in.

Saraya raises both her hands, looking like my fourth-grade teacher, Mrs. Hayes, when she was signaling for us to shut up or big trouble would result. Like no recess. Did these kids have recess? Doubtful based on what Saraya said earlier.

"No killing," she says. "For now. Michael's orders."

The children back away and straighten into a line. Their disappointment is palpable.

"Is this normal?" I ask with my voice low. "The bloodthirstiness?"

"They're training to be holy warriors," Sean says.

It's my turn to look between him and Saraya. "Why did you answer that?" I ask. "And what if a kid is no good at fighting?"

Saraya shrugs. "We're all capable of defending the city, but some may ultimately take other positions. Farming or cooking, firing the forges . . . the scholars who keep our history and maintain the library."

"Uh-oh," Luke says.

"What?" Saraya asks.

"You mentioned a library." Luke nudges me with his arm. "Go ahead."

"Can we see it?" I try not to sound too eager. She'll only say no.

"Not tonight," she says. "We must eat. The day's work is done."

On cue, the crystalline ringing of a bell pierces the air. Fitting they'd use one here. Church bells aren't just pretty sound effects, but believed by many to drive away demons and unclean spirits. It wasn't uncommon in ye olden days to inscribe the metal with messages about the specific effects like to banish storms and threats to souls.

The children and their minder file out automatically, heading off for their suppers. We wait, letting them go first. The air feels heavy with the things that remain to be said.

As the ringing stops, Sean shifts uncomfortably. He seems about a thousand percent more nervous. But then, he's having a day. "We're going to the feast hall?" he asks.

"Yes," Saraya says, and glares at him. "Why the concern— you don't want to face more of the people you betrayed?"

What could she possibly mean?

"Oh, that bastard," Luke says, and shakes his head. "You grew up here. Didn't you?"

Sean answers as if it pains him. "Yes."

I think of what Porsoth told me about encouraging Lucifer to tell Sean about his parentage. The connection hits like a blow from one of the holy weapons. "You found out on your seventeenth birthday."

"And I left immediately. There was no way to explain." Sean has eyes only for Saraya. In this case, it's mutual.

"Explain what?" She grits the words out, almost as if she doesn't want to ask. Or maybe like she doesn't want to know the answer.

"It wasn't just me," Luke says. "She doesn't know either."

He checks in with me. "No more secrets," I say.

Sean doesn't protest.

"We're brothers," Luke says, and waves a hand from himself to Sean. He puts his usual rosy spin on it. "From other mothers. I found out earlier today."

"You . . . you are . . ." Saraya's hand has gravitated to the hilt of her sword. Her extremely sharp and deadly security blanket.

"You can see why I had to leave," Sean says.

The bell rings again, one final time.

"We must go," Saraya says, and turns.

"Wait," Sean says.

"No!" Saraya barks without turning around.

By the time we reach the rope bridge, Saraya is already across. She's been filled with nothing but contempt for me, but I'm imagining a whole other side to her. And that side is hurting.

"You can get us to the hall?" I ask Sean.

"I can." He peers into the evening. Saraya's already out of sight.

"Good." I step out onto the bridge before either of them can stop me.

Luke says, "Callie, what are you doing?"

"I can make it." And by doing so, I can buy Saraya a little time to process. I pause and slowly turn my head to look at him. "It's fine."

She told me I could do it before and she sounded certain. I don't think she's a liar, even though she didn't exactly describe what Sean helping train the kids entailed. Thing is, if she didn't have feelings for him, why bother with that? It can't just be about his leaving. She clearly didn't know about his father. It's a lot to take in.

I've been there.

Luke eases onto the bridge behind me, and it doesn't budge. Well-constructed.

The three of us head across, and I purposely take my time. There's a trick to the balance without a hold for hands, but the bridge itself barely sways and is firm beneath my feet. I have to admit there's something fun about it, once I get the hang of it. I jump the last couple of steps, and I have a little window into what my life might look like now if I'd taken up Michael on his offer to join the guardians.

I can almost picture it, but I don't feel drawn to. Luke gathers me in close to him for a quick kiss. My longing is fine right here.

"You had to do that, didn't you?" Luke asks.

"I've wanted to go to Amazon Training School in Themyscira ever since the *Wonder Woman* movie came out." Jared and Mag more or less do—they go to some modern gladiator training warehouse across town. I wonder how today went back home.

"I'm sure they're fine," Luke says, guessing the direction of my thoughts.

Sean coughs and we separate. No need to rub our happy in his face. I can try to get a phone signal here in probably-Eden later. The sky is the blue of ocean depths and there are more stars visible in it than anyplace I've ever been.

I face Sean. "Let me get this straight. Lucifer visited you and told you who you are and you ran off without telling anyone—including Saraya—and became a con artist?"

"When you put it like that, I sound like a real asshole," Sean says. "I didn't want her to think I was dead. I had a lifetime of being here without deserving it to atone for."

"And a very particular set of skills, Liam Neeson–style?" I suggest.

"A face that could charm the devil," Sean says.

"Anyone except the devil," Luke says, joining the conversation. "What about your mother?"

"She died on a mission when I was fourteen. We never talked about my father."

"I'm sorry," Luke says.

Sean nods, accepting it.

Guardians are mortal, then. Unlike . . . me. I do need to find the right time to reveal that to Luke.

"It didn't feel right to stay here," Sean says.

"Did it feel right to leave?" The question's out before I can stop it.

"No," he says. "I gave up on anything ever feeling right after that day. That's why I can't be redeemed. Why you're going to lose your bet."

"And let Lucifer get what he wants?" I ask. "No way."

Luke says, "We find the Grail. If that can't wipe away a little fatherly sin, nothing can."

I hear what Luke hasn't said, that he's agreeing with Sean that being Lucifer's sons makes them inherently bad in some way. "I thought we'd covered this—you are not your father. You have a soul, a good one," I tell Luke. "And you probably do too," I tell Sean. "Otherwise none of this would bother you."

"You don't understand," Sean says. "How could you? You didn't grow up the way either of us did. My father wanted me to undermine the guardians. His entire design for me was to be his Trojan horse. It wasn't even a question for him that I'd do it."

"But he was wrong." I'm not budging on this.

"Maybe about that," Sean says. "But not about me. I was angry when I got forced out of Hell, because it was the first time in my life I felt like I belonged where I was."

Before I can argue, he's walking off in the direction Saraya went in. "Feast hall's this way," he drops over his shoulder.

"How do you hit the reset button for someone who doesn't want it?" I ask.

"You make him want it," Luke says.

I don't think I'm capable of that, but I know who is.

I've given up trying to expect what things will look like. The feast hall of Guardian City is described in none of the books I grew up inhaling. From Luke's description, we're off the map. Or between the folds, or maybe in one of those "here be dragons" sections. (That wasn't actually a common saying on old maps, but at least one famous globe does warn of fanciful creatures. I read a convincing argument once that most sea monster sightings were likely whale penises. The more you know.)

Sean is waiting outside a structure made of graceful arches of metal and crystal-clear glass, so unlike the wood and greenery everywhere else. People bustle around or sit around long tables inside. The sounds of laughter and the clatter of cutlery are audible. The air fills with a delicious smell that reminds me of . . . hot dogs.

"Are we going in?" I don't say that I'm starving. Luke is always hungry and given the way Sean descended upon the room service menu almost twenty-four hours ago he must be up for dinner.

"Yes," Sean says. "Funny that now I'm waiting for you rather than fleeing you."

"Hilarious," Luke says.

A man appears in the open entrance. He's wearing a pair of loose-fitting white pants and tunic, and has a neat, snowy beard that comes to a point below his well-lined face. And he's wearing a Cubs cap. Yes, the baseball team. He takes it off.

"Isaac," Sean says, like he can't believe it. "Is that you?"

The man strides forward, loose-limbed despite his age. "I could ask you the same thing, boy. I couldn't believe it when they said you'd returned . . . and in such company." The man stops and waits with a more polite expression than anyone else has offered us so far.

"I'm Callie Johnson, of Lexington, Kentucky." Porsoth has made a big deal of how important bona fides are when meeting someone new in this world. I just don't have any others.

Well . . . "Bachelor's in history," I add. "And this is Luke Morningstar . . ."

"Prince of Hell, at your service," Luke says. "That last part is a figure of speech."

Isaac doesn't offer his own specifics, but speaks again to Sean. "I could ask where you've been all these years, but the rumors kept me fairly informed."

"Doubtful," Sean says. His voice is soft. "It's good to see you."

"You too. Don't leave without saying good-bye this time."

"I won't."

Saraya joins us—or declines to. She stands in the opening and calls orders. "Hurry it up! Or there'll be no food left and I'm not rustling up something extra for you."

"Ball game night," Isaac says. "The best brats in Christendom await."

He turns and goes back in, pausing to set a hand on Saraya's shoulder, which she allows, before disappearing. Cheers sound from inside.

"Game night?" I ask.

Sean tips an imaginary hat. "Baseball. You may have noticed guardians have a competitive streak. They love all sports."

"An optimist indeed if he likes the Cubs," Luke says.

"You've been holding out on me," I say. "I didn't know you followed sports."

"Training," Luke says. "Research on humans. You'd be surprised what people will do if they think it'll help their team. Or after a big loss when they're weak."

"To prey upon a fan's heartbreak, now that's cruelty," Sean says.

"Who's your team?" Luke asks.

Sean scoffs. "No way I'm telling you."

"Are we eating or not?" I ask.

Saraya has disappeared. With a shrug, we head in. She's waiting, thin-lipped and tense, just inside.

"I did it," I say, "I made it across the bridge."

"How exciting for you," Saraya says.

Despite our relationship, it stings, though I understand she's simply lashing out.

The entire assembly—there must be several hundred people here—hushes as they realize we've entered. The baseball game playing on an enormous screen at the back fills the silence. Almost.

A hit *cracks* and that's enough to get their attention. More cheers break out across the room, and children go back to racing around the long tables, just as they might back home at a big family gathering. Along with swirls of pastel pink and blue cotton candy, and towering ice cream cones, apparently part of the theme night.

I turn and Sean and Luke are standing side by side. It's hard not to want to smack my head for not seeing it earlier. They are so alike in their mannerisms and the cocky way they hold themselves. Both of them are so handsome it hurts.

But there's a softness to Luke—maybe I imagine it or maybe I'm the only one who sees it—that Sean doesn't have yet. I suspect he's on edge all the time under his cool veneer.

"Help yourselves," Saraya says, and there's a distinct air of "Do I have to tell you everything?" to it.

There's a long line of serving platters and food, and we make our way over together. Luke stays quiet behind me.

"You all right?" I ask.

"Not my usual scene," he murmurs.

Fair.

We load up our plates with brats and potato salad. We tuck in and almost immediately I begin to feel drowsy and heavy.

"Do you think they've drugged us?" I ask.

"There's no insomnia here," Sean says. "You're feeling the daily rhythms. I'm tired too, and I should be way too keyed up for it to act on me."

Luke yawns. "So that's what it is. How do they pay attention to the game?"

"They're familiar with the rhythms of the day," he says. "They'll leave here and sleep well to rise with the sun. Or, some of them, for midnight drills."

A trumpet sounds then, blaring, and everyone freezes for a moment. Saraya abandons us and makes her way quickly toward the exit. Sean is on his feet in an instant, motioning for us to follow her.

"An arrival," he says.

"Michael?" I wonder.

"No," he says. "He announces himself with blazing light. You know that."

"Someone from Hell," we hear as we make it outside.

Saraya has pulled the sword from before, and it glows in the darkness now, a faint white. She jogs toward the gated walls. We trail her, keeping up as best we can.

"Could it be your father?" I ask Luke, before I realize I'm asking Sean too now.

"If he's come here, it's not good news," Luke says.

"Anyone from Hell coming here isn't good news," Sean says. He gives Luke a look. "Sorry, but it's true."

"No offense taken."

As we approach the gate where we came in, we find a flurry of activity. From inside, it's easy to see how deceptively picturesque the outer walls appear. Doves are being waved into position by women in white leathers, and archers and others are tucked into vantage points where they have good aim to target anyone who's coming.

"Humans too," I hear Saraya bark. "Three of them."

A vague thought twinges at the back of my head.

"Be prepared to kill on sight," Saraya says.

No one protests.

I pull my phone out and confirm it has no service.

"Let's see who it is first," I say.

"You have no authority here," Saraya counters.

She's right, and given how fragile she must be feeling, challenging her isn't the best idea. I do it anyway. "Michael said to help us. It seems unlikely this has nothing to do with us. We wait and see who and what this is. No shooting first."

I get a growl in answer, but I'll take it.

I turn back to the, well, brothers. "You stay here . . . unless I call for you."

Luke leans in and kisses my cheek. "I'd rather go."

"No." Saraya sounds immovable on this point.

I suspected as much and it's why I told them to stay put.

Luke nods to me. "I'll be there in a heartbeat, if you need me."

"I know."

He hesitates. "You've got something on your face."

"No," I say, my heart beating a dance, "you've got something on *your* face."

"You two are strange," Sean says, but there's no heat in it.

I cross to Saraya's side and walk out with her to meet the new arrivals. "If it is Lucifer, feel free to shoot at him with everything you've got," I say, low.

Her face angles the barest fraction toward me with what might be approval.

Doves streak from the wall through the night sky, more menacing without the light to guide them. They swoop and call and chills spread along my spine. A wind blows, the fields alongside rustling with the sound, and then I see exactly who is here.

A scholar's robe billows in the night, silhouetting one particular owl-pig silhouette. The figures with him defy belief at first. I blink again and even though this can't be good news . . . it *feels* like good news.

I take off at a run to meet them.

"Wait," Saraya says.

"Don't fire!" I tell her.

Another growl behind me, but I ignore it. The people coming toward me speed up too, recognizing me and realizing they're in the right place. We stop in front of each other, and I check behind me and verify that Saraya is waiting right where I left her.

"Mag, Jared—and Mom? What are you doing here?"

Mag gives a sheepish wave, hand in Jared's. Mom is half looking at me and half watching the looping doves in the darkness.

Porsoth comes forward, hooves solid thumps on the firm earth. "They insisted on coming when I told them, milady."

"Told them what?"

"The moon in Hell's sky, the omen." Porsoth's voice is weak, bothered. "It's turned to blood."

"What does that mean?" I'm glad they're here, but confused.

"I don't know," Porsoth says. "But it seemed imperative you

have all the help we could muster for the third day. Is the young master still well?" He leans over to peer toward the gate.

"He's waiting inside."

"I must see him."

"There's protocol first," I say.

Porsoth nods, seemingly comforted. "As there should be. Protocol is the mark of a civilized culture."

An arrow flies from the wall then. And behind it another.

Between one blink and the next, Porsoth assumes his full demonic form—growing into a stories-tall, broad, scary owl-pig. He raises a wing and bats away the guardian arrows like children's toys.

"Wait!" I shout. "Everyone wait!"

That's when the beam of light shines in an unmistakable flare and Michael lands beside us, the ground shaking as his feet hit the Earth. His wings gleam like Saraya's sword, but a thousand times brighter and us puny humans (or mostly humans, in my case) raise our hands to shield our eyes.

Now I'm the one waiting, for more arrows. For attacking troops. For Luke to fly out to my side. None of that happens before Michael speaks.

"Let us set protocol aside for the evening." The archangel Michael smiles and it might be the first not-entirely-terrifying, genuine expression I've ever seen from him. It's still pretty terrifying. "Welcome to Guardian City. I bring news."

CHAPTER TWENTY-TWO

LUKE

I wasn't lying about not wanting Callie to venture out without me. But I understood that protesting would get me nowhere. That's a lesson I finally learned on the ruins in Glastonbury.

Still, there's nothing that could keep me inside the walls once I hear someone say, "Michael's arriving—defensive posture!"

I shake off the impulse to rest this place has created and sharpen my senses in time to catch the low whistle of arrows flying. And then Saraya shouts, "Stand down!"

My wings are out and I fly too high for any new arrows to catch me—though even at the thought my thigh throbs sympathetically—and glide out over the fields to the road.

I set down moments after Michael descends in his blaze of glory. His affect to the newcomers—Callie's mother, Mag, and Jared—is positively welcoming, aside from the need for eye-shielding. He even dims his presence when he notices they can't quite look upon him. And that's with Porsoth there too, wearing his giant demon form, overkill and temptation for the guardians at once.

"Greetings, Prince," Michael says to me. His smile fades. "I hear you were injured."

"It seems I'll live," I say.

"We did not know what sort of greeting to expect here," Porsoth says. "The arrows were not a surprise, but the welcome of an archangel is. What is this news?"

"Porsoth," I hiss and raise my hand to bring two fingers together to indicate shrinking. I suspect he forgotten he's much more intimidating when he's that size.

"Of course, of course," he fusses and within a few seconds he's the more diminutive demon we're used to. "My apologies, and pardon for any offense."

Michael lifts his hand and waves the concern away. What is happening?

Callie finds her way to my side. "The gang's all here," she says.

"Now it is," Sean says. He strides up and stops beside a peevish Saraya. He nods to Callie's family. I'm dead curious why her mother is here. Almost as curious as I am about what's going on with Michael.

"Porsoth also has news," Callie says.

"Let us go inside, to the hearthfire," Michael says. Then, he pauses. "It's game night, isn't it? Perhaps we should not interrupt."

He waves a hand and the soil beside us parts in a wide crack. An eruption of sound and motion follows as reality reassembles itself to fit Michael's wishes. In moments, a cozy fire (assuming that's not holy flame) burns inside a tidy outdoor fire pit and the even cozier seating around it could give any Real Housewife's mansion a run for its filthy rich money.

Michael motions for us to sit and it's as if we're on an uneasy camping trip.

"Where are the s'mores?" Callie mutters, clearly on the same page, as she slips her hand into mine. "I'm joking," she adds, worried Michael or me—or Porsoth—might take her seriously and produce some.

Callie's mother has yet to say a word. Jared and Mag take the chairs nearest us.

"Mom." Callie motions with her head and her mother sinks down beside her.

I don't know whether wings or no wings are more polite, so I leave them out.

"As our guests, please share your tidings first, Porsoth." Michael stands beside the fire, gracious, eyes glinting.

"An ominous moon hangs over Hell, and it has taken the color of blood. We thought it best to warn the prince."

Which still doesn't quite explain how Callie's relatives and best friend ended up here, but I'm chalking that up to Porsoth's panic—and the kind of love for each other that I've had a hard time fathoming. They quarrel, they have differing opinions on important issues, and their relationships withstand it. Always.

"Ah," Michael says. "That is of a piece. We are on the precipice of a change, one I hope will be good for all of us."

He places a slight emphasis on the last word. *Us.*

The oddity of this scene hits me again and it's almost as if I'm looking down from above. There is no doubt Michael is one of the most powerful beings in the universe. Why is he suddenly holding court and using the word *us* in a way that includes everyone here, even me? I can summon only one answer.

"You've talked to Father," I say.

"Not directly about these matters, but I have heard reports." Michael folds his hands in front of him, church and steeple style. "I was aware of his experiment. He thought to prove that he could infiltrate the guardians with progeny. It did not work."

I imagine Sean hearing this. We haven't had time to fully discuss . . . everything, but I can predict how it strikes him. I'm keenly aware of how it feels to be manipulated as if the part of you that makes you *you* hardly matters.

"You play chess, don't you?" I stand and ask. "With Father. You two think we're all just playthings."

Michael's conspiratorial swagger disappears and the frost returns to his face and posture.

Saraya draws a sword and idly swings it low. "Be careful. He could withdraw his protection."

There's a note that might be concern, not only the expected bloodthirstiness.

"No," Callie says, coolly, "he promised your aid until our bet with Lucifer is done."

"You're still pursuing salvation for this one?" He points to Sean. "I'll grant it. We have larger matters to address. I had hoped that with your desire for reform, we might enter into a deal together."

"I wasn't aware angels made deals," I say. "I thought that was our area."

"You can't offer me salvation," Sean says.

"I can make it happen," Michael says. "Do not fret."

"I would need forgiveness from someone besides you."

Saraya says nothing.

Michael looks to me. "I am told Lucifer is preparing to leave. You are to be the heir. We could be friendly."

Beside me, Callie stiffens. Her hand retracts from mine. "I said no more secrets. What's he talking about?"

I've messed this up royally. Again.

"Yes," Sean says, "what is he talking about?"

I find Porsoth's eyes with mine. "Then it is true," he says.

"It's true that he's set all this up," I say. "That he believes it will go as he wants. That he intends for me to betray Sean, and Callie, and myself. That he believes I'll assume his position because he wishes it."

"When were you going to tell me?" Callie asks. "We can only help you if you tell us things."

I still. I don't understand for a long moment. I wait for the sting of her palm on my cheek. Or holy fire from Michael. For Saraya's blade to strike me down.

"You thought we wouldn't help you?" Callie asks.

"Who's we?" I ask.

"This grows tiresome," Michael says, and his wings widen, seeming as broad as the night sky and glowing harshly as a star up close. "When you come to your senses or at the end of the wager, whichever happens first . . . I will see you then."

He vanishes in a blink of light instead of a blaze. The fire in the hearth goes out and the Earth rumbles below us.

We scramble as one. Callie helps her mother. I steer Jared and Mag out of the way. Saraya, Sean, and Porsoth leap aside. We watch as the tidy fireside chat scene vanishes entirely, leaving smooth ground and then the fields, as they were. What a show of power. He didn't even need to be here.

"We is *us*," Callie says, and my knees weaken.

Her hand sweeps between the two of us and then out to

include Porsoth and her family. Even Sean and Saraya, who I'm not sure agree that they're included.

She's saying we have that kind of love. The kind where even when I screw up, it doesn't disappear. That she thinks of me the same way as her family.

"Callie," her mother says, "I think something's wrong. With Luke."

My thigh wound makes itself known. I look down and although it's night, the dull wet patch on my jeans leg is visible to my senses.

The stabbing I felt when I touched Saraya's sword returns. It doesn't leave.

My leg folds beneath me, and it's only Porsoth catching me under both arms that keeps me from full collapse.

"It seems that I'm not fine after all," I say before an immense sense of tiredness sweeps through me and takes me over.

I can't manage the words, but I can interpret what's happening. Michael has withdrawn whatever in Hell's healing had closed my wound. His message is perfectly clear. Assume control of Hell or else.

DAY THREE

ALL HELL BREAKS LOOSE

"Well, I shan't go, at any rate," said Alice; "besides, that's not a regular rule: you invented it just now."

"It's the oldest rule in the book," said the King.

"Then it ought to be Number One," said Alice.

ALICE'S ADVENTURES IN WONDERLAND, LEWIS CARROLL

The gates of hell are open night and day;

Smooth the descent, and easy is the way:

But to return, and view the cheerful skies,

In this the task and mighty labour lies.

VIRGIL, *AENEID*, BOOK VI (TRANS. JOHN DRYDEN, 1697)

CHAPTER TWENTY-THREE

CALLIE

Last night, when Sean assured me I'd sleep like the just and exhausted, I didn't believe it. Despite the magic powers of Guardian City slumber. But when I wake up, it's from the kind of drooling peace babies and puppies experience. I guess. I've never had a puppy or a baby.

Just like before this, I'd never been in love. I push up to my side and watch Luke sleep. If I could listen to his heart, I would, creepy or not.

His rest isn't peaceful. He's flushed and though they tried to convince me to let them take him to an infirmary, Saraya also admitted that holy wounds tend to run their course. The person must fight them off.

I insisted we stay together. We were shown to a nicely furnished guesthouse that looks like someone hit Bilbo's home in Hobbiton with a ray that made it normal-sized. Everyone parted ways and went to sleep.

The light through the paned window has the soft look of early morning. Day three is here.

Lucifer told Luke he has to take over the kingdom of Hell. Michael wants him to. That would make Luke the devil? Or would it? Why didn't he tell me? I want to shake him awake and demand he confess what he was thinking, but I don't.

I do gently press a kiss to his cheek and touch his chest and then I climb from bed.

My mother is already up in the small kitchen. This doesn't surprise me.

What does is that she and Saraya are sitting together like comfortable old friends, eating toast. Mom's drinking tea.

"Honey," she says when she sees me. She puts down the mug, gets up, and pulls me into a hug.

Saraya looks away, embarrassed, and rises from the table. "I'll give you some privacy."

She exits through the same hallway we entered through last night. I wonder if she slept here or in her own quarters, and what those are like. Is she surrounded by her loyal warriors at all times? If so, I bet she stayed here. She wouldn't want to talk about everything that's happened in the last twenty-four hours since she broke out the hotel skylight and crashed this not-party.

I take the chair she vacated. "I'm so glad you're here, but we didn't really get to cover this—why are you here? Did Mag and Jared make you come?" *I thought you didn't approve of any of this. Of what I want for my life.*

Mom sits down across from me. "I owe you an apology. Not for being angry at you for neglecting your job, but because you were right. This is not normal." She shrugs. "When Porsoth showed up and told us that you and Luke might be in trouble, that you needed our help . . . I realized I was being a big coward."

"Mom, no," I say. We've always shared an anxiety, fear about most things. Until I began to change.

"Yes, I was," she says. "I love all these stories about regular people who end up pulled into giant circumstances. Who fight the good fight no matter what. Except when my grown kid tells me that she wants to do that, I say no. I get worried. I ask her to go small."

"You just want the best for me."

"I do," she says. "But I should know better than to assume safest is best, by this point. You were right."

"I was?" I mean, now that she's admitting it, I want to hear why. I'm glad she's sure, because I'm wondering at this point.

"Last night, when we got here, seeing all that up close and in person . . . I understand. How could you know this exists and just pretend it doesn't? Pretend not to have a role?"

"What role though? Luke is so badly hurt. What if we're in way over our heads and there's no way out this time?"

"We have today," Mom says. "A lot can happen in a day."

That's true enough.

"I need to talk to Saraya," I say, "the Rude."

"I'll go sit with Luke until he wakes up."

A fragile sliver of hope sparks within me. My people are here. What can't we do together? But I need to get Saraya's read on this, and she's most definitely not one of my people. I have to confess that I like her. To myself. Not to her. I'm thinking she might stab me if I confessed it to her.

I scuff along the polished wood floors to the arched door. I missed an opportunity to ask Mom if this house reminds her of a giant hobbit-hole too. Maybe we're in New Zealand.

I find Saraya sitting outside on a bench and keeping watch

on a street beginning to show signs of life. Some people are already leaving home for work or chores or fight practice.

"None of them know the truth," she says.

I slide onto the bench beside her. "How do you mean?"

"They don't know why Sean left. They don't know why Michael was here last night. They don't know that we're pawns."

"They have to, right? You do whatever you're told to."

"In the name of good." Her face is solemn.

"Luke always told me there were more similarities between Team Good and Team Evil than anyone wants to admit. I guess he's right."

I'm hoping to provoke some fight, to see a glimpse of the Saraya I've gotten to know.

"I suppose so," she says.

Oh no. Wow, that's defeat.

"Since it was your arrow, is there a way for you to fix it?"

She turns to face me. "I didn't mean to hit either of them. Well, I meant to hook Sean's shirt collar and tow him down." There's the embarrassment again. "Our weapons' workings are mysterious, even to us. We've always been told that they will only prove fatal to someone who refuses to atone."

"Sounds like Luke." But I can work with it. "Sean . . ." I say. "You going to forgive him?"

"He broke my heart." The words slip out, so soft I wonder if I misheard.

I can't believe she said it. To me. "I kinda figured."

"I loved him, and I was sure he knew that even if we never said it, and then he left. He was just gone. And he became a thief." She says it with disgust. "Why didn't he tell me?"

"Why didn't Luke tell me about his dad?" Any of the times, including the most recent one. "They're afraid."

She snorts. "Afraid?"

"I think Sean broke his own heart too," I say. "He told Luke he wants to get the Holy Grail so he can give you a perfect world. Paradise on Earth. That's a pretty huge gesture."

She's shocked. "He wouldn't."

"Oh, he might," I say. "But probably not if you were to forgive him. Besides, who knows what will happen today—are we still chasing the Grail? And why?"

Something I just said echoes within me. There's a greater meaning here. I'm missing it.

Saraya says, "The healers may know more—or Isaac. I should fetch Isaac."

"Isaac, we met him," I say, recognizing the name. I'm still chasing the thought dangling out of reach . . .

"He's the chief scholar."

My mind keeps circling something about seeking the Grail. Luke brought it up again yesterday. That it could wipe away sin. Bring about paradise.

What if he wasn't after it for only Sean anymore?

"Get him," I say. "Isaac. We want everything he has or knows on the Grail legend. I have a theory."

I race back inside, confident Saraya will take my orders. This might be the weirdest morning ever. My mother is beside the bed in a chair and looks up as I rush in. "What is it?" she asks.

I throw back the covers over Luke. The bandage on his leg, fresh from last night, is soaked in red again. I shake his shoulders gently until he wakes up. "Were you going to get the Grail?" I demand. "What for?"

Luke blinks, hazy and sleepy, and I see a suggestive smile ghost across his gorgeous face before he takes in my mom now standing behind me. He winces with pain and his hand goes to his thigh.

"Don't lie. Tell me," I say. "The Grail. Why did you still want to find it?"

He lifts one shoulder, propping himself up on his arm. "If we bring about paradise, Father's wishes don't matter anymore. No more Hell. For anyone." He says it with a challenge, but then, "I should have told you. I wanted to prove to you I was capable. I'm sorry."

No, I want to say. *This is great. Sort of.* I don't say that part. I focus on the good news. "I think I know why your wound opened back up. Michael's only part of it."

"What?" he asks.

My mother frowns a question at me.

"You're the Fisher King. Well, prince. You're the Fisher Prince. And if I'm right we're going to need the Grail after all."

Everyone obviously thinks I've lost my mind, and I probably have. But this feels right. Not clear, not simple. But correct.

It figures we'd end up on a Grail quest. I blame Sean. Or Lucifer. Yes, always safe to blame Lucifer.

Our entire group is en route to the Guardian City library, because this is going to call for research. My mother is the only one I'm confident knows anything about the Fisher King part of Arthurian legend. She knows about everything. But this means I still have some explaining to do. Although given what Luke said about Porsoth being involved in some of the real events, he could have some unique insights to share. If it's possible to have studied this, and made sense to do so in Hell, I'm sure he has.

Presently he's in his large form carrying Luke, over Luke's protests and Saraya's. Small, fierce children line the street across from the library as we approach. "Kill! Demon!" I hear in a familiar voice. The woman who was with them yesterday is there as well.

The little boy breaks free and runs straight at my mother and Mag, walking side by side. He peers up at them. "You are not demons," he declares. This kid can't be more than six. "That is demon!" He points up at Porsoth.

My mother tilts her head. "He's a nice demon. He's our friend."

The boy looks entirely puzzled. The woman is skeptical. "He is?" she asks.

"Meet him and find out," Mom says.

The woman puts her hand on the boy's shoulder and turns him back to the small group.

Saraya says, "You can if you want, Vale. I have a feeling it's an all-hands-on-deck kind of day."

The woman, Vale, glances back, but says nothing. I'd swear her eyes snag on my mother for a moment, but then I'm pretty keyed up so I might imagine anything. Sean and my brother are chatting like old friends, a gift Jared has. Sean, I can tell, is using this to avoid looking at anyone outside our party or discussing what it's like being here. Jared, being a lawyer-in-training, is fascinated by Sean's legal history. I hear the word *Interpol* and suspect Jared is in Heaven.

Metaphorically.

I wonder if Luke should have agreed with Michael. Are our goals so different? But . . . whenever Lucifer tries to manipulate a situation, especially a situation involving his son—sons—it's a disaster. Case in point, Luke and his wound.

I hope I'm right about this, because if I'm not we're about to waste a whole bunch of time we don't have.

The library rises above us and it's not an exaggeration to say my heart soars. Every library is one of my favorite places in existence. But I silently promise Hell's library I won't like this one better.

The building is different in style than the rest here. Older. It has the styling of a classical Greek facade, perfectly balanced columns. I know it's the library because . . . I just do. There's some writing in a language I can't read engraved between the columns. I wonder if it's the language of the angels. Speaking of, there are three statues of graceful, fearsome angels with books in hand above the entrance. A tree heavy with round red pomegranates is surrounded by a circle of stones on the street level.

A figure in long white robes strides out to join us, beads in his beard now. "Isaac?" I ask.

"I heard you were coming, so I thought I'd greet you. I've begun pulling an assortment of relevant materials." He pauses and finds Sean. "You'll know exactly where we're going."

Sean scrubs the back of his neck. Are his cheeks slightly pink?

Saraya laughs. Actually laughs. It's not even harsh.

"What's so funny?" I ask.

"This is when you all find out Sean is—was—a huge nerd."

"I was interested in scholarship," Sean says, and crosses his arms.

"And he had a talent for it. For following me around from the time he was small, too." Isaac's laugh is a boom.

"Oh no," Luke calls down, "I'm surrounded."

I make a face at him. "You love it."

"I'm afraid you'll need to shrink down," Isaac informs Porsoth, somehow knowing that he can.

Porsoth does so in a blink and carefully arranges it so Luke's leaning on him. I slide my arm under his other shoulder.

"I'm not that weak," Luke protests, but . . . weakly.

"Lead on," I say to Sean. Sean, who's a secret nerd. Will wonders never cease?

We don't have time to spare, but I have to take a breath when we walk into the marble hall. The stacks surround us in a large rectangle with a circle of spheres with book baskets and spiral steps that range among the levels. The books stretch from the bottom up and up and up—how many levels is impossible to say. I suppose if you can hide an entire city in the folds of the map, you can hide some library floors within a building too.

Sean doesn't hesitate, but sticks with Isaac as they go for the nearest circular stairwell. "Would it be easier for you to fly up?" I ask Luke.

"But then I'd have to stop touching you," he says, low. My turn for my cheeks to warm.

The heat in his eyes, even wounded, when he realized I am with him—that *we* are with him—and not abandoning him is something I'll never get over. It's something I never want to.

Lucifer can't get what he wants out of this. He can't. We're trying to bring a little fairness to the universe—what's more fair than denying him a win?

If the sight of the library is heavenly, so is the smell. That particular combination of old knowledge and aged paper and bindings. Everything good. Rub it on my pulse point. If I were Bosch, I'd roll around in it.

"Who's watching Bosch and Cupcake?" I ask.

"Oh," Mom says, "it turns out your replacements are very responsible. I met one of their mothers and she volunteered when I said we needed to find a place to board them on short notice."

"Did she see Porsoth?" I ask.

"We told her it was a cosplay," Mag puts in. "She was super-impressed."

"One of the kids mentioned your wings and how real they looked the day before," Mom says, "so she had no reason to doubt."

"Not to mention, the average human is extremely skilled at coming up with explanations for the otherwise inexplicable," Isaac says.

Porsoth bobs his beak. "I can't tell you how many times in my early days, marauding and claiming souls, in my other form, drunks convinced themselves I was a hallucination. Humans are good at denial."

"Which makes this a special bunch," Isaac says. "It's a wonder you didn't all end up here sooner."

"We're just visiting," I say.

By this point, we've gone up three levels and Sean exits a whirl of stairs. Concealed by the first row of shelves is a nook with a large circular table in the middle and a window that lets in a generous amount of sunlight on the far side. Stacks surround the rest. The tables are covered in ancient-looking books, scrolls, and other documents that make my mouth water.

"This is the Grail collection," Isaac says. "The interesting parts, at least. Why don't you tell us exactly what we're looking for?"

I sweep my eyes over these people. My people. Plus, Sean and Saraya, who, I admit, I'm beginning to put in the same category.

"You may want to sit down," I say.

CHAPTER TWENTY-FOUR

LUKE

can't believe I'm this lucky—to have Callie fighting for me, to understand it's because she loves me. And unlucky—as a spear of pain shoots through my leg when I lever into a seat. I feel a sparkle of sweat on my brow, but I don't waste the energy to wipe it away.

Callie is standing, looking her fill at the table as we settle. Her hair's pulled back in a sensible ponytail. She's ready to do battle. Well, read old books and then do battle. I'm not as surprised as I could be to hear Sean is a scholarly prat. Another difference between us. He and Callie would've made a perfect match, I bet, in other circumstances.

I don't know why I thought that. I haven't detected any interest from either of them in the other. But there's definitely a voice inside me that keeps repeating *the good son* in my father's voice and knowing it's not me. I long for it to shut up.

Porsoth sits beside me on the right, and Callie's mother on my left. Sean's across from me. Saraya stands, leaning on her sword. This isn't her scene, but she's here. And quiet.

Mag and Jared sink down beside each other, and he drops a press of his lips to theirs.

Porsoth's hands flutter over the books, itching to dig in. "Callie, should we wait or do you have information to share? I'm eager to hear a theory that requires this bounty."

Isaac eyes my tutor, but doesn't tell him *hands off*. Solely due to Michael's commandment in all likelihood.

Callie takes a deep breath and exhales. "When we first met Sean, he told us he was on a Grail quest. He even used the word *seeker*."

"So what?" Sean asks. "It's a myth, or at least a very hard-to-confirm truth. I grew up obsessed with tales of it, and I thought you two might run a merry chase keeping up with me. I won't lie—I've always wanted to steal the Grail, ever since I left here. But mostly my plan was misdirection."

"To keep us busy, so you could get to know your brother without telling him who you were," Callie says. "I figured as much. You just weren't going about it all that well, in contrast to your other thefts."

Saraya sucks her lip, but says nothing.

Callie continues. "But you did share your goal with Luke— that you planned to bring about paradise on Earth, supposedly inspired by Solomon Elerion and how he almost succeeded at the opposite."

"Except for you," my mother says, sounding proud.

"Except for all of us," Callie says. "And Michael." She goes on, focusing back on Sean. "In this case, you claimed it was a gift, so we believed you."

Sean studies the table intently. He misses out on Saraya staring at him.

Callie shakes her head. "Long story short—in most Grail

legends, there's a wounded or maimed king, usually called the Fisher King. Sometimes there's two men, a father and son, or two brothers, both wounded, one more than the other." Callie pauses here to look pointedly at Sean and me.

I wave at her, but her words make my pulse speed. What does it mean?

Callie's cheeks have a slight flush. "The wound is almost always in the groin—in a lot of stories it's said to symbolize—"

"The loss of fertility," her mother puts in eagerly. "Yes. The wasteland, the broken kingdom."

"My fertility is fine," I say, affronted. "It's a thigh wound."

"A euphemism people have been using since the very beginning," Callie says with a grin.

"She's got you there, brother," Sean says.

I ignore him. "There's a thigh wound and the Grail heals it?"

"No," Porsoth says. "At least not directly."

Callie holds up a hand. "Finding the Grail castle is about reading the clues, yes, but also about worthiness of seeing it. Of being in the right place and usually of someone asking the right question. A knight."

"We have to find a place I won't be able to see?" *Worthy* is not a word used to describe people like me, but I want to be. I want to be worthy of her, of her trust and love. Of a life together. "And we need some knights?"

"Sort of," Callie says.

"I feel like I'm still missing the larger point here," Sean says.

"Here's my theory," Callie says, and I can see how nervous she is in the tap of her fingers against her own right thigh, in how fast she talks when she launches into it. "Some stories have a gravity of their own. Sean comes along, and even though he's going through the motions, he names himself a seeker and both he and his brother are facing different challenges. His brother is wounded—"

"Accidentally," Saraya puts in.

"Not because of anything anyone did—except, yes, fire an arrow—but because of who he was and who he was with."

Isaac lets out a low whistle. "You're saying that the Grail legend is playing itself out. And they're part of it now."

Callie nods. "Don't you see it? Right now?" She swings her hand around. "We're at the freaking Round Table. We're the knights."

"I've always wanted to be a knight," Mag says. "But what do we actually do? To help Luke?"

"We need to find the Holy Grail. We've got to play it out. Once you're in a Grail quest, you have to follow it through. This is the only chance we have. We redeem Sean. We heal Luke. And bonus, if this works, the Grail will give us the leverage to stop Lucifer." Callie pulls out a chair and sits in it, makes to pull a manuscript toward her. "So get looking."

"That's it?" Sean asks. "That's the plan?"

Her eyebrows lift. "You have a better one?"

"No," he says.

"That's what I thought. Everybody dig in. We're finding the Holy Grail or else."

I have many conflicting feelings. My heart wants to do this, for Callie. I can't stand the idea of her disappointment, if she's wrong. Or the idea of this wound slowly spreading throughout my body, of me as the wasteland Callie's mother mentioned.

As they say, what the hell? I grab a book and open it. My brain recognizes the language as French and starts decoding it for me.

There's that word again: *worthy*. I do my best to put it out of my mind.

The good son, the good son, the good son repeats at the back of it.

An hour inches past, then two. The words blur in front of my eyes. My attention span is a challenge at the best of times, and using half my effort to push away the throbbing pain in my thigh is, to put it mildly, the worst.

When Sean gets up with a book and heads into the stacks, I pry my body out of my seat to follow.

"Luke?" Callie glances up from the manuscript she's reading.

"Need to stretch my . . . groin," I say and grit a smile at her so she'll know I'm okay enough to leave for a moment.

Sean is in his element. I find him running his fingers along a row of gilded leather spines, clearly seeking a certain volume.

To be fair, I haven't seen Sean anywhere he couldn't make seem like his element. I try to picture our circumstances exchanged, his upbringing in Hell (Porsoth would've been delighted by his nerdy streak), and me here (is there a delinquent guardian school?). Then I picture how kind Isaac has been to him. And it's plain that Saraya's antipathy comes from a deep well of feeling. He lost his mother, but I bet she did love him. Would I have been a different person if I'd grown up here instead of him? Would he be different if he'd grown up in Hell?

We've both had the kind of pressure only Father can exert applied to us. That's something we do have in common.

Sean turns his head to peer at me over his shoulder. "Yes?"

"I thought we might talk." We haven't yet. Things moved so fast, our conversations have been brief and witnessed.

"Do we have time for that?" Sean goes back to his shelf.

"Are we getting anywhere in there? I'm the one with the mortal wound."

He pauses. "You don't think this will work?"

"I hope it will because Callie would like it to. And this thing hurts like you'd expect a magical wound to." I nod down at my leg. "What about you? You planning to let yourself be forgiven? You've got it way easier, brother."

Sean leans carefully back against the bookshelf. "Is that what you think?"

"It sounds like you had an idyllic childhood."

"And you didn't? In the palace?"

I have to laugh. "Are we arguing about which one of us is the most spoiled?"

"No," Sean says, "it's obviously you."

The mirth departs. A heat of offense builds within me that the wound in my leg only makes burn hotter. "Are you provoking me on purpose?"

"No, brother," Sean says. "Tell me how I've got it wrong. You grew up in the lap of supernatural luxury. You were surrounded by tailors and tutors and probably temptresses—"

He's not wrong.

"—they let you get away with being lax at all of it. That was what the chattering class of demons said, at least. Part of our father probably thought your slacking off showed character. Then, out of nowhere, you save the damned world and become a hero. How is that fair? I became a thief."

Fairness. That's what he's stuck on. He and Callie do share a lot of beliefs.

"Do you want to know what it was actually like?" I ask. I don't wait for his answer. "Father could be displeased by anything—answering too slowly or too quickly. Refusing to practice a torture technique. And when he was displeased, sometimes the technique was demonstrated on me. Or he'd send me to live with Lilith, who loves me in her way, but it's not a very motherly way. She'd have a parade of human lovers, mostly talented but dirtbag musicians, in and out of the house. She'd give me chores. And every now and again, we'd have a good day together. Then, Father would demand I return, a year, or three years, later. I wasn't permitted to know other people my age, because I was to be above them. I was a failure at getting souls, and my supervisor wasn't Porsoth, it was Rofocale. He would have happily unmade me or watched Father do it. I never knew what it was to feel something genuine that was mine, to have that feeling returned, until I met Callie. All this"—I wave between us—"all these games of his are to make me give her up and be who he always intended me to be. So, yes, I think I had it worse. You were able to walk away from his plans, the good son." Making me the bad son.

Sean is intent, considering. "Was I? How far away have I gotten? Yes, I had more people in my life. I understood love. And I had to leave it behind. Could you do that?"

I tried once, and Callie refused to let it stand. If she were eavesdropping on this . . . I allow myself to see us through her eyes.

"We are ridiculous," I say. "The pair of us. Poor-little-rich-boying each other."

"I wasn't rich."

"You were, just not in money." I sigh. "This isn't why I came back here."

"No?"

"No," I say. "I wanted to say that . . . I don't hate the idea of having a brother. Even if it is you."

Why did I say that to him? I must be developing a habit of offering up my heart on a plate to people. Callie is one thing, but Sean? My wound is rotting my resolve.

"You're not so bad," Sean says. "I don't hate it either."

More than I expected. "Good. Now let's talk about how you're going to win Saraya back."

Sean scoffs. "Back? We were never truly together."

"I've seen how you look at her. The deference. And I don't think the idea of creating a paradise for her was an idle one. You'd do it, if you could. I was ready to help you."

He doesn't deny it. "She doesn't want me. How could she, knowing what she knows now? I did think the guardians would come—I wanted to see her. Just see her. To want more would be foolish."

"I suspected you were a fool. You can't just give up." I couldn't turn my back on Callie, not for . . . a kingdom. Not for anything. That's what Father doesn't understand. I'd sooner be unmade than disappoint her. I finally have a glimpse at a future I desire.

"It can't work. It's not to be. The devil's son and the chief warrior of the guardians? Even a fairy tale would never claim it could exist."

"Have you asked *her*?"

"What?" Sean raises his hands. "Asked her what?"

No, then. "Have you asked her anything?"

I should get back. Let him sit with that question. But I came back here for one more thing. "Sean, if things . . . don't go well. Father says there can only be one heir. I don't want it to be me."

"It's not going to be me either. Tell him yourself."

"I have. But I think you know what I'm saying."

I leave before he can give me a yes or no. I don't believe I'm thinking straight, but I can hear the ticking of a clock in my ears and it reverberates with the pain in my leg. If I displease Father, if we don't find a way out of this, I have to make sure Callie is protected. That may mean severing her connection to me.

After the past few days, I'm beginning to sense a sacrifice is in order. Mine.

I turn back. "Don't mention this to her."

Sean is watching me. He doesn't agree or disagree. He pulls a book off the shelf and walks toward me, looping his free arm around me. He supports me all the way back to the round table.

Callie stops reading to watch us, the hint of a smile playing at her lips at seeing the two of us together. Little does she know.

No, I'd never give her up. Unless I have to in order to save her.

CHAPTER TWENTY-FIVE

CALLIE

We're getting nowhere, and way too slowly. We've been at this for over two hours and other than a few tidbits read aloud and then dismissed, we're no closer to an answer.

I slam my current book closed—a forgotten Grail quest story that had a weird interlude involving sheep—and bang my head on it. Then I look up to find everyone around the table giving me a concerned eye.

"Honey?" my mom asks.

We're interrupted then, as Vale, the woman from the street, enters. "Still need help?" she asks, and her eyes linger on Porsoth. He reaches over and removes a book from Isaac to consult it himself. The two of them are showing a competitive streak.

"We do," I say to Vale.

"Let's take a walk," Mag says to me. They know when I'm at my wit's end.

I nod and get up. "Might be a good idea."

I had a moment's hope when Luke came back leaning on Sean. Acting like brothers. That they're working together is good.

My mother motions for Vale to come sit beside her and she does.

Saraya is pacing, the only one of us not busy researching. The tense line of her body is what I feel like inside. We're not making progress. My plan is failing.

Mag and I walk back out to the spiraling steps. "Up or down?" they ask.

"Up," I say.

We head up together, feet slow thumps on the marble. "All the answers are supposed to be in books," I say. "I really thought we'd solve the puzzle like this."

"We will," Mag says. Then adds, "Solve it."

I've been thinking about something else too. "I want Jared's apartment. I need something to look forward to, after this."

Mag blinks, surprised. "You do? That's great. There's room for Luke there, you know."

"How about Cupcake?"

"The entrance is at the back. You can probably manage to sneak him. And dogs are allowed."

This feels so far from right now, today, but it's true. I need to imagine the other side of this.

"How will you pay your half of the rent?" they ask.

"Great question," I say. "I'll think about that later."

Mag nods.

"What changed your mind? I know what changed Mom's."

"Porsoth told us, about Luke's brush with . . ." They trail off, searching.

"Death?" I supply.

"Yeah. And how you reacted. I realized I can't actually imagine the two of you not together anymore. I knew how much it must've hurt, the thought of losing him. I . . . if it had been me . . ."

"I get it. Brushes with death do clarify things."

Brushes with death . . . Wait a second. "I have an idea," I say and pivot back the way we came.

Mag follows without hesitation, and we pound back down the stairs. "Glastonbury," I say as we burst back onto the landing and hurry to the table. "What have you found about it?"

"We've already been there, though," Sean says with a slight, pretty frown.

"That's where the wound occurred," I say. "What if we left in too big a hurry? What if we just didn't find it?"

Isaac and Porsoth are elbowing each other, some light squabbling going on between them. "I told you that one was promising," Porsoth says.

"I suppose you had a point," Isaac says. He leafs through the stack in front of him and produces a document, then slides it over to Porsoth.

Vale's and my mother's heads are close together over whatever book they were reading. Mom says something to her and I see the first ever smile on the other woman's face. They look up expectantly at Porsoth.

Interesting.

"Are you going to put us out of our misery?" Luke says. "Can we stop this?"

"Perhaps, if I can locate the correct line. Wait," Porsoth says, and stabs at the page with a finger at the end of a wing. "Ah, here it is." He clears his feathered throat and then reads aloud, "'The castle exists in shade and shadow, protected by the thorn of flowers and the red waters. Its guardians are legend.'"

Yes, that could be important. "Why didn't you say this before?" I ask.

"I tried," Porsoth says. "I was informed it was too obvious."

"I said I was sorry," Isaac says. "Well, I'm saying it now."

Sean says, "You think it means the Grail is back in Glastonbury."

"Sometimes things hide in plain sight," I say. "Or I guess in this case, are hidden from plain sight. But that *has* to be a reference to the Holy Thorn and the Chalice Well."

Luke gives me a look.

I explain. "The Holy Thorn is said to have been created by Joseph of Arimathea—"

"Him again," he says.

"Striking the ground with his staff. It created this special flowering hawthorn people still visit. And the well of the Red Spring runs with water tinted like blood."

"From the iron content," my mother says. "Ferric acid residue."

"The natural world is made to reflect the wonders of creation," Vale says.

"Yes!" I say to be encouraging. "But iron aside, it's said to be a hint of the blood the Grail once held. Or the rust from the nails of the cross."

"Why are all these stories so gross?" Mag asks.

Jared says, "An excellent question."

"How do we find it this time, if we couldn't before? And what does 'Its guardians are legend' mean?" Sean asks.

Good questions. Inconveniently good questions. "There's also the White Spring, and that's got to mean something too."

"Calcite deposits," my mother says, more softly this time. Vale smiles at her with encouragement.

"But it's not mentioned in that text," Porsoth says.

"Which could be a clue itself," Isaac adds.

"'Its guardians are legend.'" Sean repeats it again.

"Could it be a reference to the legends themselves?" I ask.

"The ones so strong they're repeating themselves with us?" Luke asks. I can tell by the strain in his voice that the wound isn't getting any less painful.

"No. Wait." I hold up my hand. I close my eyes and envision Glastonbury. The ruins. The grounds around the ruins . . . "I think I know what it means. What did that phrase come from?"

Porsoth owlishly blinks. "It's an account from—"

"The monks," Isaac says. "Who used to be at the abbey. It's never been published. It's part of our private collection, recovered by a guardian centuries ago."

A monk at Glastonbury Abbey. There's one thing at it we didn't go see, because I didn't think it was really them. But what if it doesn't matter? What if their presence *is* the clue?

"Lady Guinevere and King Arthur. Their so-called graves were discovered by the monks. On the same grounds as the abbey," I say. "'Its guardians are legend.' It doesn't get more legendary than those two."

Everyone is quiet and I expect disagreement. Instead Luke lifts his hands, smiles at me, and claps. Genuinely claps. "Stop it," I say, embarrassed when Jared and Mag join in. "We've got some ruins to revisit, stat."

"Finally," Saraya says. "We get to do something."

The group bursts into conversation. Luke presses his weight on the table with his hands and levers himself up. He sidles over to me, putting one hand around my waist and his nose against my cheek. "I think you deserved the applause."

"You would," I say.

He kisses me, soft and sweet, and it shouldn't make me worry. It's a lovely kiss. But I worry anyway.

What follows is a flurry of activity. Knights go on quests together, and I insist everyone comes. Except Isaac, who says his place is in Guardian City, and stays behind. He and Porsoth exchange a handshake, and then Porsoth ducks his head in a slight bow. "May the light shine on you in your time of darkness," Isaac says in farewell.

Now we're in a supply barracks, empty of guardians because everyone else is working or training.

I have my arm tucked in Luke's, propping him up. I'm sticking close to him, because I need the reminder that we still have time. Saraya is busy gathering anything she thinks we might need, other than reinforcements. That turns out to be way more weapons than I'd have thought, but about par for her. She sticks a crossbow into a large satchel.

For that matter, I guess Sean knows how to use them too. He's quietly helping her. She directed my mother to a kitchen area, where some food is being packed to take.

It's already midday and we're almost ready to leave. I continue to worry that I'm wrong, about all of this, and that Luke's kiss had something weird in it. An apology in advance? He's being quiet and I don't like it.

But pressing him in front of everyone won't get me anywhere. I'll choose my moment. We're going to get through this, because we have to. Leaving Guardian City does feel like being cast out of a sanctuary. Being back on the map feels like it will be symbolic in a way that isn't exactly good.

"Back on the map is back on the clock," I say.

Saraya is practically vibrating with her joy at being in motion. "We're ready," she says, fastening the bag, which Sean then hefts over his shoulder.

"Do you think you're strong enough to make us hard to notice when we get there?" I ask Luke. "Those security guards are going to flip if not, but we'll deal with it."

"I'll muster the energy," Luke says. "I'm wounded, not dead."

The Fisher King loses his capacity to function slowly is what I don't say. No reason to plant that in his head. He's called the Fisher King because it's all he can do in a lot of stories—in the ones where he can even leave the castle—cast out a rod and catch a fish or two. Not that Luke couldn't serve some *A River Runs Through It*–era young Brad Pitt with a fishing rod, but the image is ridiculous.

"Do people go boating in Hell?" I ask him.

"Why wouldn't they?" he counters. "You could forget everything, or get roasted alive, or hang out with Styx."

"Did I tell you she said hi?" I ask Porsoth. "She was worried about you."

Porsoth fidgets. "I, ah, saw her before I left."

Luke and I exchange a smile, and I almost tow him away right then to interrogate him. *What are you thinking, devil's son? What have you decided to do? Or not do, my secretive love?*

I leave it for now.

But I decide to ask him something else. "I'm thinking of getting an apartment. Taking over Jared's."

"You are?" he looks at me searchingly.

I swallow. "Mag says it's big enough for two people."

"They do?" he asks.

"Yeah, they do. And a goat and a dog."

Luke does a slow blink. "Are you asking if I'll move in with you?"

"I'm asking if maybe, once this is over, you might want to move in together. Yes." Not that it's what he's used to, with his palace apartments. "But you don't have to answer—" What am I doing? What has gotten into me?

"I want to," he says. "Yes." He leans in and speaks into my ear. "I'll need to make sure it has the right kind of shower, however."

I swat him. "You could magic the right kind."

"True." He straightens and says, "Let's get going. I have something to live for."

I force him to look at me. "You always did, goofball."

He straightens with a wince. "I am not a goofball."

Mag and Jared come in then, hefting two packs full of whatever my mother's put together. She's behind them, along with Vale. Mom has picked up a plus-one. "You are both goofballs," Mag says.

I stick my tongue out, because I'm mature. Then, I ask, "How are we going? Is there a non-searing-pain way of travel?" I clarify. "Not for me, for everyone else. I'm with you," I tell Luke.

I hope he hears the truth of it. I'm with you, even when it hurts. Even when it's hard. That's what love means.

"I'd never want you to hurt on my account," he says. "Especially if there was another option."

Saraya throws her arms out wide and bares her teeth in a smile. "Everyone huddle up," she says. She tosses a glance at Luke. "You too."

"Me?" he asks, surprised.

"If Sean can travel this way, so can you," she says with a shrug.

Sean says, "She has a point. It's a lot more pleasant."

"I'll go on ahead," Porsoth says, and he's popped out before anyone can protest.

The rest of us ring our arms around each other in a tight circle, turning ourselves into an echo of the Round Table. Here we go.

Saraya chants, low, and Sean joins in. The tones vibrate and then the world around us joins too. I catch Mag's wide eyes and see how tightly they grip Jared and then I don't see anything. We fly and float, weightless, among stars. There's no screaming. No pain. We don't move at a hurtle, the way I do with Luke when we zappity. We meander through time and space.

And when we stop, we're still linked together on the brilliant green of the abbey grounds.

Time to find an invisible castle.

CHAPTER TWENTY-SIX

LUKE

ack where I almost died, I find that I'm weaker and stronger. My leg aches with a constant sharpness that pushing away physical sensations doesn't mute. And if I send those away, that means distancing the touch of Callie too. I can't bring myself to do so.

I let it hurt.

She asked me to move in together. On Earth. Her world, our place.

It's hard to envision. It feels like a movie I heard demons discussing during their version of pop culture happy hour. But that doesn't stop me from wanting it as badly as I want this pain gone. Possibly more.

The day is warmer than yesterday, the afternoon air thick and humid. I extend my powers around us, sealing us inside an envelope that should make us stick out less. Tourists turn in our direction, then away again, shaking their heads. Did they see something?

Being here is materially different this time. I concentrate

to put my fetching finger on why that is, and realize how to describe the source of my discomfort. Harder to spot or not, there's a palpable sense that we're being watched. That eyes are on us.

And if they aren't the eyes of the tourists around us, whose are they?

"Do you feel that?" Callie asks and, by turns, everyone nods, even Porsoth. He sails up to us with his scholar's robes whirling around him.

"Not just me, then," I say.

"Definitely not," Sean says.

"There is something here." Porsoth fusses with his collar. "Something uncanny. Eldritch."

Saraya unsheathes her sword.

"Not yet," Callie says, and Saraya doesn't even bother to threaten her. Those two have gotten practically chummy overnight. "I didn't think anyone actually used the word *eldritch*."

"Only when horrors feel near," Porsoth says. "Or when torturing Howard Phillips."

Ugh, I hope we're not about to discuss Lovecraft. Nothing creepier than that guy, even dead. No second chances forthcoming for him. I think of Agnes and wonder how she's doing. She must be convinced we'll fail, with Porsoth having abandoned Hell to come to us and a blood moon in the sky. Little does she know that—at this point—getting her a fresh start might be the easiest of our tasks.

Callie won't give up on her. Or me. Which means we have to successfully do all of this.

And if we can't, Sean better keep his promise to me.

Mag spins in a slow circle, taking the abbey ruins and lovely environs in. They give Jared a dazzling smile when they face him. He and his mother are goggling too.

"Yes, there's something kind of creepy-feeling about this . . . But it's all so beautiful," Callie's mother says. She seems almost shy as she explains to Vale. "I've never been out of the U.S. before." A couple pass by us a few feet away, talking loudly about lunch. "There are British accents everywhere! It's like we might see the TARDIS at any second."

Vale, who I'd previously taken for constitutionally stern, smiles at her.

"I think we might see something a lot weirder than the TARDIS, Mom," Callie says. "At least before this is over." She puts her hands on her hips. Planning Callie is back in action. "Should we split up? I can't believe I just suggested that, after all the yelling I've done at everyone who ever does on-screen . . . But should we?"

"No," Saraya says. "Splitting up the party is *always* a bad idea."

I don't point out that she did it earlier when she sent her guardian squad in after Sean. And they ended up as our allies in result. Then again, that could be what she means.

She goes on. "We should keep close together. That way our defenses are at hand. At least until we find the Grail castle."

I don't want to be the bummer, but someone has to ask. "And how do we do that?"

That term *worthy* comes back to me yet again. If that's the key that fits in the invisible lock, we're in big trouble. I doubt anyone in charge of revealing this thing would count me as worthy in any sense of the word, soul or no soul.

"Shouldn't it be our castle now?" Sean says. "If we're the Fisher King twins? Can't we demand it show itself?"

Callie tugs on her lip, thinking. "Yes. It should recognize you. Maybe. If that's how this works?"

"Should we walk around calling for it like a dog?" I lift my voice a hair. "Here, castle castle castle . . ."

"What if it's a metaphor?" Callie's mother asks. "The castle?"

"How can a metaphor house the Grail?" Callie shakes her head. "Luke's wound isn't imaginary. It's got to be some sort of real."

Jared is nodding *cool cool cool* style. "Some sort of real. Sounds like a description of reality from a conspiracy theory handbook. Should we consult the internet?"

Mag pulls out their phone with a shrug. "Why not?" They tap in an unknown string of search terms.

Porsoth has been standing, stroking his beak-chin in that way he does when he's deep in thought. "I am attempting to recall the commonalities in the stories of the knights. Usually, there was an encounter that led them to the discovery of the castle. Whether they knew what it was at the time or not."

"An encounter." That's . . . spectacularly vague. As is the rest of his sentence.

Callie wears a frustrated frown. She's swiveling to check out different directions, lifting her hand and squinting when needed. If she still had my powers, steam would probably be emerging from her ears in a steady stream.

"What if we split into two groups—so not a full split-up. One with Sean, the other with Luke," Callie says. "One group can comb the grounds here, and the other can try the Chalice Well and White Springs shrine."

"I already said no splitting up." Saraya dismisses the idea.

"Let's start where we are. You can spread out a bit, but stay within my view."

I don't know what threats she thinks we'll face here in idyllic Glastonbury that need her weaponry or Vale's (or brother Sean's—wait, I just got his priest costume joke, invoking our father). What things we might encounter that are worse than us. But those unseen eyes are still present.

Doing as she says, we separate slightly into pairs and threes and Porsoth on his own and begin to weave our way through the grounds, closer to the ruins. I cast my senses to their limits—both to insulate us and to detect anything unusual. Other than the prickly unseen stares, I don't.

Mag and Jared disappear inside the walls of the ruins we visited before, but . . . "Let's avoid going over there," I say.

Callie takes my hand. "I just realized I never wanted to see this place again either." She's quiet for a moment as we loop wide around the side. "Luke . . . you aren't keeping any more secrets, are you? You're planning to fight this? To not let your father win, right?"

Each question slices through me with the ease of a holy blade. She senses that I'm not convinced we'll get through this. That I'm not convinced I will. She's the most perceptive soul I've ever met.

Worse, I don't know that I can answer truthfully. The answers might not exist yet.

"Would I do something that stupid?" I ask.

"Like disappoint your father?" she asks. "I hope so. He doesn't own you. No one does."

I hear *not even me,* and want to disagree. *I'm yours.*

"Someone should tell him that," I say.

"Luke . . ." she says, a warning.

"I promise I'm trying," I say, "to beat this." *Beat him.* I'm not sure it's possible. He's the king of Hell. I don't want to be like him.

My wound sings and shrieks, reminding me that it's trying to have its way with me. Figures I'd make the hottest possible date and stumble into a legend instead.

"If you do decide to do something stupid, please tell me first." Callie sniffs. "I can talk you out of it."

We round the last set of lower stone ruins in front of us, and come into an open green. Why couldn't Sean have decided to climb *these* puny walls earlier? There's a brown historical marker ahead. Callie stops and points.

"There," she says. "Let's go read it."

That's my girl. Better plans through reading.

We speed up to get there first. The rest of the group trails along behind us, some faster, some slower. In a few steps, Saraya strides even with us. "Is that important?" she asks, nodding ahead.

"I'm not sure," Callie says. "But maybe."

We approach it, getting up close and personal. The grass here has a grave-shaped rectangle of stone setting some of it apart, but the marker confirms that no bodies rest within it. A spray of yellow flowers is positioned against the bottom of the sign telling the story of what happened to King Arthur and Guinevere's supposed resting place. The official story goes their bodies were originally found on the grounds in 1191, and then were moved in 1278 to a more permanent black marble tomb with another king and queen—alive— watching. When the abbey dissolved in 1539, the tomb went the way of extinction. Not even ruins left.

"I bet they were pissed off, being moved around so much," I observe.

"And then basically disinterred for good," Callie says. She

gives me a sly glance through her lashes. "Remember the first tomb we entered together?"

The site of our first kiss? Yes. I remember. "Burned in my brain. You want to be buried in pajamas."

"Or a ball gown," she says.

"Really?" I raise my brows. "When did that change happen?"

"I'm keeping my options open."

"Ugh," Saraya says. "Stop it. You're embarrassing."

Callie and I exchange another glance.

Sean has joined us and skims the text on the marker. "I think they're enviable, not embarrassing."

Saraya grunts again, an *of course you do* grunt. I don't point out he said much the same thing about us early in our acquaintance.

Sean watches Saraya, without her noticing, and I want to shake him and tell him not to wait too long. Jared, Mag, and Callie's mother join us.

Porsoth trundles up last. "I remain certain there *is* something here," he says. "I remember Morgan the Fay used to say that the hills of Avalon were filled with secrets, that they were in the ground beneath your feet."

"The ground beneath our feet," Callie says. "Humor me."

She looks at the long body-like shape of the grassy grave labeled as Guinevere and Arthur's initial resting place and then she lowers to her bottom. She stretches out on top of the grass, lying there. Her stormy eyes gaze up at me, and she reaches up and motions for me to join her.

Oh, it hurts, the way my leg protests, but I choose not to care about that. I settle down beside her with as much grace as I can manage.

"Did this just get weird for anyone else?" Jared asks.

Mag elbows him.

"What do you see?" Porsoth asks.

His face. The faces of the others. The clouds drifting by above us.

"Close your eyes," Callie says.

I do.

For a long moment, there's only sounds—birds and breathing and Callie's heartbeat if I strain to find it beneath all that. There's the smell of the grass, like the scent of green itself. A note of dirt beneath it, beneath us.

And below that . . . Secrets. Faint voices reach my ears or they could be inside my head. I can't quite make out the words.

But something is happening, that much is plain.

Callie's hand reaches out and takes mine. Her fingers are chilled despite the warmth and sun on us. There's the whispers of giant trees speaking to each other. The echoes of conversations long past. A wind filled with ghosts, cold as the grave, floats over us.

I realize the sensation of the sun is gone.

"Oh my god," Mag says. "Sorry if that offends anyone from Guardian City."

I open my eyes, and there's a man in full armor charging toward us on a fast horse through a sudden mist. The ground shakes, the sound of the horse's hooves loud enough to rattle my jaw. I grab Callie's hand and pull us both upright, forgetting my injury.

Until my leg folds beneath me. My wings extend from my shoulders and I might fly once my balance returns . . .

The knight keeps coming.

Saraya has her blade up, but she hesitates. I lift slightly off the ground, not enough. The horse is going too fast. The knight's lance is too steady. Sean dives at me to get me out of its path and takes a hoof to his own leg.

"Fuck!" he shouts.

I watch as he falls to the ground and the rider canters past like they were in a tournament. "Nice ambush!" I call, my heart thundering in my chest.

Sean rubs his leg.

Now we're both wounded.

"Are you whole?" Saraya demands from Sean. She has her sword up, and is clearly doing the math on taking on a ghostly knight with a sword and this amount of backup.

"I'll live," he says, and I can tell he's pleased she asked. Asking means she cares.

Don't wait too long, brother.

The knight wings the horse around and slowly clops back toward us. "What is your business here?" the knight asks, voice feminine.

"Where is here?" Callie asks. "Just to be sure."

"You have breached the grounds of Camelot," the knight responds.

We made it. Callie's intuition found an entrance.

"We're here to visit the castle," I say, breathless. "We seek the Grail."

"My apologies," the knight says. She drops the lance on the ground. "I thought you intruders. It has been years since a rightful seeker came—the last visitor was some sort of actor."

She pushes up her visor and removes her helmet, holding it at her side. Her face is lovely but skeletal and decayed. Long white-blond hair flows down her back.

"The Lady Guinevere," she says. "At your service."

"I think I'm going to pass out," Callie's mother says.

CHAPTER TWENTY-SEVEN

CALLIE

My mom's near-fainting unfreezes us from the shock of Lady Guinevere, bad-ass knight from beyond the grave. Vale catches Mom beneath her arms and cradles her against her strong body.

My mother cranes her neck back and says, "Thank you," to Vale in a starry-eyed way. I'm pretty slow on the uptake and my mother has gone on two dates—total—since I've been old enough to remember. One was with her D&D dungeon master and forced her to retire her fifth-level wizard priestess and another was with the librarian at the branch we don't go to much anymore. She said she "just didn't feel anything click" both times.

From the way she's looking at Vale there's some major clicking.

"Do you think . . ." Luke whispers to me.

"I hope so," I say.

She deserves happiness. I'll worry later whether it's feasible for her to have a girlfriend from Guardian City. The possibility is too wonderful. If Luke and I can make us work, then they'll figure it out.

Jared catches my eye and I can tell he's thinking the same thing. Mag claps their hands under their chin. "This is delightful," they say.

Vale helps Mom steady on her feet. Mom flushes and refuses to look at us.

Lady Guinevere continues to tower over us on her mighty steed. At least we're in the right place.

"Can you show us to the castle?" I ask.

"Oh no," Lady Guinevere says, imperiously. "Seekers must find it. Those are the rules."

With that, she puts her helmet back on and thunders off into . . . the thick woods that now surround us. "I don't think we're in Glastonbury anymore."

"At least not present Glastonbury," Porsoth agrees. "But this landscape seems rather familiar."

"That's one way to hide the Grail," Sean says from the ground, rubbing his mid-thigh. "Out of time."

I go to my mother and put my hands on her shoulders. "Don't think about the maybe-time-travel and what it means, it'll break your brain." I lower my voice. "I approve."

She ducks her head, meaning she's definitely aware of what I mean. She waves me off. "I'm fine now. I just had a moment of . . . That was Lady *Guinevere*."

"As a skeleton or a zombie or something, yes," I say, as if I'm used to this kind of thing. I never will be. "She went into the woods. Should we follow?"

Saraya steps over to Sean's side and gives him a hand up. I think he might say something to her, but he stays quiet. His step has a catch in it when he tests walking on his leg. Note: phantom horses make real impacts.

"How do you feel?" I ask Luke.

"Like my leg's on fire." His voice is casual and I wonder how much the effort costs him.

Vale raises her hands. "I can carry him?"

"I'll be all right," Luke says, jaw clenched.

A raging wind blows around us, like it's urging us on toward the trees. The branches sway in its force, their shadows moving below. It's like every fairy tale scenario meant to warn you to keep out of the dark woods.

"Time may pass differently here," Porsoth says, "than in Glastonbury proper. We shouldn't tarry. The sire will not take it well if you're late."

Lucifer and his ridiculous deadline. "Yeah, we wouldn't want to keep him waiting," I say.

"Not if you want to win," Luke says.

Oh, I do.

"Agnes was willing to give up her chance for you," I say to Luke.

"She wanted to come with me to Earth," Porsoth says. "But she can't leave the borders."

"She'll be able to," I say, putting as much confidence in it as I can manage. "Soon."

I loop my arm under Luke's again to help support him and steer us toward the thick forest. Over my shoulder, I see that Sean manages to walk on his own, but Saraya is right beside him. She'll jump in if he has trouble. Those two have got to just talk already.

Mag holds up their phone before putting it away. "I think the actor she mentioned was Nic Cage."

"What?" my mother asks. "Really?"

"He came here looking for the Holy Grail, drank from the spring."

"Not to steal the Declaration of Independence?" Jared jokes.

"We don't think he found it?" Mom asks.

"No." Porsoth is the one who answers. "I suspect all this exists only to protect the Grail. The legends say that it is eventually claimed and so then its servants are likely freed from their pledge to protect it."

"We're going to put dead Lady Guinevere out of work?" I ask.

I don't want a zombie queen with a grudge roaming Earth.

"I really couldn't say," Porsoth answers, considering. "You should ask her."

Questions, right. We have to be careful. In most of the stories, there's one question to be asked that results in healing. I only wish I knew who has to ask it to heal Luke. And now, I suppose, Sean too.

"I can dispatch her, if necessary," Saraya says.

We all know better than to question Saraya, but personally I'd rather not put it to the test.

The forest has a fairly defined path through it, which we stick to. The trees are old, canopies high above us rustling in gusty, chill breezes. Occasionally, we hear hoofbeats ahead in the distance. We never catch up to them though.

Time creeps past, and the path goes on with no sign of ending. Eventually, we stop for a water break.

"Does anyone else feel like we're doing something wrong?" I ask.

"We're taking the path of Nic Cage, aren't we?" Mag asks. "And getting nowhere."

Luke lets out a groaning sigh. His leg must be screaming. "I hate to say this, but maybe we should leave the path."

"Why do you say that?" Mom asks.

"If I were going to all this trouble to hide something, I certainly wouldn't create a path to it."

The woods are foreboding and dark around us. No part of me wants to venture into the wild of them, and risk getting lost. But Luke is almost certainly right.

"Bread crumbs!" I say it way too enthusiastically.

"What?" Luke asks.

"Did the kitchen crew pack something we can use to leave a trail? So we can get back out, if we get lost in the forest?"

"Oh, yes," Mom says. "There's a baguette." She drops one of the packs and pulls out a halved baguette, hefting it in victory.

"This should work," Mag says, taking it. "I haven't seen or heard any animals out here."

"You are correct," Porsoth says. "We are alone. There are no other living things here."

Not the most reassuring phrasing. There could be plenty of dead ones. I keep this thought to myself.

"Here we go then," I say and I let Luke take the first step into the thick woods. We have to stagger our group to wind between the trunks. That sensation of someone watching us from before returns. We might be getting somewhere. There is a sense of comfort in not being on our own; we have numbers.

"What's that?" There's a stone shape ahead, barely visible through the undergrowth. The castle already?

When we reach it at last, Sean advances and brushes moss off the huge stone sculpture. It's an angel, fierce, blowing a trumpet skyward in one hand and clutching a sword in the other.

"Promising," Luke says, like it's not also terrifying. But he did grow up in Hell, so. The two aren't as different there.

"We keep going," I say.

We continue to thread through the trees, and there are more statues. A dragon's head. Another angel, mouth open in a scream. A creature that looks like it might be a distant cousin to Porsoth, with the head of a snake and the body of a leopard, parts of other animals folded in too. This has to be the Questing Beast, a creature from Arthurian legend.

The trees begin to thin, the light changing. The mist becomes something more like sunlight through dust. There's a gleam, an otherworldly quality.

In a clearing, the largest stone shape we've seen waits. It's an enormous monster's head, much bigger than any of the other statues. All gaping mouth. The top of the opening makes it more than possible we could walk inside. Words are engraved below it.

"What does it say?" I ask Luke. He's got a thin sheen of sweat coating his face. His jaw is tight with effort.

"*Answer in truth or be lost,*" Porsoth supplies.

"You mentioned a question before," Luke says to me.

"Yes," Sean says, "but is this thing going to ask it? Or do we whisper in it or . . . ?"

Excellent questions that I also don't have the answers to. "Maybe Luke and Sean should go inside?"

The mouth is a cave of some kind, formed intentionally by whatever sculptor built these.

"Not alone," Saraya says.

"Of course not," I say.

When no one else protests, I link my arm with Luke's. "We'll go first."

"Wait!" Mag rushes forward and tears off a hunk of baguette

to offer me. "In case you need to leave a trail or something." I don't mention that I'm tempted to eat it, but take it and stuff it awkwardly in Luke's jacket pocket.

"You're ruining my look," he says.

"Are you kidding? You're basically a hot man with carbs, aka every woman's dream, now." I pat his shoulder. It's true. And he is well aware how stunning he is even sans bread. "Are we ready?"

I loop my arm back through his. Saraya looks at Sean, but doesn't offer to help him as they move beside us.

In we go. The leaves underfoot crunch as we walk forward, hesitating on the last step from ground to stone. The gaping mouth is wide enough that the four of us can enter at the same time and we do.

Luke gasps in a shock of pain and grips my arm hard enough to hurt. I support him—barely—as he leans on me more heavily.

Sean makes a similar noise of discomfort. Saraya says, "I don't like this."

Even though we just stepped out of the light, we're completely surrounded by darkness. It's like we've been swallowed by Jonah's biblical whale, dropped into the deep pit of its belly.

"What if we *weren't* supposed to walk into the giant mouth?" I ask, despite it being my idea.

Saraya makes a noise and her sword begins to glow. The light is enough to show that we're inside a passage. I turn and see that behind us is nothing except darkness and blank stone.

"Looks like the only way out is through," Sean says.

Luke says, "That's a design choice."

"We will go forward," Saraya says. "And you will all do exactly as I say."

Our voices reverberate in the space. The darkness seems to

surge against the small glow of Saraya's sword. I'd know if we were underneath something, right? My fear would automatically detect the danger and kick in. But what I feel isn't the blind panic I get in confined spaces. A tiny blessing.

"You okay?" Luke asks. "Not hyperventilating?"

"Not yet," I say.

Saraya slices forward into the black. The rest of us follow, staying quiet. Our breathing is the only sound besides our footsteps. That is, until the voices start.

"I sought the Grail for vanity . . ."

"I wanted power . . ."

"I ruled cruelly, and would have forever . . ."

"I desired to be a god myself . . ."

Most are masculine, but others sound feminine. It's a litany of brief cautionary tales, a list of bad reasons for taking on the Grail quest. I imagine it's meant to turn us around. The ghosts of those who failed might have returned here because they wanted to be close to the magic of the Grail.

That must mean we're getting close too.

But it also sinks in how many people must have come here over the centuries, seeking the Grail for this reason or that, and been denied. Do we have any chance? And if we don't, what does that mean for Luke and Sean? Do they end up stuck here, Fisher Kings in residence?

I thought figuring out the pattern was the important part. Obviously, it's getting out of here with the success to leave and not be stuck in regret.

"There's a light ahead," Saraya tells us a second before we see it.

There is in fact a ring of light that signals the end of the passage. It waits there, inviting, as we move cautiously closer.

We've almost reached it when a strange creature moves into the opening, partially blocking the illumination with its strange silhouette. A narrow head transitions into a four-pawed body. A chorus of barking echoes around us, despite only one figure before us. The yelps and growls are like a pack of invisible hounds.

I remember where the Questing Beast got its name. People assume it's because of the constant hunts to bring it down. But, no. It's because it sounded like thirty hunting hounds. Sometimes called the Bizarre Beast, for obvious reasons.

"Back?" Saraya asks quietly. The creature isn't moving in our direction, not yet.

I turn and can't see anything. I reach out and my hand hits a stone wall. "No going back," I say. "There is no back anymore. I think . . . that's the Questing Beast."

"Another challenge we must pass." Saraya lifts her sword a fraction higher. "Stay behind me."

"Wait, Luke, could you put it to sleep?" I ask, raising my voice over the increase in its full-throated baying.

"I can try." His voice is tight with pain, but Saraya lets him move forward to stand beside her in the passage.

We walk closer to the creature, me tugging Sean along, because I don't want to get stuck in the wall as it proceeds along behind us. The rules here are too mysterious to take chances with.

The beast waits until we're almost on top of it before it moves. We can see the slither and slide of its snake's tongue on a serpentine head, as it watches us get closer. Its leopard body is lean and graceful. The piercing sound of the barking seems to come from inside its stomach. Each new round of yelps in stereo makes the hairs on my arms prickle.

The beast squares off in the opening. "Now?" I suggest as it launches forward. Luke puts out his hand and shouts, "Sleep!" which he doesn't usually have to do. Usually he just lifts his hand and whoever it's directed at conks out.

Here, the command does nothing. The creature slows, toying with us. It stalks us, weaving forward from one side of the passage to the other, taking its time. Saliva drips from snake jaws, which is . . . weird. The barking and yipping from inside it continues without pause.

"I'm going to try to strike it down," Saraya says. "Stay back."

"There is no back." I reach behind me and confirm again.

She lifts her sword high overhead. My mind is shouting at the volume of the barking to find another way. Even a monster is filling its role. This is an animal. I don't want to slay it. I don't want it slain.

I settle on what's probably the dumbest and riskiest thought I've had. But I have to try.

"Wait," I say again and reach into Luke's jacket. I pull the baguette hunk free and stride forward quickly.

"No," Luke says, and someone grabs at the back of my shirt.

I dangle the baguette in front of me. "Hey there, beastie," I say. "Nice beastie. Do you want some food? Some bread, maybe?"

"Callie . . ." Luke's voice is strained.

The snake's head slips back and forth, weaving, eyes glittering in the dark, and then its leopard paws take two steps closer, then two more. I hold out the bread, shaking it a little.

I'm not prepared for when it lunges forward and—

Almost delicately takes the baguette from my fingers. The Questing Beast sits back on its haunches and chews in a way that shouldn't work with a snake's head and then releases a sigh with the profound happiness of thirty hounds in it.

"I suppose you're here for the cup," it says with a slight hiss on the *s*'s. Then, "I don't hate that journey for you. Come. This way."

The creature pivots, smooth as silk in motion, and leads us toward the light.

I could fall over. I need a moment. Or ten.

The others join me. Saraya is gaping. Luke grins through his pain, eyebrows raised, proud.

"You bribed the Questing Beast." Sean shakes his head in awe. "Well done."

The beast pads back where we can see it. "I said this way, *please.*"

CHAPTER TWENTY-EIGHT

LUKE

Of course, *of course*, Callie charmed the so-called Questing Beast. Callie and animals, always best friends. I'm surprised she didn't make a pal out of Guinevere's fearsome steed. I bet we're among the few to get this far, and I'd be willing to gamble the others were bullies about it, based on those voices on the way in.

I'm not as bad as them. An unusual thought for me.

We emerge from the passage—which seals into a brick wall behind us—into a, well, castle. Not the normal drafty medieval dump either. The interior isn't as luxurious as the Gray Keep. But there's no plain stone walls here, no grim light. A blazing fire burns in the hearth, and tapestries depicting knights and battle unicorns and angels hang on the walls. A table is set with a feast.

A man in king's robes with skeletal features and a crown sits at the head of it. He stands and waves us forward. This must be King Arthur.

There's a clatter at the other end of the hall as a door is

flung open and Lady Guinevere enters, having swapped out her full suit of armor for a pair of leather breeches and a chain mail shirt. The Questing Beast pads forward to meet her and gets a pat on its snaky head.

She takes the seat at the opposite end of the table from Arthur.

She doesn't acknowledge us until she's settled. She does so by removing a sharp knife from a sheath looped around her hips, slicing off a generous pat of butter in front of her and grinning at us as she applies it to a hard roll. She hands the treat off to the beast.

"I hear you discovered the creature's weakness," she says. "You won't discover ours."

"Should we sit down?" Callie asks, low.

King Arthur's voice booms out, a contrast to his desiccated appearance. "Please, join us. This is the next stage in your quest."

"So it is," I say, well aware of the history of slaughters over the dinner table. Guest rights are violated often by our kind. What do you think inspired the Red Wedding? I sketch a bow. "Luke Morningstar, prince of Hell."

King Arthur pauses. "I've met your father. A despicable sort."

Understatement of the millennium.

"He's my father too," Sean puts in. "I'm Sean, not-Morningstar."

Callie does her best curtsey. "And this is Saraya the Rude, of the Guardians," she says, indicating Saraya. Who rolls her eyes at the name, but nods. "And I'm Callie. Of, uh, Kentucky."

"Interesting party composition, wouldn't you say, my lady?" Arthur comments.

"Certainly, my lord," Guinevere says. "But here to seek the Grail, as usual."

"Some of us don't care about the Grail," Saraya says.

"None of us do," Callie clarifies. "We only care about healing the wounds of Luke and Sean. They've gotten sucked into your story."

There's a pause. I realize the Questing Beast took its roll and left. I can't begin to guess if that's a good sign or a bad one.

"Our story?" King Arthur says. "Oh no, no. Perhaps it's a story we got sucked into as well. We serve the Grail."

"Damn it," Callie murmurs. "We better sit down. Who you serve is the classic question, so that can't be it," she says, and I have no clue what she means.

I do as she says, pulling out her seat with the manners I've observed and not the ones taught to me.

I reach forward to take a slice of the roast and Guinevere snorts. "You think to feast?" she asks with disbelief.

"I thought you were inviting us to the table."

Sean sits down beside me. "It did seem that way."

"Oh, it did," King Arthur says. "But this food is poison to your sort." He pauses. "Kidding. Or am I?" He chortles with his head thrown back. I'm afraid his mandible will fall out of the thin decayed skin left over the bone.

"I've rather lost my appetite," I say. "What's the next test? Where's the Grail?"

"Why, it's in this room," Arthur says, and takes a drink from his cup. He lifts his free hand and sweeps it from left to right. "You have but to discover it."

I understand the propensity of the supernatural sorts to play games. It's a long time to be alive. These two and their creature must be set in a pattern that is rarely disrupted. Father is always claiming boredom. Half the time I suspect it's why he left Heaven in the first place to create Hell. For entertainment purposes.

"If you have the wounds, the Grail has chosen to give you a chance," Arthur says. "Difficult as it is for me to countenance."

"What polite hosts you are," Callie says, thick with irony.

Saraya fills a goblet with ruby wine from a carafe, sniffs it, and downs it. "Not poison," she declares and smacks the glass back onto the table.

Guinevere shrugs and looks down her nose at Saraya.

"We can figure this out," Sean says. "Simple process of elimination."

"Remember, it might not be a cup," Callie says. "Despite what the beast said."

"Could be a dish," Sean says. "Or a platter."

We all examine the table. The number of serving platters and dishes may as well be infinite.

I think back to the first church where Sean went looking for the Grail, how we gazed on the fancy chalice encrusted with stones and he said there was no magic present. I didn't have the benefit of my senses then, but I do now.

I catch Sean's eye. "Race you?" I ask, meaning which of us can detect the magic object in the room first.

His cockiest grin emerges. "You're on."

Seems there's a little of Father's gambling streak in us after all.

Callie and Saraya watch as we push back from the table. Sean wanders around slowly with his hands lifted. I close my eyes and cast my senses out.

"There's . . . nothing." Not a single magic thing sings more loudly to me, despite this entire place clearly being steeped in it. I turn to Sean, who nods agreement. "Same here," he says.

"You're cheating," I say to Arthur.

"Did you truly think it would be so easy? The Grail's magic is hidden, but it *can* be discovered."

"You can do this," Callie says with a pleading note.

The entire place is magic. Just like Hell, where I grew up. Since the Grail is hidden, maybe *that* is what will make it visible.

"Let me try something," I say to Sean.

Guinevere and Arthur lean against the high backs of their chairs, grinning death's head grins.

I ignore their expectation of failure. I'll have to face that from Father soon enough—assuming we get out of here.

The table is too obvious, isn't it? It's laden with objects that might be the Grail, meant to tempt someone into the wrong choice. No one has to explain that we get one chance at this.

I walk the perimeter of the room, my leg like a dowsing rod, aching sharply. Instead of looking for the magic thing, the thing that emanates power, I look for the thing that feels different, a blank spot. I trace the tapestries with my fingers—a unicorn standing with angels against dark knights, a forest scene with a pale-haired beauty who might be Guinevere before she traded dresses for breeches. And there's one depicting the table of a lavish feast . . . Not unlike the one on the table right now.

I study it closely, comparing.

Sean appears at my shoulder. "It's this table, isn't it?"

The number of dishes and platters seems to match. We take the time to compare, starting at either side. The scene matches almost exactly.

"What is it?" Callie asks, worried.

I reach out and touch the lone spot on the tapestry that doesn't mirror the actual table. It's blank. I wouldn't be surprised if my hand sank into the reality of the image and came back out with the Grail. But it's going to be simpler than that.

"I see," Sean says, and nods to me.

King Arthur is wily, but so am I, the prince of Hell.

"You almost outsmarted us," I say and turn back to the table. I believe I know exactly where I'll find the object that doesn't match with the illusion of this place.

I pass Callie on my way toward Arthur. "What are you doing?" she asks.

"I'm retrieving the Grail," I say.

Sean goes the other way around, so that we end up flanking King Arthur.

"Are you going to let that go or do we have to take it?" I ask.

The simple cup of aged, battered metal is gripped in his hand. My wound strains toward it.

"It is yours now," Arthur says. "You have shown yourself able to see it, and that makes you worthy."

He sets the Grail down and pushes it toward me. With a greedy glance at Sean, I pick it up.

"Take a drink," Callie says.

There is liquid inside. My leg throbs, hopefully for only a moment more. I put it to my lips and drink. Its magic bursts forth, shining like a sun. How it was hidden given the amount of power it holds is for a wizard or witch to guess; it would take a magic almost as powerful as its own to conceal it.

I wait for my wound to heal. For the pain to stop.

Nothing changes.

"You try," I say to Sean with a frown.

He circles behind King Arthur, who sits with hands folded, observing us.

Sean picks up the cup and takes a sip. He waits a moment, grimaces, and shakes his head.

"What's wrong?" Callie asks.

"It's not working," Saraya says.

"It is the Grail," I say, "but it's not healing us."

"Ha." Guinevere snorts. "Healing from your wounds can only come from within. From a question and an answer in the Grail's presence."

"But they must be the correct question and answer," King Arthur says.

Sean strokes his chin, then lowers his hand. "There's only one question I care about," he says. "I'll ask that."

"Usually the person with the wound is asked the question, not the other way around," Callie says.

"I'm asking this one," Sean says, "no matter what. I got some decent advice that suggested it."

Sean crosses to where Saraya is still seated at the table. "It's a question for you," Sean says.

She stares up at him, unreadable.

"I've been thinking about what Callie and Luke started this trying to do, to give people second chances. It seems like the most important thing in creation, that possibility. So my question is this . . . Can you give me a second chance?"

Saraya gives the wine carafe a long look, as if she might drain it. Then she rises and extends her hands to Sean. He takes them and the room is heavy as we wait.

"Yes, you can have a second chance," she says. "Fool."

Sean's smile spreads and he straightens visibly. "It worked," he says, and hugs Saraya and picks her up off the ground to demonstrate.

I expect her to stab him for the liberty, but she only smiles back and then says, "Put me down."

He does, still smiling. He finds me. "What is *your* question, brother?"

I have no idea. All my questions are about how I could ever possibly have what I want—a life with Callie, escape from my father's control, the pain in my thigh gone though I suspect I deserve it.

"I think I know what to ask," Callie says.

"But Sean asked me," Saraya counters.

"It matters only that the question and answer meet the Grail's approval," Guinevere says.

Callie reaches out and I put my hands in hers. I stare into her eyes. What happens if this doesn't work? What if *I'm* supposed to ask the question?

But I still don't have one. I'm the question mark here, the one least likely to come out of this breathing easy.

"I know you're thinking of doing something stupid. When I asked you, you were lying to me."

"I wouldn't call it lying." I don't want to disappoint her. I'm afraid I'm about to.

"I want you to think deeply about your answer. It must be true. I think . . . There's only one way to be free of your wound. Only one chance we get through this."

"No pressure?" I keep my voice light, but nothing has ever felt as serious as this.

"You're up to it," Callie says. "Here it is." She swallows, then, "Whose life will you live?"

Whose life will I live?

I couldn't have anticipated this question. My mind scrambles around the edges of the question, trying it from different directions, attempting to solve for the one answer that will be

true. Faces cycle through my mind, Father's lasting the longest. He would say the answer is his, the life he wants for me.
He would expect me to answer Callie that way.

She told me to think deeply and so I do. I think about what
I want. A life with Callie, yes, but what else? If I've gotten this
far, maybe I am worthier than I assumed. If I'm worthy of Callie's love, then maybe I'm worthy of my own.

I close my eyes and I think the question: Whose life will
you live? I answer on instinct, straight from the gut.

"Mine," I say.

Callie looks expectantly at me when I open my eyes. The
Grail clatters on the table, almost as if it's doing a dance. The
pain in my leg is . . . gone. Just gone.

"I will live *my* life," I say. "It worked."

The barking and growling symphony of the Questing
Beast returns, claws scrabbling on the floor as it races in. "I
tried to stop them, but the demon had a boon from Morgan,"
it says.

King Arthur rests his head in his hands. "My sister strikes
again."

Mag bursts into the room first, from the direction of the
Questing Beast. "We're here to rescue you!"

Vale leaps in front of them, brandishing a sword.

Porsoth trundles in slower, and bows to the king and then
the queen. "Apologies, my lord, my lady. I did know Morgan
once upon a time and, ah, she was convinced to offer me
admittance." He pulls at his scholar's collar like it's too tight.

Jared and Callie's mother spill into the room next, stopping
in the threshold.

"Perfect timing," I say. "We're healed. Which means it's
time to blow this Holy Grail Popsicle stand."

"Aren't you at least impressed that we got inside?" Mag asks. "Porsoth was dashing in summoning zombie Morgan the Fay."

Porsoth shifts from foot to foot, slightly embarrassed. "I simply traded on our long-distant past together."

"She was *into him*," Mag says.

"Styx better not find out, then," Callie says, and they grin at each other.

I knew Porsoth was a terror in his heyday, but not that he was such a ladies' man.

"We *should* take our leave," Porsoth says. "You are in grave danger of being late."

As everyone gathers, the exit far more straightforward than getting in apparently, Callie pulls me aside. "You're not a fool, so don't do anything foolish," she says. "Remember what you just said. You're going to live your own life." She kisses me, relief in it.

But I suspect our nightmare is far from over.

"Everything is good?" Callie's mother asks.

Callie looks around. "I think . . . we did it. Didn't we?" She directs that at Sean.

"Yes, that's all the redemption I ever needed," Sean says. "You definitely bested Lucifer's challenge."

"I can't wait to tell Agnes that I told her so," Callie says.

My sense of foreboding isn't shared and I don't know how to explain it to the rest of them. "I'm not sure you should return to Hell with us," I say to Sean.

"That's part of the terms," Sean says. "I heard him say so. I'm coming."

"Me too," Saraya adds.

I was afraid of that.

"The rest of you can't—the humans," I say. "You wouldn't enjoy it."

"He's right," Callie says. "You don't want to have to deal with Styx."

Vale nods at Callie's mother, Mag, and Jared. "I will see them home."

"Good luck, sweetie," Callie's mother says, and comes over to touch her forehead against Callie's and give her a quick hug. She follows it with a hug for me. "And you too, Luke. You make her happy."

I'm so touched I can't quite manage to respond. I'm not sure whether what she said is an order or a statement of fact.

"Go give the devil his due," Mag says.

"How long have you been sitting on that one?" Callie asks them.

"They came up with it yesterday," Jared says.

Callie laughs and her love is clear. She has these people who would do anything for her, even help save me. And maybe I deserved saving.

It's a funny thought.

"You should leave this place," King Arthur announces. "Our business is concluded."

"What will you do?" Callie asks. "The two of you, I mean?"

"We will do as we have always done, and sleep until we are called awake by the mighty angels," he says.

"And then, if needed, we will fight," Lady Guinevere adds and bares her teeth.

Sounds familiar.

We may have won the bet, but Father will not be so easily swayed on the bigger prize he has his eye on—an immediate successor. I pluck the Grail from the table and find it fits snugly in my pocket.

The Holy Grail is a small, dull metal cup that has been hiding in plain sight for centuries on a ghostly table. And it's my ticket out of Father's clutches, if I can play it right. If not, I will live *my* life in one way: lonely.

And alone.

CHAPTER TWENTY-NINE

CALLIE AND LUKE

We stand outside Camelot one moment, and the next there's only the green, now dark field of the Glastonbury Abbey. My mother, Jared, and Mag have just left with a chanting Vale.

"How are we traveling?" I ask our remaining squad. "The easy way or the hard way?"

"Er, probably not the best idea to antagonize Lucifer by coming in using the guardian method," Porsoth says. "Even if you do deserve comfort."

"We'll be vulnerable briefly if we travel the other way," Sean says.

"I'll travel solo," Saraya says, "and that way I'll be able to protect you."

"How will you find us?" I ask.

Saraya gives a sly smile. "Once Sean left the borders of Hell, I could track him anywhere. That means I can follow. I'll be right behind you."

"Okay, then," Luke says, "that's settled."

"You're not alone in this," I say, reminding him. "I've got your back. We all do."

Luke's eyes lock with mine and I think he might confess . . . whatever it is that's going on in his brain. He doesn't. He slides a hand to my cheek, then down to my shoulder, and the length of my arm to my hand. I tip forward to chase his touch.

"Here we go," he says.

The shrieking dark surrounds us in an instant, screaming and threatening to turn me inside-out, as usual. I'm so nervous about what's going to happen that I manage to nearly block out the pain of zappitying. Nearly.

We end up on the outside portico where Lilith and I arrived the day before. I hang my head, hands on my knees, and breathe through the disorientation. When I stand up, Saraya lands alongside Sean. He's adjusted too.

The moon hangs low and red in the sky. Should it still look that way?

Agnes races through the door, the guards shouting after her. "Hurry!" she says.

"She's right. We've not a parsec to spare," Porsoth says, and sets out for the Keep's entrance at a fast trot.

There's nothing to do but go along with him.

"We did it, Agnes," I tell her as we jog.

"You did?" she says with a frown on her small face. I imagine it's hard for her to believe it.

We should feel like a conquering brigade returning. Sean *was* a challenge, but we met it. Agnes is getting her second chance. Problem is, I can tell Luke doesn't feel victorious. His somber mood casts a pall over any excitement about showing up Lucifer. The man I love has his reasons, I'm positive. I take comfort that even if he won't share them, they're about to be revealed.

And I'll be there to keep him from forgetting what he promised. His answer had to be true for the Grail to take it. He *will* live his life. *His*. No one else's. He needs to understand that life can be good. With me.

We make a quick, quiet journey through the corridors until we pause outside the throne room. The fingerless, antlered soldier from earlier stands sentry. "Announce us," Luke orders him.

"Lukas Astaroth Morningstar," the sentry calls. He hesitates and looks at the rest of us.

Porsoth clears his throat.

"That'll be plenty," Luke says.

"Enter," comes Lucifer's chilly voice.

Luke raises his hand as if to say, "see?"

"We're right here with you," I say. "Don't forget that."

Sean says, "She's right."

Saraya grunts what sounds like agreement. It's touching, honestly.

Luke hesitates again, then turns and strides into the throne room. Here we are, back where this endless date began. I can't regret it, though.

I follow Luke, with Sean and Saraya next. Porsoth and Agnes slip in last, and go to stand by Lilith and Rofocale. Luke's mother is relieved and grins, then gives a smokier grin to Sean that's very her. Rofocale is his usual brand of disapproving.

"Why, son," Lucifer says, "you brought me a going-away present. You shouldn't've. Just his head would have been plenty."

I realize with horror that he means Sean's. Saraya pointedly steps in front of him.

"Not a present," Luke says, "the proof we won our side of the wager. You're not still going on about leaving, are you?"

"Yes," I jump in, before Lucifer can. "You wouldn't go back on our deal, would you? Sean's soul is free and clear and he's ready for his second chance."

"There will be no second chance for him." Lucifer's wings stretch out, intimidating because he sits so still otherwise. "There can only be one heir, son, I told you." He stands then and leaves the throne. "This is yours, son. You have but to claim it," he says, nodding to the ornate black chair.

Luke is unmoving. He's on the precipice of a decision. I don't think I got that before this instant. I couldn't imagine Lucifer leaving Hell, but, for once, he doesn't seem to be playing a game. What's Luke going to choose? And is Lucifer truly giving him a choice? I doubt it.

Think fast, Callie, there must be something you can do to stop this.

Luke reaches into his pocket and removes the Grail, placing it flat on his palm to show it off.

"Now, this, this is a present—but it's not for you, not exactly." Luke's lips turn up in an ice-cold grin. "It's a get-out-of-being-the-heir-free card and I'm ready to play it."

Gambler up, big gamble in progress. Callie's giving me the most puzzled expression, as if she has no idea what I'm going on about. This is my one move, and I hope against hope that it works.

"You found the Grail," Lucifer says. "Interesting. You prove a more worthy heir than I thought. Please tell me that bore Arthur is dead."

"Sort of?" Callie offers. "Luke, what are you doing?"

"I was about to ask the same question," Sean says.

"I could simply kill you, spare," Lucifer says to Sean.

Saraya pulls her sword. "Try it."

"You do realize I'm still king and could summon Hell's armies?" Lucifer asks. "I, too, am an angel, just like your master."

Saraya has the briefest of hesitations. She lifts her chin. "Go ahead."

Mother decides to enter the fray then. "Why can't you simply go in peace, Lucifer? New heir, do you have any interest in Hell's throne?"

"I do not," Sean says.

"Let him be on his way," Mother says.

"And neither do I." I summon my wings to underscore the point.

"Now, Luke, don't be so hasty," Mother says. "You've always known this could all be yours one day."

"No one ever asked me if I wanted it," I tell her. "I don't. Give it to Rofocale, for all I care."

"Sire," Porsoth starts, "I do not think that would be in the best . . ."

"No." Lilith speaks up. "Not happening."

Rofocale might want to protest, but he swallows it.

Lucifer's wings spread wide and with two beats, he hovers in front of me. The elevation allows him to stare down at me, menacingly. It's a vantage he's always liked using with me. But I refuse to cower.

Ignoring him, Callie comes in close to my side. "What are you doing?" she asks.

To not give Father her attention when he's bringing the full command of his presence to bear . . . That's not something that's easy to do. I wonder if he has to give any of his powers up, how long he plans to be absent.

"I'm saying no," I tell her, which is true.

I toss the cup an inch or so in the air and catch it. "I'm told that among the many powers this has, one is to make a paradise of any land. There will hardly be a need for a devil without any Hell."

Father's jaw works, his rage palpable. Have I outplayed him? Is it possible? Sean's idea was a good one, but he intended to make it a reality in the wrong place.

The cursed sentry from the door breaks in and announces someone new. "The archangel Michael," he shouts, clearly petrified.

The glowing angel who tried to bully me into the job the other night strides in to join the party.

Lucifer turns in disbelief. "I didn't realize I'd invited *you*," he says.

"Greetings, Lucifer," Michael says. "One of my guardians is here"—he peers at Saraya and Sean—"make that two of them, and therefore I may be present. I hear you are preparing to leave."

Sean blinks. His reinstated status must be news to him. I slide the Grail back into my pocket.

"What are you doing here?" Callie asks Michael.

"I can understand why dealing with these upstarts might get old," Michael says. "They are tiresome."

"You are *not* tiresome," I tell Callie.

"My son is threatening to make Hell a paradise," Father says, and sighs. "I simply desire a walkabout."

"That would be a bad idea," Michael says to me. "You two

wanted to give people who deserved it extra chances, from what I understood. It would remove that possibility. Whereas, you could take over and then do what you like."

Callie's going to be swayed by this, but I stay firm. "I won't be the heir."

Her mouth opens, but she doesn't argue. I suppose I always knew that if she was confronted with the true depths of my self-interest, she'd balk.

"I intend to live my life," I say, quietly. "Even if it's alone, it will be on my own terms."

"What do you mean, 'even if it's alone'?" Callie gapes at me, then snorts. "You still think I'm going to abandon you, don't you? It's never happening."

My heart experiences an inconvenient jolt of electricity. I believe her. I start to hope.

"You truly don't want to rule?" she asks.

"Never. I don't want to risk being like Father, and I have no desire to run the Kingdom. I don't think I'd be any good at it."

Callie takes this in, nodding. "Okay, then."

"Someone must rule," Father says. "That is a simple fact. It must be you, Luke."

"That's not what you said," Callie says, and I can practically see her mind generating possibilities. "You only said *someone* must rule . . ."

She looks at me and I watch as her grin spreads wide as a sky. She turns to Father. "I'm someone. I'll do it."

I stare into Lucifer's ice-block eyes, hard and dismissive, and I repeat it. "I'll do it. I'll rule."

Lilith approaches us. "It's not the worst idea," she says with approval. "It would mean our son stays here as well."

Luke puts his hand on my arm. "Callie, you don't have to do this for me. If you really want me to, I'll . . ."

"No," I blurt. "No, I don't want you to. I would never want you to do something you so obviously do not want to do. But . . . how would you feel about helping me? I'd do all the hard parts." She stops and winks. "You just have to look pretty."

"I am good at that," I say. "But I don't think you understand what you're saying."

"I could help, too," Porsoth says, "as a trusted, dear friend."

Lucifer gives a thundering beat of his wings to silence us. "Excuse me," he says.

"No, let her talk," Michael puts in.

Sean and Saraya watch the proceedings like a tennis match—maybe literally given how into sports guardians are. Lucifer stays quiet. I seize my chance.

"Pros," I say to Luke, lifting my hand to count them off on my fingers, "to prove I'm thinking this through. I'd have a new job, since I'm currently unemployed. I bet it comes with room and board, for both of us. Pygmy fainting goats and dogs totally allowed. I can do all the reforms I want for as long as we're in charge. We can . . . stay close to our friends back home. I don't see any cons."

"There's a big con," Luke says, sounding like he wishes he didn't have to voice it. "You're human. I'm not even sure it's possible."

Oops. "Did I forget to tell you? I'm not human, not anymore. Not all the way, at least."

"What?" Luke demands.

"I'm like your mother—in that one specific way," I say. Lilith beams. "Porsoth confirmed it. I'm immortal-ish. Something about traveling back and forth so often. I think I'd be good at this. I was able to use your powers—does the job come with those?"

"Some of them," Lucifer answers in a growl.

"And you're not freaked out, about not being exactly human?" Luke asks. "It must be my fault."

I don't know how to get him to understand. "The trouble we get into together, it's the only thing I've ever been good at. It's the only thing I want to do for the rest of *my* life."

He looks at me hard, like he's trying to see whether it's a lie. *It's not. It's the only true thing.*

"The demons would revolt," Rofocale snarls.

"I don't think they would," Porsoth says, pushing back hard with some vibrato in his voice. "They would quite like the change, I suspect. And I can get the ones who challenge her on board."

"There must be other cons," Luke says, but he's hoping. I can see it. He's hoping this works out. "You're positive this is what you want?"

"I want it. It may be the first time I've known exactly what I want to do with my life." I put my hands on my hips and speak directly to Lucifer and Michael. "I want to rule Hell. And I want Luke not to have to do this or anything else just because Lucifer wants it. Ever again."

It shouldn't come as such a surprise, given that I've been hanging out in churches lately, but I find that I'm doing something most people would describe as praying. I'm praying that this happens. I never wanted to stay here and be Father's bad soldier. But to get to stay here with Callie, while she does something that makes her happy? To live the life I want beside her? Yes, please.

She would make a great queen, and it never even occurred to me.

"Lucifer?" Michael says.

"You want that walkabout," I say. "Don't forget."

Lucifer is quiet and I envision a lifetime spent scheming to get Callie what she knows she wants now. If I have to go to war against my father, I'll make it part of my life. Mine. She gave me that knowledge, the desire to live for myself. I owe her everything, but there's no collecting of debts. Not with love.

I finally stood up to my father.

"Fine," Lucifer says. "You can have one hundred years. Then we'll discuss it."

Callie's eyes are wide. Father stalks over to Mother, kisses her, and then leaves.

"One hundred years," Callie says. "One hundred years, is he serious?"

"He wouldn't have left otherwise," Porsoth says. "Oh, what a happy day. We have so many celebrations to plan! Oh, and your coronation! You will be radiant."

Michael has quietly taken off too. Sean and Saraya are still here though.

"Didn't see that one coming," Sean says, and claps his arm around me in a brotherly half hug.

"Don't be strangers," I say.

"Yes." Callie snuggles into my side and her face is filled with joy. "Please come visit. Often. Or we'll visit you."

"You're going to be the queen of Hell now," Saraya points out.

"It's just a job," Callie says.

Oh, wow, Hell is not going to know what hit it.

"Then we'll see you soon," Sean says. "Thank you both, for everything."

Everything being Saraya, the obvious center of his universe. "Anytime. Well, hopefully never any of that again," I say, "but you know what I mean."

Saraya and he rope their arms around each other's necks and, with a last wave from Sean, they leave our borders. I feel it as they go.

I look at Callie and see she does too. "But I want wings," she says. Then clarifies, "Of my own."

"It might be possible," Porsoth says with a hoot. "I'll consult the spellcasters immediately."

"I can pull the relevant library volumes," Agnes puts in.

"Don't you want to go now?" Callie says. "You can."

"I'm not ready," Agnes declares with a vaguely maddening shrug.

Callie and I glance at each other, but don't say anything. Something else occurs to me and I reach into my pocket to check. Yes. I'm right.

"Sean stole the Grail," I say.

Callie claps her hands together and her delight at the fact is the absolute best thing I've ever seen or ever will.

EPILOGUE

CALLIE

Coronation day is here. *My* coronation day, as queen of Hell. Luke has insisted that he be called prince regent, at least until the day we tie the knot, so that it's clear who's in charge. Turns out my hyper-controlling nerdy self? Loves being in charge.

Porsoth and I have spent days in the library going through arcane regulations and discussing tweaks. Rofocale has been assigned to oversee the first group of second-chancers. He's come around surprisingly quickly. Porsoth says he always liked me, and I'm aware that's a lie. But he even takes orders from Luke without complaining directly.

Agnes has been working with Porsoth, putting off leaving, which I didn't expect. She said this feels like a second chance already—but that she reserves the right to leave if we get too annoying. I have not pointed out the irony that we did all this for her and now she seems happy where she is. A true Agnes move.

We've also managed to figure out a handkerchief method

so my family can come visit when they want. Mom's bringing Vale as her date today. We told Jared to let his apartment go to some nice, fully human couple. I hope they're happy in it.

A low whistle sounds behind me, and I'm grinning when I spin elaborately to show off the swirling black brocade skirt of my gown. The tailors of Hell have worked on this goth confection for six weeks and it's almost too exquisite to wear. It's not exactly *me*, but Porsoth reminded me that I'm also an office now and I have to look the part "today of all days."

And I like it. I especially like the way Luke looks at me, breathtaking in a perfectly tailored black suit. Bosch and Cupcake scamper in from behind him, where they've been hanging out in the outer chamber of our apartments. They do an excited circle around me and then head back through the door. Watching the demon staff treat them like royal pets is so much fun.

"You are a vision," Luke says, like he just recovered the ability to speak.

"Keep going," I say and twirl once more for good measure.

"Oh no, you're turning into me," he says.

I wrinkle my nose at him to prove I am *not*. "You've got something on your face," I say as he walks over to me.

He slips his arm around my waist. "No, you've got something on your face."

"Porsoth will murder me if I mess up this dress," I say.

"You're the boss of him now. And of me," he says, and leans in for a kiss. It lasts long enough that it goes from "quick kiss" to "we're starting something" territory. I push the heavy drape over the window aside to peek out. The plains are still covered by demons on their way to the Gray Keep for the ceremony.

"You know, sometimes I want to say it, the words," I say. "I love you."

"And I love you," Luke says. Our breathing mingles. My skin feels hot, like I could take it off the same way I'd take off this dress. "So," he says, "do we have to be on time?"

I pause to consider. "No," I say. "I checked with the woman in charge. We definitely do not."

He laughs and scoops me up in his arms, elaborate skirts and all, and heads for the bed. Our bed. Our life together.

It's only the beginning.

ACKNOWLEDGMENTS

No book is easy, but writing this one during the pandemic was especially difficult. My first thanks have to go to Tiffany Shelton and Jennie Conway, my above-and-beyond understanding editors, who never freaked out about my needing a little (er, a lot of) extra time. Jennie, you guided me over the finish line with this book and I'm forever grateful. Let's get the whole St. Martin's rock star team in there while I'm at it: Kerri Resnick for that amazing cover, and the super fabulous marketing and PR team: Mary Moates, Erica Martirano, and Kejana Ayala. Working with you all is a pleasure.

To the Friday Zoom bunch—C, Richard Butner, Ted Chiang, Kelly Link, Gavin Grant, Karen Joy Fowler, Molly Gloss, Barb Gilly, John Kessel, Jim Patrick Kelly, Kristin Livdahl, and assorted guests—for being a bright spot every week and for general commiseration about writing. To my dear friends Kami Garcia and Sam Humphries, same; Kami, there's no way I'd have finished this without you. To the Moonscribers, my beloved writing group, and to the exceptionally great writers at the Lexington Writer's Room for a sense of community.

My agents, Jennifer Laughran and Kate McKean, are both the best and never steer me wrong. It's a gift to have you in my corner.

The pets—Puck, Sally, Izzy, Phoebe, and Stella—you don't help write the books, but you are essential to my writing them—even if you can't read this. Christopher Rowe, you continue to be the best part of my life. Thank you for the writing patio and everything else.

And as always, to you, dear readers, booksellers, librarians, and other lovers of books: the hugest of thanks for taking this journey with me.

ABOUT THE AUTHOR

 WENDA BOND is the *New York Times* bestselling author of many novels, including the Lois Lane and Cirque American trilogies. She wrote the first official Stranger Things novel, *Suspicious Minds*. She also created *Dead Air*, a serialized mystery and scripted podcast written with Carrie Ryan and Rachel Caine. *Not Your Average Hot Guy* was her first romantic comedy for adults.

Her nonfiction writing has appeared in *Publishers Weekly*, *Locus*, *Salon*, the *Los Angeles Times*, and many other publications. She has an MFA in writing from the Vermont College of Fine Arts. She lives in a hundred-year-old house in Lexington, Kentucky, with her husband and their unruly pets.

She believes she may have escaped from a 1940s screwball comedy. She writes a monthlyish letter you can sign up for at her website (gwendabond.com), and you can also follow her on Twitter (@Gwenda).